wrong Crowd

LISA HELEN GRAY

Edited by Stephanie Farrant at Farrant Editing
Cover Design by Cassy Roop at Pink Ink Designs

wrong Crowd

chapter one

My mum had been buried twenty-four hours, and before I could even let it really sink in, to mourn the mum I wish she was and the person she *really* was, I was being carted off into the unknown.

I glance over to my aunt Nova, my mum's twin sister, someone I didn't know about until two nights ago.

I take a moment to appraise her appearance. She couldn't be more different to my mum if she tried. In her fancy clothes—pink silk top, loose and flowing, and beige suit trousers—she reminds me of a teacher or someone official. Someone I didn't like at my old school. I think it's why I don't trust her. The flashiest thing Cara Monroe had owned was her heels; her clothes screamed slut and were beyond tacky.

Although the two had similar features, Mum had looked ten years older. Her face had weathered and wrinkled from all the drugs and alcohol she pumped into her body. Nova's skin is smooth and looks soft to the touch. It makes me wonder if Mum had been that pretty at one point.

A lot of men would comment on her looks, giving her advice on what do with her hair, her makeup, her clothes. It never made a difference though. She had abused her body for far too long.

Who knows why.

Mum also had bleach-blonde hair, whereas Nova's is dark, yet lighter than my jet-black hair, which almost looks like it has a blue tinge to it.

The other thing that cuts the two apart is the fact my mum was dirt poor and Nova is clearly rich—if her handbag, car and clothes are anything to go by. She has this presence that screams money. My mum couldn't even claim benefits; they cut her off after she refused to get another job last year—not that she could get a job most of the time. We've been squatting in our flat ever since, scrounging by, using food banks and homeless shelters to eat, and she'd always screw men to get her money or fix. They didn't even know what they were in for before coming inside most of the time. Not until she had robbed them clean and threatened to tell loved ones what they got up to behind closed doors.

Why did she make us scrounge for leftovers if she had a twin sister who was rich? It's the one thing that seriously bothers me. It makes me hate her.

"Ivy, I can hear you thinking. You can ask me anything, you know," Nova says, her voice sweet, soft; nothing like my mum's scratchy voice. I avoid her gaze and look back out of the windshield.

"Why didn't I know about you?"

"Your mum didn't want you to. We tried to see you as a baby, you know."

News to me. I didn't even know we had any family, but according to this lady, I have an uncle and grandparents. None are here in England. Apparently, they're in the States on business.

When I don't ask her anything else, she takes a deep breath. "I had my housekeeper go out and get you some more clothes."

My stomach bottoms out, and I look at her in horror. "I am not wearing your fancy as shit clothes," I snap. I like my jeans, my tank tops, and my boots. They are the nicest things I own, and only because one of the ladies at the food bank took a liking to me and offered me help where I needed it.

A small smile plays at her lips, but I don't know what she finds funny. "There's going to be rules."

"Let's go back to the clothes," I order. Fuck the rules. I've raised myself for as long as I can remember, and rules didn't come into the equation. Mum never set any. She never cared enough about me to do it.

"Don't worry. I told her to get whatever she wanted with regards to underwear and pyjamas, but for clothes, I did inform her you like jeans and jackets. I'm not saying there won't be anything fancy when you get home, but there will be something you like."

"It's not my home," I snap defensively.

"It is for as long as you want it to be."

"I turn eighteen in a month."

"I thought we had a deal," she murmurs, and I sink further down in my chair.

I hate my mum. I hate that she died and left me. She left me with a debt owed to a drug dealer and with no money to pay it, no home, and a bag with a few items of clothing. I'm stuck. And getting a job with the state my clothes are in would be impossible in our area. I had tried many times before, fed up of starving and freezing to death. They took one look at me and decided there and then that I wasn't worth it. They probably thought I would steal from the cash register or bring trouble.

When Nova found all of this out, she tried to talk me into going back with her, informing me I was family and she wanted to get to know me. I said no, not trusting her. But then she offered me a deal. I could go live with her, get a part-time job so I could save my money up, and have somewhere warm and safe to sleep, as long as I agreed to try school for a year. If I made it the full year, she would give me ten thousand pounds to start my life with. And on top of all that, she would give me a monthly allowance.

I wanted to say no at first, wondering where this woman got off on throwing her cash around. But I'm not stupid—far from it. If I want to get out of the life I'm in and away from the exact path my mum made, I need out. If she wants to waste her cash on me, she can go for it. I know I'd survive without it, but I'm tired of surviving. I want to finally live my life.

"We have a deal," I tell her. "But I told you, there is no way I'm getting into that fancy as fuck academy, college, or whatever it is."

"Language," she scolds. "And you already have. It's a private academy. It will give you choices, and it's different from other colleges. And I'm good friends with the family who own it, so stop worrying."

"Whatever," I mutter, looking back out the window.

The dirty streets littered with rubbish and women hanging on corners left us hours ago. Now we're driving down roads with houses bigger than my old school.

When Nova pulls up outside a huge gate, I can't help but freak out a little. She really is rich. Even though I knew it, seeing it is another matter altogether.

She waves to the guy sitting in the small building beside the gate. He leans out the window. "Good evening, Nova."

"This is my niece, Ivy," she tells him, her voice cheery. "She's coming to live with me."

I watch the guy bend down to see into the car where I'm sitting, and I can see the surprise written on his face. I snort, looking back out my window.

"Nice to meet you," he says. Fake. All of them are fake.

Nora ends their little chat. "Have a good night."

The gates open, and as we pull off again, I look at her. "You have your own security guard. *Who are you?*"

She rolls her eyes. "No, I don't. This is a gated community, Ivy. They are there for all of us."

"All of you?"

"Yes. The two houses there at the top of the hill; one is Monroe Manor and the other is Kingsley Manor. Our families are the ones who bought this land and built on it. Over time, more people built and here we are. A small community for the rich."

The houses we pass are huge, yet when we weave up the curvy hill, two large houses, built side by side, come into view, and there is nothing to stop my eyes from bugging out.

"Holy fuck!" I gasp.

"Language," she scolds.

A lady who looks to be in her fifties is waiting inside the garage. She's wearing a grey polo shirt and black suit trousers. Her hair is pulled back in a tight bun. She steps forward the minute Nova shuts her car off, and I quickly get out, following her to the back of the car and snatching my backpack from the boot as she reaches for it.

"I can take your bag, Miss Monroe," the lady greets me.

"No." It's all that I own. I'm not optimistic about this working out. I don't belong in a place like this. I feel like dirt they trod in through the door.

She goes to take my bag again. "It's perfectly fine. I'll take it straight to your room."

I take note of what is in my bag, and although none of it's valuable, it's all I have, and she's not taking it away. The house feels like it's getting bigger as I take another step closer. There is no way I am going to make it here. Nova might dress me up, but it will only take another of her kind to take one look at me and realise who I am.

"Ivy, this is Annette, our housekeeper. She has her own home at the back of the property but is here from five a.m. until six p.m."

I don't say anything, and when she sees that, she blows out another breath and gestures for me to follow her. I do, taking in everything as I go. I didn't know what to expect when she told me I was going to live with her. I met her the day before yesterday and I still don't know what to think.

This house is really something though. She told me she lives alone, so why does she want all this space? I can't believe just one person lives here.

There are open rooms everywhere, all decorated in neutral colours, like something you'd see in a magazine.

The room we walk past next has a grand fireplace, the beige marble gleaming. It doesn't look like the fireplace is used though, only there for show. The sofas are grey, two two-seaters facing each other, with a glass coffee table in the middle. I don't get a chance to look at anything else before we're entering the kitchen, and my mouth opens with surprise. I marvel over how clean it looks, the white cupboards and white and grey marble gleaming.

I bet there's food in those cupboards too.

If the outside doesn't scream money, this kitchen does. I don't need to be an expert to know it's been decked out with all the finest furnishings.

"Down there we have a cinema room and a games room. Feel free to check it out tomorrow," Nova explains as she points to different doors. "We have an outdoor pool that's heated throughout the year. You'll find swimsuits in your bedroom. Living room, dining room, another living area and the conservatory," she adds, and walks me to a set of stairs. "The other rooms down here don't get used. "We have seven bedrooms. Mine is on the other side of the house, along with my office. I've kept you on this side to give you more privacy."

I have to stop her there. "More privacy? I could walk around this place naked and not even risk bumping into someone."

Her face scrunches up. "Do not walk around here undressed."

I smirk, hiking my bag up higher on my shoulder.

She opens a door to the right, letting it swing open, and takes a step back. She looks at me, and when I don't move, she rolls her eyes. "Go. This is your room."

I try to hide my nerves as I take a tentative step inside. Two lamps on either side of the bed have been left on, casting a warm glow around the room. I swallow, taking in the clean sheets and fluffy pillows. It's also a king, something I've never seen before. Back home I had a single-sized bed that was held up by some old library books.

The walls are cream, and Nova has kept them plain. There's a huge window with a reading nook beneath it. The chaise will come in handy when it rains, which is meant to happen over the weekend. There's a huge seating area to my right, and a table next to it with a vase of flowers on top.

There's a desk next to the window, and my eyes bug out when I see the laptop, mobile, and set of keys.

"The mobile is under contract and my numbers are programmed into it. The laptop is all set up to the Wi-Fi and is yours to do schoolwork on. The keys are for the front door, garage door and backdoor. If you are ready to start your driving lessons, I do have someone who can begin teaching you within a week, so you can take your test."

This sounds too good to be true.

I step back over to the bed, running my finger along the soft cotton sheets. When my gaze finds two doors on the other side of the room, I look over my shoulder, raising an eyebrow at Nova. She takes her first step into the room, pointing to the first door. "That's the bathroom. It's yours and yours alone. Second door is your wardrobe. Would you like Annette to fix you something to eat before you go to sleep?"

My stomach grumbles, but there's no way I can eat right now. I'm too nervous, and if I'm honest, I miss my mum. No matter how shitty she was or however fucked up, she was still my mum. I knew what to expect and that was nothing. With Nova, she has the power to give me more than I ever dreamed of having, and then take it away in her next breath without a care in the world. We don't know each other. We have no emotional ties. Yet even though I'm not completely convinced I won't end up going through life alone, she's here and she's family. I might as well suck it up. The minute she shows me a different side to her, I will be gone, and she'll never see me again. I might not understand why she is doing this for me, someone she doesn't know or has cared to know, but she is. And I haven't missed the way pain will flash through her eyes whenever she watches me, either. It's there, even when she tries so hard to hide it. I just don't know why.

"No. I'm good, thank you."

"If you change your mind, head down to the kitchen and help yourself to anything. In fact, I'll get her to make you a sandwich and pop it in the fridge."

I nod, not feeling my confident self right now. She must see it because she only takes a step back, her gaze lowered. "All right. I'll let you get some rest."

I hear her reach the door and let out a breath I didn't realise I was holding. I feel tears gather in my eyes, but they don't fall. I didn't even cry when they announced my mum was dead. I didn't feel much of anything. I did get a sense of relief, and with that followed guilt. Even at her funeral I didn't cry. I couldn't. I just felt helpless.

Sighing, I scan the room once more. Even the carpet looks expensive. It kind of makes me angry, but I don't know who at. At Mum for knowing she could have this or an aunt who had it and didn't share it. It just seems unfair that this was here. Hell, I would have been happy to sleep in the garage.

I have so many questions, but I don't know who to trust. Mum isn't here to answer them, and there has to be a reason she lived in shit and didn't come crawling back. She had no problem when it was one of her male friends, so why not her own twin sister? It wasn't a pride thing. My mum never had any.

There are secrets here. Secrets that can reveal why I only found out I had an aunt two days ago. Nova hadn't explained anything to me, just said Mum disappeared.

So, whether I can trust Nova or not, still has a big fat question mark around it.

I can't help but compare the room to our old home. It's bigger than our entire flat, that's for sure. However, it's how clean and well-kept it is that makes me feel uncomfortable. I'm not used to it. And I guess a part of me is scared to be in case it's ripped away. You can't miss something you never had, which is how I spent my whole life.

Fuck it.

I'm here and I don't have anywhere else to go. By now, the council have taken over the flat and are gutting the place. Nothing inside was worth saving, not even the bathroom tiles that were thick with grime because we couldn't afford cleaning supplies.

I quickly take a peek up and down the hallway to make sure Nova isn't hovering before shutting the door quietly behind me. I survey the room in all its glory and drop my bag down by the end of the bed.

The bathroom door is my first stop, peering inside and gawking at the magnificent marble. Everything shines, even the ceiling with its spotlights poking through. It has a huge walk-in glass shower that has a bench inside. Looking closer, I see there's a box with a million buttons and dials inside. It'd better come with a simple hot or cold button, otherwise it will never get used. There's a huge white, cast iron bath to the left, not too far away from the his and hers sinks. Bottles of stuff are set in place on the countertop, along with fresh towels, and a dressing gown is hanging up on the back of the door.

I quickly do my business before heading over to the sink. As I wash my hands, I examine the countertops for a toothbrush and toothpaste. There's nothing. Only bottles of hand wash, shampoo, conditioner and body wash.

I dry my hands with the hand towel hanging over the lip of the sink and notice there are drawers just to the side. I go to pull one open, but it doesn't move, so I shove it. "Damn thing!" I curse. Something clicks and it slowly falls open.

Mouth agape, I notice more toiletries inside, along with a toothbrush, toothpaste, moisturisers and, thank God, a brush. I've had to use my fingers for the past few weeks since mine completely fell apart on me.

It doesn't take me long to wash up. I had a shower this morning in the hotel Nova made us stay at after the funeral. I think she wanted me to say goodbye to it all after Mum's funeral, which is why we didn't go back to the flat. Not that I'm complaining.

Heading back into the bedroom, I go to grab the oversized T-shirt stashed in my bag, but something stops me. I like my things. They're scraps of cloths to other people, but to me, they are the best things I own.

Sighing, I head over to the wardrobe. There's no harm in finding out what damage her housekeeper did.

I have to step back when the doors open.

Holy fucking shit.

"This isn't a wardrobe. This is a fucking bedroom," I murmur, wide-eyed. In the middle of the room is a massive white, suede, round pouffe. "No, it's a fucking clothes shop."

To the left is a row of T-shirts and tops. I run my fingers through them, my nose scrunching up at the pink blouse.

Never going to wear that.

Most are black tank tops, a few T-shirts and other tops that I kind of like but would show too much skin and look ridiculous with my skinny body. My hips might flare out a little but there isn't any meat on them. My mum gifted me with her large breasts, ones that have gotten me into trouble with the men in our block of flats a few times. In my defence, I was a kid and they were staring. It was only fair they got a black eye or a knee to their balls.

The row of tops stop, and in the middle are shelves filled with trainers, some white as snow, some black, some pink, and some cool as fuck boots. I pick up the black pair with laces to the ankle, admiring them. I might have had doubts, but I know there is no way I'm going to pass up wearing these.

On the other side is another row of clothes, these ones coats, jackets and other stuff. I say 'stuff' because I ignore the row of handbags on the thinner set of shelves. I do, however, see the backpack shoved at the bottom, like someone was trying to hide it. I reluctantly grin.

Continuing to walk around, I come to some drawers. Opening them the same way the bathroom one opened, I flick through them. Bra's and underwear are in the first one, bikinis and swimsuits in the second. In the third and fourth is a bunch of sleepwear. I ignore it for the moment, knowing I'll be going back to it for something to sleep in.

There's another set of drawers next to it, but I don't bother looking through them.

The right wall is stacked with jeans first, all in different shades. They look too neatly stacked for me to pull a pair out to check if they are okay or not. I skim past the dressing table, even though the girl inside me does want to know how those skin products feel. I also see another brush.

I roll my eyes when I come to the next row of clothes. It's all dresses. Yeah, I won't be wearing them either.

I head back over to the drawers and push the drawer with the nightwear in. Most of it is thin silk. I pull out the first set; a burgundy colour with black lace around the edges. I hold the silk top up, biting my bottom lip.

What the hell. I've got nothing to lose. I quickly change, marvelling at the feel of the material against my bare skin. The shorts fit snug over my round arse.

I yawn, but I know I won't be able to sleep. It was hard at the hotel last night with no noise whatsoever. I even tried to turn the television on for some white noise, but it wasn't the same as the cacophony of sounds I was used to.

I have a book stored in the bottom of my bag that I can read until I'm sleepy.

I pause when I walk past the mirror, doing a double take of the girl staring back at me. My black hair is tied back with a bobble, but I still notice it has a shine to it that it never had before.

The pyjamas make me groan and aren't something I'd ever pick out for myself, but I can't help but think I look good. My cleavage shows and my legs look longer.

After ten minutes of trying to figure out where the wardrobe's light switches are and then turning them off, I head back over to my bag. I grab the old, withered book I got for free at a car boot sale before flicking one of the lamps off and leaving the other one on.

I grab the throw from the end of the bed and drag it over to the chaise. I stack the pillows against the wall and get comfy, wrapping the blanket over my legs, even if the night air is stifling tonight. It's another reason I'm glad it's meant to rain over the weekend, not that I believe it will happen. They've been saying it for weeks. We're having one heck of a summer.

I'm barely into the new chapter when a squeal gains my attention. I jump, looking through the window at the manor across the way. Most of the lights are out, but one is on in the bedroom opposite.

I shouldn't look, I know it, but when two bodies—two very naked bodies—come into view, I can't look away.

Holy shit!

The guy's headboard is against the window and they're standing at the end, so although the girl's back is to me, giving me a good view of her arse, he's facing me. I could get caught.

If he didn't want someone watching, he should have shut the fucking curtains and turned off the fucking lights.

From what I can make out, he has dark hair—

Oh my God. He lifts the blonde by her hips and throws her down on the bed. I gape at the quick glimpse I get of his athletic body. I'm sad when he crawls up over her, wanting to check him out a little bit more.

A small puff of air escapes between my lips when he grabs onto the headboard with one hand, his other still somewhere on her, and begins to thrust, hard. I can see the bed shaking from here.

My cheeks flame as I watch them, but I can't look away. I don't *want* to look away. I've had one sexual partner in my seventeen years, and although I have nothing to compare it to, it was good. The guy had experience and knew what he was doing. This guy though… he looks like he mastered in sex.

Heat pools between my legs, and I take bets on which one lives there. With my luck, it's the girl who doesn't mind people watching her while she gets fucked.

Or…

I freeze when he lifts his head, and although it's too far to be sure, I know he's looking at me. He could be looking at his reflection in the window, but I'm not that lucky. I can feel the heat of his gaze all over my body.

My lips part, and after a moment, he smirks, then thrusts harder inside the girl. Her scream echoes through his open window and my eyes widen in shock.

Quickly, I throw the blanket off me and run over to my bed, facing away from the window.

Knowing my luck, the hot guy who just caught me watching him have sex lives there.

Crap!

chapter two

The next morning, I take a long, warm shower and grab some clothes out of the wardrobe. Annette either has good taste or she got a sales lady to help her, because most of these clothes are the shit.

Instead of my usual jeans and T, I grab a pair of denim shorts that come to mid-thigh and pair them with a T-shirt that has 'New York' written across my chest area. It looks good. Real good. It feels foreign to have options, to have something that feels so nice against my skin instead of the usual rough material that scratched me.

I didn't see them before, but I grab the closest pair of flip-flops. I've never worn them before, but they're actually comfy. And it's not like I can wear my ratty pumps with clothes this nice.

After what happened last night, I couldn't sleep, so I went mooching through the rest of the drawers. I mostly found girly shit, which is why when I found the dark purple nail polish, I sat and painted my fingernails and toenails. I never understood why the girls at school would do it until then. It made me hate my mum a little bit more for taking another thing away from me. It made me feel feminine, something I'd never felt before in my ratty clothes and lack of girly products.

It's nine, too early to be awake when I was up most of the night, but I woke up with a strange feeling, like someone watching me. I could feel the tingle down my neck. As I rose from the bed, there was no one in sight. It still made it impossible for me to go back to sleep.

I retrace my steps from last night and, thankfully, find the kitchen with only one mistake. The voices echoing outside the entryway have me pausing.

"Why is she here?" the menacing voice asks. "Did you learn nothing from your sister?"

What?

I take another step forward, but Nova's words stop me.

"She's my niece. I don't want her anywhere else. She's nothing like Cara was," Nova argues.

"What about the money? She has rights to that money," the man tells her. "Does she know?"

"She doesn't know, and even if she does, why would I care? She can have it."

"You really have a problem with boundaries, don't you, sweetheart?"

I jump at the raspy voice in my ear. A startled squeak escapes me and I turn to face the guy from last night. Don't tell me how I know, I just do. He's more handsome up close; strong jawline, perfectly shaped lips and dark green, smouldering eyes that girls could get lost in. However, peering closer, I see a void in them I hadn't noticed at first glance.

I can see why the blonde didn't have a problem fucking him with the lights on and curtains open. I'd want to see him too. He has broad shoulders, and his black T-shirt clings to him, giving me a peek of a tattoo wrapped around his bicep. I'm willing to bet my soul his bad boy physique looks better up close and personal.

"Who are you?" I ask.

He looks over my shoulder, pasting on a fake smile. "Nova, morning."

"Ivy, you're up." She sounds surprised and looks kind of fidgety, which makes me question what I just heard even more. Why were they talking about me? And why would he be worried about money? I don't have any. "Morning, Kaiden. I see you've met Ivy, my niece."

"Or she met me," he replies sweetly. He stands so close to me his shoulder is touching mine, and I can smell his woodsy scent. It's enough to make a girl drop her panties. "Isn't that right?"

"Um..." I struggle with what to say, his presence making me dizzy. I've never had this problem before. The old Ivy would have snapped some snarky comeback and walked out of the room. Not this Ivy. She got hit with his beauty and lost her ability to speak.

"Annette is making breakfast. Come on in and take a seat."

I go to follow her inside, highly aware of the large figure looming next to me. I'm pulled back by the hoops of my shorts. I glare up at the handsome devil but don't make a sound, wanting to escape Nova's attention.

He scrutinises every inch of me, his top lip curling in disgust, yet his actions show something different when he runs his finger down my neck. I try to swat him away, but he chuckles low and deep, moving his finger back as he runs it across my cleavage.

My chest rises and falls. Whether it's from fear or want, I don't know. I try to take a step back, his presence doing too much for my libido.

"Get off me," I hiss, glaring up at him.

"Don't think I don't know you were watching me last night. Tell me, did you enjoy the show?"

"Get off me," I hiss louder when he doesn't let go of the loop in my shorts.

He shakes his head, like he's disappointed in me for speaking. "Never forget your place, Ivy."

The way he says my name sends a shiver of fear down my spine, like he knows exactly where I come from, *who* I come from. I watch him swagger past me, his stride assertive and dominant, and the deviant in me wants to lash out, kick the back of his knees or something. Anything to put a stop to that smug swagger he's got going on.

Even with the bad vibes coming off him, I can't help but glance down at his denim-covered arse. I'm a girl after all. All plump, tight and round. He really works those jeans.

Yum.

Shame he's a fucking jackass.

I follow him into the kitchen, and the second I do, Nova tenses, her gaze briefly going to the other man in the room. I ignore Kaiden, eyeing the man watching me with disdain. He's older but looks good for his age. He has light brown hair and dark, soulless eyes. They're almost black and it creeps me out.

"Ivy, I presume."

"Yes," I reply, not bothering to ask who he is. His eyes flare with annoyance, but I don't care.

"As I'm sure you know, I'm Royce Kingsley. I live next door."

I inwardly snort at the entitlement rolling off him. He really believes I should know who he is and either be impressed or awed. I'm neither.

I'm bored.

I ignore him, turning to Nova. "Can I go into town to apply for a job?"

"A job?" Royce asks, like the word is foreign to him. My gaze flicks to Kaiden, and I notice he's just watching me, something working behind those eyes.

"Yes. *A job*. It's where people make money."

"We don't work low-paying jobs," he shoots out snottily. "And I doubt you have the expertise to get anything better. We will not have you ruining our reputation by getting a job as a cashier."

Is this guy for real?

Nova looks uncomfortable about the subject, and I know what Dickhead just said is true. "Nova, you said I could," I remind her.

"Maybe you should take some time to get caught up with studies. We could go to the Academy, take a look around."

I raise my eyebrow. "I'm free to go out, right?"

She sighs, not looking at Dickhead. "Yes."

"I'm going out."

"Wait! I have something for you," she tells me, running to her bag sat on the side. I watch as she pulls out her purse, then walks over to me, handing me a bunch of twenties.

What the fuck does she think I need this for? I have clothes upstairs, food in the cupboards, and right now, that's more than I've ever had in my life. If she thinks she can buy me, she has another thing coming. I'm getting a job. She promised.

"Take this until your debit card comes. I ordered it yesterday," she explains, and I take the cash, not wanting to refuse in front of strangers. I can feel my face flame. "Kaiden, would you be a dear and drive Ivy into town?" Before he can reply, she continues. "Make sure you have your phone, and when you're ready to be picked up, call me."

Wait, what?

"No. I can walk," I tell her, my voice rising a little too loudly.

Her expression can only be one of horror. "No! One, you don't know where it is, and two, it's a little bit far to walk."

"I'll run," I deadpan, not wanting to be alone with Kaiden.

"I'll take her," he says, his voice scratchy.

"Where are the boys?" Royce asks.

"Out," Kaiden replies shortly before looking at me. "I need to be somewhere, so you should go get your phone. I doubt you've got it on you."

I shiver from the way he looks me over, like he's picturing me naked.

I go to refuse, but Nova pushes me back towards the stairs. "Go. Have a look around in town, then come back and I'll show you around the property more."

Mutely, I nod and head back up the stairs. I grab the new phone I turned on last night and head back down. Kaiden is waiting for me, charming Nova like the devil isn't inside of him.

She can't really believe his act, can she?

"Ready?" he rumbles. I nod, then give Nova a chin lift before following him out. He walks across the gravel road, over to his house, where a sports car beeps as he remotely unlocks it.

I don't even know what kind of car it is, but I know it must have cost a mint. Up until now, Kaiden didn't scream rich, just an entitled prick. Even the way he dresses is normal, not what I thought someone with his money would dress like. He seems just like the lads I grew up with, except he clearly knows how to shower and dresses like he owns it.

"Get in," he demands, and I quickly shove myself inside, strapping myself in.

It has that new car smell, and apart from a pack of cigarettes in the compartment under the touchscreen tablet, everything is clean.

Probably hires us poor folk to clean it every day.

I'm pulled out of my musings when he gets into the car, his movements graceful and fluid. He pulls his Ray-Bans down, covering those forest green eyes so I can no longer get a read on him.

He turns the music to a rock station before wheel-spinning out of the driveway. I cling to my seat, my heart racing.

Mum never had a car. The first and only car I got into was Nova's. I flinch when he drives too close to the fence bordering the road.

We pass more houses bigger than the school I went to. They get smaller as we get closer to the gate, and I wonder if that was intentional on the architect's part. Most likely.

He doesn't waste time by chatting to the new security guard, just drives on past like he owns the place.

He kind of does, I remind myself.

As he drives, I glance at the scenery. It's green, with lots of trees and more pretentious housing. I've not seen any run-down houses at all.

Not long into the drive, he pulls over onto the side of a dirt road in front of a gate leading onto a field.

"What are you doing?" I ask, glancing around. There's no sign of civilisation, and a shiver of fear runs down my spine.

"What are you doing here? What's your game?"

"In this car?" I ask, dumbfounded.

I can't see his gaze, but I know it's on me. I can feel the burn on my skin. "No, here with Nova. You're what, eighteen soon? You didn't have to come with her."

Not liking his tone, I sit up straighter in my seat. "It's none of your business."

He smirks, leaning forward in his chair. "That's where you're wrong. It is my business."

I tilt my head, meeting his gaze with a challenge. "How's that?"

"You want money, princess, I'll give it to you. I'm sure I can think of ways for you to pay me back," he drawls.

I lean forward until I can feel his hot breath on my face. The nerve of this guy. "I don't know who the fuck you think you are, but you don't fucking know me."

"I don't?" he asks, not pulling away. I don't either, not wanting to give him the satisfaction.

"No!" I snap. "How dare you!"

"No, how dare you think you can come here. *You*." My back straightens at the way he says 'you', like he knows me. Which is weird because I've never met him before. Pretty sure I'd remember. "Daughter of a whore. You should know, whatever fucking game you're playing, you won't win. I'll fucking destroy you, ruin you."

"Game?" I ask incredulously, not denying my mum is a slag. She was. "I'm not sure what Nova told you, but she wanted me here."

"Yeah, and you came willingly, wanting to sink those fingers into money that isn't yours. But we both know why you're really here," he tells me cryptically.

"Fuck you," I snap, having enough of talking in circles. I feel like I'm missing a crucial part of the story. Before I have the chance to argue any further, he leans closer, his lips a breath away, and I freeze, my mouth going dry.

"Great arse, great tits. Might even be able to get past the rest of you for just those. I think I've even got enough change on me to pay you." He slides his Rays up on his head and glares at me with disdain.

My lips part at his words. Pretending he isn't getting to me isn't going to work much longer.

The moment he touches me, my skin begins to burn, and I try to move back. I'm frozen to my seat when he brings his nose to my exposed neck, running it along my jaw and up to my ear.

"You'd like that, wouldn't you? Do anything for a few quid," he whispers harshly. I jump when he cups my breast, and then slap his hand away.

"Get the fuck off me."

He chuckles dryly, eyeing me up and down, making me feel naked and exposed. "Yeah, money-hungry slut. Get out."

"What?" I gasp, trying to wipe off the effects of him touching me has left. I meet his gaze to see if he's being serious, but he's showing nothing, his expression blank.

"Need me to dumb it down? I said, get the fuck out. I've said what I needed to." Short, curt, and he means it.

"You're gonna leave me here? I don't even know where *here* is," I screech at him.

He sighs, turning the car off and opening his door. I panic when he walks around the other side, and I'm almost tempted to lock the doors and jump in the driver's seat. But I have no idea how to drive.

He can't really be doing this.

He opens the door and leans in to unclip me, purposely making his fingers brush over my breasts, before dragging me out of the car. I'm in a haze, so I don't fight. He really is going to leave me here, wherever here is. On my own.

"Kaiden, let me go," I start, coming to terms with what's happening. I'd beg, but that's one thing I'll never do, especially not to him.

He slams the door shut behind me before pushing me against the car, which, hot with the summer heat, burns into my back. I wince.

"Listen. Know your place when you're here. You don't belong. Never will. Don't go snooping into things you have no business being in. And last warning: we'll be watching you."

"Are you fucking serious," I yell.

He stares at me dead on, no emotion behind those forest green eyes as he replies, "Deadly."

"Wait," I yell, going to grab his arm. He shoves me off and I trip, falling to the floor. My arse and palms sting, almost bringing tears to my eyes. *Almost.*

I've not cried since I was little and learned that it got you nowhere. I didn't even cry when they told me my mother died, or the day she was cremated and buried.

"Never touch me," he snaps, looking deadlier than I've seen him yet. I knew he was dangerous, but this is more, and I know I'll have to watch my back if I'm to stay here. "Just like your mum, down on her back."

His leaving comment hardens another part inside of me, and I get up from the floor, dusting myself off. I lean down, picking up a rock, and before he can pull off, I aim at his back window and throw. It smashes from the force, and I grin to myself before picking up another and walking over to it.

I reach the back of the car with a smirk on my face, and slowly, I dig the stone into his red, flashy paintwork and run it along. The door opens and he slowly gets out, and my back straightens. I expected him to get mad, to yell at me, but this seems much worse. I don't cower though. Instead, I stand taller, showing him that I won't be pushed around like some new toy Daddy bought him.

"Never, and I mean, *never*, lay a fucking hand on me again. Never speak to me that way either. Stay out of my way, and I'll stay out of yours. I'm here a year. I'm sure someone like you doesn't feel that threatened by a nobody like me."

His glasses are back on, so I can't read what he's thinking. Even his body language isn't giving anything away, which makes it all the worse.

He takes two steps to reach me before leaning down, his face so close to mine. "You'll regret that, princess."

He doesn't say anything else to me, just folds himself into the car and screeches off, his tyres kicking up dirt, causing stones to hit the bottom of my legs.

My hands shake as I sit back on my haunches, wondering what the fuck I just did. He's not like the guys I'm used to. He's in a league of his own.

A dangerous one.

And I just seriously pissed him off.

Shit!

chapter three

I'm fuming by the time I make it into town. My feet are killing me. I'm pretty sure my blisters have blisters.

He wasn't just a jerk; he was a fucking wanker.

And to make matters worse, this isn't a town. It's a few shops in a small area surrounded by a few town houses. It's like I've hit a place where there is zero population in the middle of nowhere. There are no charity shops, no banks, no take-out joints, nothing. Just a corner shop, a flower shop, and a couple of others that hold no appeal to me.

The amount of horse shit I saw on the way over made me want to puke. It was worse than the dog shit that would litter the streets where I lived before.

I sit on the steps of the church, eating a breakfast bar I grabbed from the corner shop. A corner shop that literally sells fags, booze, and a few bits and pieces. When I asked where a Tesco or a Morrisons was, the guy looked at me and laughed. Actually laughed. He said folk—yes, he actually used that word—had their shopping delivered.

I guess rich people didn't want to get their hands dirty by going to something as small as a grocery shop. Heaven forbid they get caught in the condom aisle.

Grabbing the phone Nova bought me, I flick through the contacts and decide to text her. If I speak to her right now, I'll lose my mind. She let me go with that—that… moron, and what's worse, she acted like the sun shone out of his arse.

I'm thinking a year here is going to be harder than I thought. There is nothing here. Nothing I can do to keep my mind off things. There isn't even a skateboard park—not that I have a skateboard anymore. The one I snatched after finding it abandoned at the park near me, broke last summer. This is an endless place of nothing. I might die of boredom.

Nova texts straight back to say she's on her way.

I wait, watching the few people walk by. This is nothing like the place I lived. There're no bags of rubbish outside on the pavement, no gangs of kids on the street corners causing mayhem, and everything is clean. I swear, the pavements are cleaner than the carpet in our old flat.

I've never seen anything like it. Hell, I didn't think a place like this existed. I kind of miss the noise of traffic, kids causing trouble and couples arguing. Silence isn't something I'm used to.

And then there's Kaiden, a new brand of male. I've never encountered a jerk like him, and I've met plenty.

"Are you lost, dear?" I turn to the old lady walking her two Beagles. She has to be in her fifties or sixties, easily.

"Depends who you're asking," I mumble, taking a swig of Coke. It's getting hotter and sweat is running down my back.

"Ah, I've been there. You don't live around here," she states, and I guess I have a plaque on my forehead that screams, 'Doesn't belong'.

"Nope. I just moved in with my aunt. My mum died," I tell her.

She walks up the steps after tying her two dogs to the end of the rail. "You don't look too upset about it."

Is she for real? Why is she talking to me?

"I'm not."

"Weren't sad to see my mum go either. Best thing to ever happen to me."

That piques my interest. "How's that?"

She helps herself to one of my chocolate bars, peeling off the wrapper. I fight the smile threatening. She really gives no shits. I kind of like that about her.

"Was a mean woman. Should never have had kids. Couldn't hold a job either, not that I think she ever had one."

"You don't look like someone who grew up poor," I murmur bitterly. In fact, she's dressed in a pantsuit, even though she's only walking her dogs. You'd think she was on her way to a wedding; which she could be, for all I know.

She laughs. "I was. I just didn't let that control my life. Most people who grow up in poverty feel like they deserve to be there, so they never try hard enough to get themselves out."

Her words hit me like a train. It wasn't too long ago I was thinking the same thing. I don't fit in here and to be honest, back home, I was settled. I knew my life was never going to get much better; the most I'd get was a job that paid a good wage.

"What if that person really does belong there?" I ask curiously. I've got no idea why I'm talking to her, but it's not like she's given me a choice. That and she's the only one I've seen today who hasn't given me side-eyes or watched me like a hawk. One woman, who was pushing a pram with her kid inside, moved to the other side of the road when she saw me coming.

"That's BS."

"BS?" I laugh. The words leaving her mouth are hilarious.

"No one belongs in a life like that. Is that what your life was like before your aunt?"

"I guess, in a way. I've only been here a night," I confess, still wondering what the fuck is wrong with me. Usually, by now I've told the person to fuck off and leave me alone. I'm not really social. My mum, on the other hand, was, and I think that's why I'm not.

"Where are you staying?"

"Anyone ever tell you you're nosey?"

She laughs, finishing her—no, *my* chocolate bar. "You seem like someone I can be around."

At her shrug, I watch her for any catch. "What, you want to be bingo buddies?" I snark.

"Testy," she remarks. "No. But when I see a beautiful girl looking sad and lost, I want to brighten her day."

"So, you feel sorry for me?" I didn't mean for it to come out so harshly, but it does. "Sorry."

"It's fine. I am curious though… Why hang out here?"

I sigh. "Like I said, I've been here a day. And my aunt Nova said it was a town."

She laughs at my expression, patting my knee. "If you want shopping malls, cinemas and all that, it's another thirty-minute drive. There is a bus that runs every twenty minutes going to and from," she informs me. "Wait, by any chance are you talking about Nova Monroe?"

"Jesus, it really is a small town. And yes," I inform her.

"Bad time of it that one," she murmurs.

"What do you—"

"Ivy. Mrs White," Nova calls through her open window.

"Your aunt has my address. If you want, you can come help me on the weekends."

"Help with what?" I ask, holding my finger up to Nova.

Mrs White grins at me. "Strawberry picking. My husband's arthritis is acting up so he's not been able to help me much. I could use a young, fit girl like you. Wouldn't be able to pay much, but you have to start somewhere."

I have so many more questions, but Nova calling my name again has me standing up.

"I'll ask her. Thank you. My name's Ivy, by the way."

"You're welcome. And call me Elle. Mrs White makes me feel old."

"You are old," I tell her without meaning to. I groan. Did I mention I was dragged up, not brought up?

"Call me old again and I won't invite you to bingo night. It can get rowdy, I tell ya."

"Take your word for it," I tell her, and this time I can't help but grin.

As I reach the car, Elle calls me back. "If you do turn up Saturday—early—you might want to wear different shoes."

At that, the throbbing comes back, and I wince. "Will do."

"That was quick," Nova comments as I get back in the car and pull the belt across me.

"There's nothing here," I whine.

She chuckles. "What was you talking to Mrs White about?"

She tries to act natural, but there's something else there; worry maybe?

"She asked me to help her on Saturday."

Seeing her visibly relax in her seat has me raising an eyebrow. Yeah, definitely hiding something from me.

Which reminds me of Kaiden.

"Nova, what is Kaiden to you?"

"What do you mean?" she asks, looking briefly at me.

"Just—you seem pretty… close."

"I've watched him grow up. I'm his godmother," she tells me, and I all I can think is, *great*. There's no way she'll take my side over his when I tell her what the jerk did. Might as well keep it to myself. "Which reminds me. He came back after dropping you off." I snort, interrupting her. Bet he didn't say *where* he dropped me off. "What?"

"Nothing, carry on."

"He and his brothers—"

"Hold the fuck up. He has brothers?" I ask, wondering which one is more of a nightmare; my old life or this new one.

She laughs, nodding. "Yes. Twins; Ethan and Lucca. They are your age."

"Oh God," I moan, resting my head back against the seat.

"Anyway, they came over earlier and Kaiden made a good point. He said it would be good for you to get to know them since you are practically living on top of each other and will be starting Kingsley Academy come September. The twins are having a party Saturday night and will have a few friends from Kingsley Academy attending. They want you to go."

"They actually said that?" I ask, not believing a word. She's clearly pushed them into it. Or paid them. And twins… God, what the hell am I gonna do if they're bigger dicks than their brother?

"Yes. They popped by as soon as Kaiden arrived home. They seemed excited."

"I bet," I mutter. "I'd rather not."

"Ivy," she warns. "It won't hurt you to get along with them. Please, just try. If you don't like it, come home. You'll only have to walk across the garden."

"Can I think about it?"

I notice we're getting closer to Nova's housing community. I'm hoping I can relax in my room or maybe somewhere in the garden. Alone.

"No."

The kick out of it? If I want a better life, a start to get me somewhere, then I need her. I'm not naïve enough to say otherwise. I know I can make it on my own, but it comes at a cost. It comes with being scared to go to sleep at night, too hungry to even think about food because it just makes you hungrier. But I'll do it if I have to.

Right now, I don't, and I will take the help she's offering, just as long as she knows I'll never ask for anything.

"Oh, I had Annette's husband grab an old bike out of the garage. If you want to use it to get into town, feel free."

"Where does Mrs White live?"

"Did you see the house we passed five minutes ago?"

"The one near the field with all the horses?"

"Yes. She lives there with her husband. She used to own the land the horses are on, but they gave it to their son and daughter-in-law when it became too much for Mr White. She has her garden though, and it's famous for her strawberries."

Since that house was only a few minutes away, I could use the bike to ride there. Because one thing is for sure, I'm not hanging around in that house all day.

"I'll use the bike to go there then. She said she couldn't pay me much," I tell her, but it's better than I've had.

"You don't need to work there. I thought you were just helping her out, which is great."

"You said I could get a job," I remind her.

"I didn't think you would. You don't need to. I can give you money while you concentrate on school."

"Kingsley Academy hasn't even started, and I want to make my own money. I'm appreciative of your help, Nova, I really am, but I'm not some money grabber."

We pass the same security guard as earlier, and he waves us in.

"I didn't say you were. I'd never think that."

I gaze out the window, not looking at her. "But I would."

"Just think about it," she tells me, but it sounds like an order, one I won't follow. She'll learn that quickly.

We pull up outside her garage and, unconsciously, I begin to examine the house next door when I get out. Unlike the other houses in the gated community that are spread apart, these two are close together, like the occupants, at one point, were best friends and it got passed down through generations.

But it's not just that. Nova's, although clean and pretentious, is nothing like the one next door. You can see there have been updates made, and the stone pillars just make them look more snobbish. I mean, who do they think they are? Royals?

"Still got a problem with minding your own," a deep voice rumbles.

I startle at Kaiden's voice yet narrow my eyes when my gaze lands on him.

"What did you say?" Nova calls out, bringing her head out from the back of the car, her hands filled with a small laptop case.

"I said, mind your feet. They look sore," he calls back, stepping closer.

Nova looks confused for a moment, staring down at her feet before looking at mine. "How long were you gone? Your feet look sore, Ivy."

No shit. And it's all thanks to that arsehole.

I smile sweetly at him. "They'll be fine. Thanks for your concern." I peek behind me and a sly smirk reaches my lips. "Nasty work someone's done on your paintwork. Pissed off the wrong person?"

"Ivy," Nova gasps, before looking at Kaiden. "Sorry about that."

"Don't apologise for me," I bark snottily.

Kaiden just smiles, and it's so fake I want to puke. "It's okay, Nova. Clearly someone mistook me for someone they could fuck over."

Her nose scrunches up. "Don't go getting into trouble, Kai. I'm sure the police can handle it."

"Where's the fun in that?" he tells her, but his gaze is burning into mine.

"Right, I need to get some work done. Ivy, if you want a late brunch, let Annette know. I'll be in my office."

I watch her leave before turning to Kaiden. "You're a dickhead for leaving me there on the side of the road. It took me an hour to get into town because I didn't know the way," I snap.

"Keep running your mouth and I'll find something to fill it."

The calmness in his voice sends a shiver down my spine. I straighten, stepping away from the car.

"*Find* being the key word, right?" I say, looking down at his crotch to emphasise my meaning.

"Oh, I'm going to enjoy breaking you."

He walks off, leaving me standing there, breathless. After a minute of him being inside, I stick my middle finger up, feeling pathetic. He's not even there to see it.

When footsteps near, I look up to find Annette walking towards me with a tray of food in her hand.

After staying in my room for two hours, I got bored and decided to check the place out. After getting bored of that, I grabbed the tatty book from my room, a seat cushion from a deck chair in the garden and headed outside to sit under the tree.

The place really is beautiful. Even the air smells different here. It feels clean, fresh, something I've never smelled before.

Nova mentioned last night that Annette lived at the back of the house with her husband. She was right; the small bungalow sat just to the side of the property in the main garden, which has a freaking pool. I ventured further, stepping through the arched, freshly trimmed bushes and into a clearing where a massive pond is. I was far enough away from the house to not feel like an unwanted guest and far enough out of the way of the deep, dark pond.

"Ivy, I brought you out a sandwich. I wasn't sure what you'd like so I just went with one turkey and one cheese."

"Um, thank you." I take the tray from her, and I thought she'd leave. Instead, she grabs a blanket from the bag I hadn't seen she was carrying, laying it out on the ground.

"I wasn't sure if you had anything to sit on. I can see you have. I was worried about you sitting in an ants' nest."

Wouldn't be the first time, I muse as I place the tray on the blanket and grab a turkey sandwich.

"How did you know I was here?" I ask curiously.

She smiles gently. "I saw you head out this way. It's a beautiful spot."

"It is."

"I'd best be going. I need to take Miss Monroe her lunch."

"Thank you—for the sandwich," I tell her, holding up the sandwich higher.

I take a huge bite whilst trying to get back into the book. It's boring as hell, but it's the only thing I have. Maybe when I get paid, Nova will take me to the library.

If they have one.

I've not even finished the first sandwich when more footsteps near. I look up, scrunching my eyes when two identical looking lads walk towards me with so much swagger it's almost cringeworthy. They work it though, both hot as hell.

I guess this is Lucca and Ethan, Kaiden's brothers.

Both look like the man I met this morning at Nova's breakfast table. They both have light brown hair, unlike Kaiden's dark hair, and the same facial features as their father, just younger and better looking.

I can't see the colour of their eyes because both are wearing shades. I do scan their physiques over once again. They're in shape, both have a good amount of muscle.

Yet they seem more laid back than Kaiden in their shorts and tank tops.

When they get closer, both of them grin at each other.

"Lucca and Ethan, I take it?" I mutter when they're close enough to hear.

Their grins spread wider. "She's heard of us already," the one wearing the red shorts chuckles.

"Something like that," I tell him, trying to figure them out.

They might seem friendly, but they look unpredictable.

"Thinks she wants a go?" Blue shorts says to his brother.

"Slags always want a go," Red shorts replies.

"Would you like me to leave you two alone?" I ask sarcastically, deciding to get up and head inside.

I begin to shake off the grass that has somehow managed to get on my legs, when they step closer.

"W-what are you doing?"

They begin to circle me, and I start to feel dizzy.

"What are we doing, Lucca?"

Ah, so Red shorts is Lucca and Blue shorts is Ethan. Good to know. Let's hope they keep to the colours every day.

"Having some fun," Lucca replies.

I go to step forward when they give me an opening, but Lucca pushes me against Ethan.

"I heard she likes it rough," Ethan whispers in my ear.

I jump away, glaring at him. "Fuck off."

"Tell me, little one, just how rough do you like it? Because we tag team. Although, someone like you is probably used to having every hole used."

"I said, fuck off!" I snap, yelping when Ethan pushes me into Lucca.

I try to shove off, but Lucca grabs me around the waist, holding me to his body, one of his hands grasping my tit.

Another hard body steps up behind me, pressing his dick against my back, and butterflies flutter in my stomach.

"Go, now," I yell, trying to get free, but with another pair of hands gripping me in place, I have no hope. Ethan's fingers run along my stomach where my top has risen, and my mind begins to race. I've encountered arseholes before, even fought off advances from grown-arse men Mum brought back with her, but this… this is something else. I wasn't expecting this.

"No!" I yell, trying to fight them off.

"Do you think it's passed down?" Ethan asks cryptically.

"You wondering what makes *her* special too?"

"Must have a magic pussy. Wonder if her daughter does too," Ethan drawls, his fingers now running over my denim-covered sex.

I squeak, getting pissed off with all the cryptic comments going back and forth. Both have charming characteristics and confidence, with a big ego that would make people believe them over me if I said they were terrorising me. Not that I'd grass. But you can believe your sweet arse I'd get revenge. And if I get caught, no one will believe me over them.

When he moves his fingers back to my top, exposing more of my midriff, I slap his hand away and shove it back down.

Wrong move.

Lucca is drawn to my cleavage that has popped out more from shoving my top down.

"We should have a taste."

"Kaiden would be pissed if we played with his new toy," Ethan replies, but doesn't sound upset over it.

"Fuck this," I snap, and before Lucca can get any more handsy, I knee him in the balls. He drops to his knees, grasping his junk.

"Fucking bitch," he wheezes.

Ethan begins to laugh, helping his brother back to his feet before they both turn to me.

"You're tougher than we thought."

"You think this is a fucking joke? You just sexually assaulted me," I snap, grabbing my book from the floor. Annette can get the rest of the shit herself. I storm off, ignoring their laughter.

"Love, we did you a favour."

I spin around at Ethan's voice, and I know it's his because his is deeper, whereas Lucca's is raspy.

"Did me a favour?" I ask in disgust. God, I need to get drunk.

He grins, eyeing me up and down. "You need to be strong for what he has planned for you. We were checking if you were—that and we're arseholes."

"What are you talking about?" I ask, tugging my hair from my face.

"Kaiden," Lucca tells me, still catching his breath.

"Are you fucking kidding me? This is about your brother?"

Ethan laughs. "Love, you have no idea. We were going to fuck with you either way, just the usual, but you pissed off our brother. And when he gets mad, he gets even and then some. I'd watch it if I were you."

"Why can't you all just stay out of my way?" I snap.

He shrugs. "You don't belong."

Oh, no, not this again. "You guys need to grow the fuck up. You make it sound like I bribed my way here and am holding Nova under protest. I'm not. She invited me here."

"You really don't know, do you?" Ethan asks, scanning my face closely.

"Know what?" I yell, throwing my hands up. "I've been here a day."

Lucca looks at Ethan and shrugs. "If I were you, I'd keep it that way."

I scream in frustration when they walk past me.

"Oh, and Ivy… great tits."

"Fantastic arse," Ethan finishes.

Anger boils inside of me and I storm in the direction of the house. There are secrets here, and I intend to find out why. There's no guessing it has to do with Mum and why she isn't a part of this life. It's also the reason those boys have gone out of their way to make my life hell.

If they think I'm going to roll over and cry, they're wrong. If Kaiden wants to fight, he's got it. I'll fight back.

First though, it's time to find out who my mum really was.

chapter four

IT'S MY FIFTH DAY HERE AT THE MANOR. Five days with my aunt, trying to get a feel for her. All I've figured out about her is that she loves her work as a lawyer and has worked from home since I arrived. Whether that's to keep an eye on me or because this is normal, I have no clue. If I were to guess, she wants to keep an eye on me.

I'm losing my mind though. The weather is scorching hot and I feel like I can't breathe. I've gone for a walk around the property but haven't gone too far due to the blisters that have finally gone down today.

"Fuck this," I mutter, getting up from my bed. Shoving my phone in my back pocket, I slide on a pair of pumps and head out.

About an hour ago, Nova went out to run some errands. Whatever that meant. She didn't take Annette with her so it can't be shopping. I snort at the thought of my aunt walking into a Tesco. She'd stand out like a sore thumb.

I walk through the house until I get to the side I've not ventured down before. Annette explained it's the side where Nova sleeps and keeps her office. Thinking that is where I will find answers, I push through the door to the office.

The desk sits in the middle of the room, the chair facing the door. Shelves and filing cabinets line each of the sides.

I step over to the shelves, seeing some pictures. Nova has her arm wrapped around an older couple, standing somewhere close to the beach.

Must be nice.

I've never been to a beach, never been on holiday. A holiday to me was not having to listen to my mum have sex in the next room.

Another picture captures my eye and this time it's one of my mum and Nova as teenagers, maybe fifteen or sixteen. They're standing in front of two horses, Nova smiling at the camera, yet Mum has her head tilted towards the ground a little. Even seeing them so young, I can tell they were polar opposites. Nova is dressed to the nines whilst Mum is wearing a skimpy top and low-riding jeans.

I pick up the picture, scanning my mum all over. I was right; she was once beautiful, even though she still had that hard edge towards her.

Seeing my mum like this, in that environment, bothers me more than it should. I'm about to leave when a picture sticking out between two books catches my eye.

I pull it out, seeing a group photo with Mum, Nova, three men and two other women. Mum looks completely different. Her hair is a light brown colour with flecks of blonde in it. She's beaming at her sister, who has her arm tucked around her. I'm mind blown, completely in shock. Even her clothes are different to the ones she is wearing in the other photo and it can't be that much older.

She looks stunning.

For the first time, I take a closer look at the other people in the picture. The one on the other end is a tiny girl with dark blonde hair that looks knotted. She's so tiny that the large lad with his arm wrapped around her shoulders, shadows over her. Next to them is another couple, and the man looks vaguely like the guy I met downstairs my first day here. Royce, if I'm remembering correctly. He looks just as intimidating in this picture, the same cunning look in his eye. A dark-haired woman is curled around him, looking so in love it's kind of sickening.

The dark-haired man with his arm wrapped around Nova's waist looks familiar too. I just can't remember where to place him. Which is weird, because I'd remember meeting someone like him before.

Seeing this is like a slap in the face. I really didn't know my mum. Something happened between this photo being taken and the one with her sister beside their horses.

A door shutting echoes in the distance, and I shove the photo back on the shelf before racing out of the office.

I need to get out of here. I need to breathe.

"Ivy, is that you?" Nova calls up the stairs.

I hit the top of the stairs just as she takes her first step. Flushed and panicked, I move past her, unable to look her in the eye. She follows behind me.

"Can I borrow that bike?"

"Um, yeah, it's just inside of the garage door. Ivy, is everything okay?"

"Yes. I need to get to Elle's house."

"I thought you might have changed your mind," she says, but I don't look at her, needing to get out of here. "Don't forget the party later. I expect you to be there, Ivy. It will be good to make friends."

I snort as I lift a leg over the bike. *Friends.* They wouldn't know the meaning. She's meant to be a lawyer. Shouldn't she see past the façade they put on?

"I'll try."

"Ivy," she warns in that snotty tone. "You'll go. Kai stopped me before I left earlier to remind you to wear a swimsuit."

"Whatever," I yell and peddle my way out of there as fast as I can. I'm nearing the bottom of the hill when a car I recognise speeds up, nearly knocking me off the road. "Wanker!"

Laughter fills the car as it comes to a stop, but I ignore it, following the road down to the front gate.

♡

I SKID TO A stop outside Elle's house—well, I'm hoping it's hers—and take a look around. It's big, but nowhere near as big as the enormous houses back in the gated community. This looks homier with its perfectly planted flowers and seat swing at the front.

Who am I kidding. I don't even know why I'm here. The lady is old and probably won't even remember me. I don't know her, either, yet she's been the only one open with me since I arrived. Even Nova closes up during conversations, and it bugs me.

I go to push off when Elle stands up from behind the hedges, tipping her sun hat up. "Are you going to stare at my home or come and help me pull these weeds up?"

"Um..."

"Child, come and help."

At her order, I swing my leg off the bike and lean it against the hedge. I push through the gate to find Elle back on her knees, yanking out weeds.

She pats a foam board next to her. "Don't stand there all day, girl. Get pulling."

Slowly, I kneel on the foam and take the gloves she hands me. I look to her side, noticing it looks like fresh soil around some beautiful yellow and blue flowers. My side looks a mess.

"See these," she tells me, pointing to some dry, ugly looking leaves. "They're pretty much dead. With the heatwave this year, we've had to water them a lot more. Which means weeds still grow."

"Which ones are weeds?" I ask, feeling stupid.

"Much easier to tell you which aren't," she says and points in a pattern of where the flowers are planted. "Now, pull the rest out. I'll start turning soil over once you've done it. Shouldn't take us long, then I can show you the strawberries. They're ready early this year."

"Do you only grow strawberries?" I ask, pulling out a weed.

"No. I grow everything. Next to my strawberries, I grow the best watermelon around."

After that, we keep quiet, only talking when really necessary. My skin is burning, sweat is pouring off me, and my throat is dry.

"Come on. Let's take a break before we do the plants," Elle says, dusting the dirt off her knees. I wipe my forehead with the top of my arm. I'm sure I've got dirt all over me, not just my bottom half.

Elle follows the path to her back garden, and I follow her, my body dragging as exhaustion hits.

Bloody heat.

"Take a seat in the shade," she orders, pointing to the table and chairs under a sun umbrella. Happily, I do, feeling my bones crack and muscles groan.

"Who are you?" a deep voice growls. I stand up quickly, seeing an older gentlemen marching up the path.

"Um, I'm—"

"I'm calling the police. We don't have anything valuable," he snaps, eyeing me with disdain.

Everything here is valuable, it's just not valuable in money. I keep my thoughts to myself and tighten my lips at him.

Elle steps out, her smile brightening when she sees the man. "Ed, meet Ivy, Nova Monroe's niece."

"She doesn't have a niece," he says, not taking his gaze from me.

"Yes, she does. This is her. Now lose the frown. She's a guest," she orders him, handing me a glass of what I hope is iced lemonade. I waste no time in gulping it down, not stopping to take a breath. "I'll go get you another."

Her laughter fades as she moves back into the kitchen. I turn back to Ed, glaring back at him. If he thinks I'm going to suck up to him just to change his perception of me then he's wrong.

"One thing goes missing, girly, and I'll be phoning the police."

"Carry on. I'm not a thief," I snap.

"Not what gossip around here is saying."

"Excuse you, but I've been to town once in the five days I've been here. All my time has been spent at the house I can assure you. You shouldn't listen to idle gossip. If I were going to steal, I would have done it when I was hungry or when I needed some shampoo, not when I have more than I've had in my life."

He watches me a minute before shrugging and taking a seat at the table. I slowly sit down opposite him, wondering what he's going to do.

"Never listened to town gossip. Uptight people around here don't know what's going on inside their own houses, much less someone else's."

"So why did you—"

"My Elle is a good woman. She's had a tough life and has been walked on by some of the people around here. And no offence, love, but you look like someone who is ready to murder the next person they see."

"Here you go," Elle says, bringing out a jug and filling my glass up.

"Thank you," I tell her, drinking it more slowly this time.

"How did it go, sweetie?"

Ed looks to his wife, rolling his eyes. "My heart is fine, Elle. I keep telling you that. All is good."

"I'll ask Lewis later."

He groans. "Woman, I'm fine!"

"I'll ask Lewis," she confirms, looking from him to me. "Now that we have five minutes, do you want to tell me what's bothering you?"

I look between them. "Nothing is bothering me."

Ed groans as he lifts up from his chair. "My game show starts soon."

"You mean you need a nap?" Elle calls out after him.

"Woman, I rest my eyes."

"Yeah, yeah," she mutters before bringing her gaze back to me. "Now, spill."

"There's nothing to spill."

She raises her eyebrow at me. "A girl like you always has something to spill. You're hot gossip around here."

"So I've heard," I mutter dryly.

"Look, we might not know each other, child, but you can trust me. Something tells me you don't trust a lot of people in your life, and around here, that will get you eaten. Everyone is out for themselves and you need someone on your side."

"And you're that person?"

"Not if you don't want me to be," she tells me, and I can see the truth on her face.

I sigh, leaning back in the chair, feeling the sting of sunburn on my back. "I don't know my mum."

"I thought your mum died?" she asks, her lips twisting in confusion.

"She did. But I feel like I didn't even know her. She was a shit mum, didn't really care if I was fed or clothed, yet I loved her just enough to put up with it and learn to take care of myself." I take a deep breath, not used to confiding in anyone. "Since I've come here I feel like people know more about me than I do, more about my mum. It's like there's this black cloud over her name, but everyone is talking in riddles. Then earlier, I found a photo of my mum. She looked so different, so young and happy, and I've never seen that side to her. Hell, I didn't even know we had other family members. It's always been just us."

"She was a happy child," Elle agrees, and my eyes widen.

"You knew my mum?"

"Girl, everyone knew your mum. She was a sweetheart, always helping out at church, school clubs and social events. You name it, your mum was involved."

Perplexed, I can only stare into space for a moment, digesting everything she just said. "My mum was a drunk, a smackhead and a bum. We were poor as dirt and have been squatting in an old block of flats, scrounging for food. That doesn't sound like my mum."

"Not sure what happened—we were busy with the stables—but she seemed to change overnight. Gone was the sweet girl everyone knew and in her place was a young woman, rebelling at everything."

"You don't know what happened?"

She doesn't meet my gaze. "It's not for me to tell you, child. Ask your aunt. There were a lot of rumours around at that time."

"When did she leave here, this place? I don't understand; if she had all of this, then why did she leave or not ask for help?"

"That, I don't know. We watched her lose herself over the years. By the time all of her friends got married, had kids and stuff, she got worse. She didn't hang out with them, mind you. She rarely hung around here at all, but a few days before she left, everyone felt the tension. We knew something bad was happening. Then she was just gone. It took a month for us to realise she wasn't coming back. She'd taken off from time to time since finishing school, but never for that long."

"She just left and no one said anything?" I ask sceptically.

"Yes. Rumours were going around, mind you. One was that she had died, that Royce Kingsley killed her."

"Royce Kingsley?" I ask, listening now. He was one of the guys in the picture.

Her lips twist. "Yes. He was in their group of friends, but a bad seed that one. And Neil Tucker. Both of them had the wool pulled over everyone's eyes, but I could see them for who they really were."

"I don't—I don't understand."

She places her hand on mine. "I've probably said too much. Just be careful of Royce and Neil. Your mum wasn't born the woman she died as. She was forced to be it, and if I were to guess, it was to protect herself the only way she knew how."

She stands before I get the chance to ask any more questions, and I have a trillion of them. However, I have more to go on than I did when I woke up this morning.

Something happened, something so bad my mum changed who she was and turned to drink and drugs to cope with it.

I just need to find out why or who.

I guess I'm going to a party after all.

chapter five

I STAND AT THE BACK GATE OF THE Kingsley's property, fidgeting with the edge of my ripped denim shorts. I've never been to a party before, not like this. The parties I went to involved a bottle of cheap beer or cider, sitting in the park. We played music from our phones or just hung around chatting shit, while the lads looked for trouble.

This party is something else. Music is blaring, and I can hear girls squealing and giggling. I can hear splashes as well, which is why I headed this way instead of going through the front door. My first idea was to go that way so I could ease into the party and maybe pretend to get lost—which wouldn't be an overstatement since their house is huge—then snoop around.

Then my mind drifted to Kaiden. Something tells me he's the kind of guy who would be seeking me out. The front door would be the best place to do that, which is why I avoided going that way.

Which leads me to here. Our main gardens are fenced off with perfectly trimmed evergreen shrubs, but the rest of the land behind me is shared.

Pushing open the gate, my eyes widen at the scene in front of me. Girls in barely-there bikinis, some not even wearing the top half, are laying around the large pool and hot tub. All of a sudden, I feel overdressed, and before I was panicking about being underdressed in only my denim shorts and white tank top.

People are drinking, smoking, and if I can believe my eyes, one table are snorting up coke.

This is not how I expected one of their parties to go. At all. Kaiden doesn't seem the type to be social. However, this is the twins' birthday, so maybe they are.

Yeah, I really need to get out of here, but first, I need to find answers that might be in that house.

Finding the wide double doors that lead into the house, I take a step in that direction, when a tall, dark figure steps out in front of me, startling me.

"Sorry," I excuse myself, going to step around him, but he sides-steps me, caging me in.

"What the fuck are you doing here?"

Is this guy for real? Wait, is there anyone who doesn't know who I am?

"Was there an announcement on Facebook or something? I'm flattered and all, but this is too much. Now move out of my way," I snap, moving around him.

He blocks my path again, glaring holes into me with those dark eyes of his. "I said, what. The. Fuck. Are. You. Doing. Here."

"Who are you?"

He blinks, grabbing my biceps. "You don't get to ask questions, bitch. Now, why the fuck are you here? Come to score? Get laid? 'Cause I'm telling you, no one is buying what you're selling."

This guy is a serious fucking jerk. I take a step forward, poking my finger against his chest. "What the fuck is wrong with you people? You don't even know me to talk crap about me. Who the fuck do you think you are?"

He smirks, but his eyes roll in disgust. "Trust me, we know who you are, and who I am doesn't fucking concern you."

I don't like the tone in which he says it. I don't. I push past him again, and he lets me, but I don't get far before he's gripping my bicep, hard enough to leave a bruise this time. I shove him off, ready to knee him in the balls.

"Watch your back. Your kind aren't welcome here," he sneers.

"I must be an alien," I snap, wondering what kind I am. There is no way they know where I've come from, and even if they do, it doesn't make me a different species. For rich guys, they are pretty dumb. "And word of advice, the last person to touch me without permission is probably still icing his precious jewels."

He glares for a moment longer before storming off, shoving his shoulder into me. I fall to the side and collapse against a table, spilling drinks and glasses. The crowd cheers when they hear them break, and I close my eyes in embarrassment.

Getting up, I wipe the drink from my hands. I thought I could do this; get in there and look around before leaving. I can't though. I've been here five minutes and a wolf came out to play.

"Seems you've pissed the prince off." I look up to the girl who just spoke and groan. She's represents everything Barbie, with fake boobs, dyed hair and clearly showing signs of having work done on her face.

"Looks like," I snark. I'm pissed about the alcohol on my top—not because it's going to stain, but because it's got that smell I loathe.

"You really should watch your back. You'll never fit in here."

I look up from wiping my top and tilt my head at her. "Because I don't have fake boobs, blonde hair and plaster my makeup on?"

Her eyes narrow into slits and her lips press together in a firm line. "No, because you're a nobody. You'll never be one of us, even if you are living with Miss Monroe." She cackles, eyeing me like a peasant. "You've got balls coming to this party, I'll give you that. But don't, for one second, think that they want you here. They hate you. Everything about you."

"Katrina, don't you have a hole to be filled?"

I look over my shoulder to see both twins step up behind me. I'm kind of pissed I'm relieved to see them. I was seconds away from making a fool of myself.

She pastes on a fake smile for the twins. "Don't be so crass, Ethan."

"Don't be such a bitch then."

Her top lip curls at him. "You're sticking up for her? Does your brother know? Grant?" She smiles sweetly now, a cunning look to her. "Maybe I'll go tell them how you're entertaining the guests."

Ethan and Lucca just sound bored. "How about we tell Grant how we caught you sucking Jamie's cock last week in the front of his car."

"Screw you, Lucca."

They laugh as she shuffles off, her arse cheeks hanging out of her bright pink bikini. Could she find one smaller?

Thank God that's over. I can't do this though. I might be a bitch at times and hard to get to know, but these guys are ruthless. I didn't come here to be a punching bag for whatever problem they have with me.

"Where you going, love?"

I groan when the twins twist me back around. "Home, so get out of my way."

"Who did that?" Lucca asks, seeing the forming bruise on my arm.

I rub it like it's going to disappear. It clearly doesn't. "No one. Now move. I'm going."

They look at each other before pouncing on me. Ethan, I think, swoops me up over his shoulder and slaps my arse. "Nope. You need to have a drink with the birthday boys. It's not every day you turn eighteen. And we start school again soon. Don't be boring."

"I don't drink," I snap, bringing my fists down hard on his back.

Lucca grins, walking behind us. "Who doesn't drink?"

"*I* don't," I snap. "Now, put me fucking down before I bite you."

He quickly deposits me on the floor in a secluded area at the side of the building, glaring at me. "Put those gnashers away, Monroe. Fuck, you're feisty. Just stay and enjoy the party."

I lean back against the wall. "I don't know anyone." I feel like a sulky teenager. I groan, wishing I did drink. After watching what it did to my mum, I stupidly tried it once to see why she did it and never drunk it again. I was ill for fucking days.

"You know us two," Ethan offers.

I eye him suspiciously. The other day they were tearing me a new one and now they're acting like we're best friends.

"That's not really a good example, Ethan. You both sexually harassed me the first time we met. The second time isn't looking good for you two either, since you manhandled me over here."

Just then, a girl in a scrap of material covering her sex and tits saunters over, swinging her hips side to side. Her bleach-blonde hair is up in a high bun, but she starts twirling a fallen piece when her gaze lands on the prize.

The twins.

Jesus, do they bleach everyone's hair around here or what?

I snort, nearly choking when I try to cover my laughter, when she nearly trips in her heels. The guys adjust their junk, and I roll my eyes. Typical males.

Blondie's gaze turns into slits when she sees me next to them. Guess she doesn't like someone next to her prize.

"Boys," she purrs. "Would you like to *come* for a *dip* in the pool?"

Both Ethan and Lucca turn to each other. They seem to be communicating something because Ethan draws his attention back to Blondie. "You want us to fuck you, is that it?"

"It'd be good," she drawls, sucking her bottom lip into her mouth.

She can't be for real. And in front of me.

Wait, both of them?

What world have I walked into?

"Maybe. Why don't you suck our dicks first, let us test the waters, so to speak," Lucca replies, his voice low and seductive. A shiver of surprise runs up my spine at how blatant they're being. Who talks to girls like that?

Do they even remember I'm here?

I look from them to Blondie, wondering how she's gonna react to being disrespected like that. She pulls her shoulders back and her face morphs into excitement. "I'm willing to do *anything*."

I gag—I can't help it. They aren't fucking made of gold. *Does she have no shame?*

"What are you looking at?" she snaps when she hears me.

I tilt my head, gazing behind her. "Just your dignity drowning itself in the pool."

She has the stupidity to look behind her. The boys begin to laugh, causing her attention to go back to them.

"Shall we go somewhere private?"

"Here's good. We're private enough." Lucca grins, licking his lips.

She only spares me a brief glance before dropping to her knees in front of him.

"You can't be serious," I snap, not looking down.

Ethan winks at me. "Feel like helping her out, go for it."

"You're going to do this—out in the open? What kind of party is this?" I hiss.

"One where guests aren't allowed upstairs. If we want to fuck, we'll go there, but she's sucking our dicks, not riding them," he tells me, like it's normal. Probably is for him.

I hear the sound of clothing hitting the floor, and I have no idea what possesses me, but I look instead of running away. She has her hand on the base of him, and I squeak when his hard dick disappears into her mouth. He moans and I jump, meeting his gaze. He's watching me, smirking while the blonde bitch bobs her head on his dick.

"Oh my God," I groan, rushing away. "Fucking hell."

"Come on, Ivy," Lucca calls, laughter in his voice. "You're used to seeing stuff like this, aren't you? Or is it different seeing it from a bird's-eye view?"

"Arsehole," I yell, moving through the crowd and ignoring their taunting laughter.

I scan the area, avoiding the pool at all costs, when I notice another couple going at it under a canopy. They're alone in there, but anyone could see. I can see.

This is too much. I'm out of my element here. I knew parties could get rowdy, but not like this.

I move faster when the girl starts to scream and find a quiet area in the back. I take a seat on a stone bench, shoving my face into my hands.

"What was I thinking," I groan quietly.

Footsteps sound near, and I slink further down the bench and out of the light.

"What the fuck is she doing here?"

"Grant, she doesn't know," Kaiden replies, and hearing his deep voice sends a shiver down my spine.

"Like fuck she doesn't. Apple doesn't fall far from the tree."

What the hell does that mean? I'm nothing like my mother.

"Yeah, probably. But I'm telling you, she has no idea. Still, she's tainted blood. She doesn't belong here."

"Then she won't see me coming for her," Grant growls.

"Where *is she?*" Kaiden asks.

"Probably fucking some poor sucker who doesn't know what she is." He takes in a deep breath. "Are we still doing this tonight?" Grant asks, and my ears perk up, yet a sense of foreboding hits me.

"I planned it, didn't I. Payback's a bitch," Kaiden replies, his voice scarier than ever. "Let me go get my brothers and we'll get it done."

"I'm just going to take a breather," Grant says, and I begin to panic when he gets closer. I stand up, pretending I didn't hear him, and walk with my head down.

"Not so fast, you little fucking slag. Were you spying on us?"

I shrug his arm off me, but he just grips me tighter until I wince. "How much did you hear?"

"What don't I know?" I ask, instead of trying to play coy. I deserve answers if they're going to treat me like this.

His smirk is ugly and dark. "Everything apparently, but I don't believe a fucking word of it. You come here and we're meant to believe it's a coincidence. I won't have the spawn of that whore blowing things up again."

"What the fuck are you talking about? I'm here because my mum died."

For a moment, I think I see a flash of remorse, but it's masked within a second and his eyes darken further. "Good."

I rear back because he's genuinely glad she's dead. "Excuse me?" I breathe.

"You're just like her. Gonna flash me a bit of boob?" he snarls and goes to lift my top. I slap his arm away, trying to step back, but he follows. Dread fills my stomach as he comes at me again, this time gripping the neckline and pulling so hard I hear the material tear.

"Get off me," I scream, fighting back. He wraps his arms around my waist, so tight I struggle to breathe. I kick and slap at him, but it's like he doesn't feel any of it.

"You want it, just like your mum," he whispers in my ear. I lean forward, biting down on his shoulder. He yowls out in pain, dropping me to the floor. I take a second to gasp for air before running away from him.

I hear him following me as I skate around another couple making out, bringing me closer to the large pool.

He grabs my arm, spinning me around and spitting on me. I scrunch my face in revulsion and slap him without thinking.

"You expect me to pay to fuck *you?*" he yells, throwing his hands up. I'm frozen, watching as everyone stops what they're doing to watch us. "Anyone else want a go? Because I wouldn't touch the skank. She begged me to take her up the arse."

A chorus of no's and name calling reaches my ears. Tears brim the edge of my eyes, but I don't shed them.

"No amount of money would make me sleep with you," I snarl back. "Katrina already warned me how shit you were. Which is why she fucks Jamie. You don't do the job," I tell him, using the knowledge I learned earlier.

It's rolling around in his head. I can see it—the thoughts and betrayal—right before hatred is back and he's taking a step towards me. "Do you think anyone would blink if I fucked you, right here, right now?"

"It would be against my wishes. There's a word for that. It's called *rape*," I snap.

"Yeah, sheep cries wolf," he snarls back.

I step back, closer to the edge of the pool, and my face pales when I notice how deep it goes. He sees it, my fear, and before I can tell him I can't swim, he pushes me into the warm water and panic seizes me.

I choke on water, my arms flapping around as I sink lower. My chest burns and black spots dance behind my eyelids.

I'm going to die in a pool of fucking water. Just as I finish the thought, hands grasp me under my armpits and begin to pull me up.

I cling to the body that saved me, but it's short lived when we reach the surface and I meet the eyes of the one who put me here.

He smirks, pulling me flush against him by squeezing my arse. I can't even let go, because I'll be back under there if I do. I struggle to catch my breath, still in a daze, when I feel him rip my top up.

I scream, trying to pull away, not caring if I drown. It would be better than what he said he'd do earlier.

"No," I cry out hoarsely.

"Baby, you're rubbing yourself up against me. My dick is so hard," he murmurs, and I feel him unclip my bra. Tears fall as he easily removes it. I've never felt so weak in my life. "Got to show everyone how good I really fucking am."

"Hey, it's not nice to share," Ethan says, and I feel a new pair of hands grip my hips, pulling me away. I don't even care that every pair of eyes around the pool can see my tits right now. I'm just glad I'm away from Grant.

chapter six

"Give her back. I'm not done," Grant barks.

Ethan spins me around and shoves me in the arms of someone else. I don't open my eyes, just cling to the warm body that smells of musk and spice, my arms and legs wrapped around him. My bare breasts press against his chest, and I feel my stomach flutter for reasons other than panic.

"You're done," Kaiden rumbles, his tone final as his chest vibrates against mine.

I want to die of mortification because I've just been spared from a demon, only to be thrown into the arms of the devil himself.

Was this their plan? Did they have all this arranged, knowing I couldn't swim? When I heard them talking earlier, they were saying something about a set up.

I feel tears of anger burning at the back of my eyes because I can't figure out what is going on here, why they are doing this to me.

My mum could never break me, no matter the challenges she threw my way. But these guys… they have the power to destroy me.

I just know I won't go down without fighting. It's not in me to give up. After all, I lived with my mother all my life.

"I'm done when I say I'm done," Grant tells him.

It's not just the hard, ripped body that tenses, but the atmosphere around me.

"Get a drink, man, and cool off," Lucca orders from close by. Should have known he'd be with his twin. So not only did everyone get a glimpse of my tits, but these guys got up close and personal.

"No!"

"You're done here," Kaiden tells him and starts moving through the water. I cling tighter to him, squashing my breasts, but I'm not going back under that water.

He doesn't say anything as he walks out of the pool with me still in his arms. My skin prickles from the cool air, causing me to shiver.

I tense, waiting for him to drop me to the ground and let everyone have a good laugh. He doesn't though, instead keeping one hand under my arse and another around my back.

My face is still shoved into his neck, my eyes firmly closed. We're moving through the house now, heading upstairs, and I begin to panic.

"I want to go home," I whisper, still not loosening my hold on him.

"Did you want to go with no top and soaking wet?" he asks sharply.

I pull back, glaring at him. "I didn't ask to be shed of my clothes, Kaiden. I didn't ask for any of this." I'm near the point of yelling now, but he doesn't care, just arches an eyebrow, looking bored. He glances down, and I notice my mistake too late. His gaze darkens with lust, surprising me. It's gone within a second, and he pulls his hand from my arse. I cling to him again, squishing my tits against his bare chest.

"Why are you naked?" I groan.

"I'm not," he mutters dryly as I hear keys jangle. "It's a pool party, and I'm in shorts."

I don't say anything as he steps into a room, locking the door behind us. "Um, I know you guys think I'm a slut, but I'm not. I'm not going to sleep with you."

He grunts, dropping me to the floor. I cover my breasts, but he doesn't really look. And I'm glad, because I so don't want him to see how hard my nipples are.

His head tilts to the side. "Don't be shy now. If I wanted to sleep with you, you'd be begging me to fuck you, Ivy."

I notice he didn't deny them thinking I'm a slut. It shouldn't hurt, but it does. He's categorising me the same as my mum, and I'm not her.

"No, I really wouldn't," I tell him, my chest rising and falling as I check him out for the first time. "You guys can't seem to take no for an answer. Not every girl wants to fuck you."

He has a tribal tattoo on his shoulder, going down to his elbow. He has another on his rib cage, though I can't make out what it is, but I do see scripted wording by its side. His large, muscular chest and tight six pack is where my attention is; right down to where those low-riding shorts hang on his narrow hips with a sculptured V.

He clears his throat, smirking, and my cheeks flare with heat. He scans my body from head to toe, and I know if I was wearing clothes, he'd totally be undressing me with those eyes. The dominance rolling off him is evident. It's then that I realise I'm staring again. I look away, pressing my arms harder against my chest.

He moves closer, enough for me to feel the body heat coming from him, and I have to force my body to step back instead of seeking out the heat.

He looks down at me, his gorgeous face and those dark, mesmerising eyes doing something to my stomach. His fingers begin to dance on my hips, leaving a trail of goose bumps in their wake.

His body brushes against mine, and I gape at him, feeling light-headed. He tilts his head forward, bringing his warm, soft lips to my neck, and my body begins to heat up.

I drop my hands, gripping his shoulders to steady myself. I can feel his breath coming in shallow pants, but it's like he's trying to hide his reaction.

His lips move to my ear, pressing lightly as he glides them across my jaw. I'm a panting mess, clinging to him. I'm wet—probably fucking soaked.

His fingers slide up my ribcage, towards my breasts. He twists my nipple between two of his fingers and my core tightens.

"Mmm," I moan, feeling high.

What am I doing? I can't seem to tell him no or to stop. I should be pushing him away by now.

He lets out a throaty chuckle before lowering his head, sucking my nipple into his mouth. I sway, dropping my head back. I'm so turned on right now I think I could orgasm from just his mouth on me.

He lifts his head, his eyes hooded. He cups my throat, his thumb pressing lightly over my jugular. Something is working in that mind of his, an array of emotions flying across his face.

Then it's like a cold mask appears and everything about him hardens.

"See? I can fuck you any time I want. I don't need to take it, to force it. Difference is, I don't fucking want you," he snarls, pushing me back.

I wobble backwards, humiliation and embarrassment washing over me. "You bastard," I hiss, shoving at his chest.

"What did you expect—that I'd want to fuck someone like you?"

"You don't even know me," I scream, then blink at the words I just said. "You all think you know me. You don't. I'm not a slut. I'm not my mother. I'm just a poor girl from a rough estate whose mother just died. I have nothing—nobody. I can't even fucking swim. That is all there is to know about me. I've led a boring, hard as fuck life. So don't pretend you fucking know me. I've met gang members with more manners than you guys."

He seems to pause on his way to his walk-in wardrobe. He looks over his shoulder, heat still in his eyes.

"You don't know anything," he tells me.

I throw my hands up, realising it makes my breasts bounce too late. "'Cause no one around here is a straight talker. You all act like I'm a mind reader."

"We don't trust you," he admits.

"I don't fucking trust you, either, but do you see *me* making *your* life difficult?"

His jaw clenches so hard I hear his teeth grind together. "You being here is making all our lives difficult. Now take this shirt and get the fuck out of here."

I take the shirt he hands me and pull it over my head. I'm still wet, so the top clings to me in places. When I look up, Kaiden is by the far window—not the one facing my room—staring out.

I open my mouth to say... I don't know what I want to say. His biceps bulge as he grips the window ledge, his head bowed.

With one last inhale, I leave the room, shutting the door quietly behind me.

The house is pretty much a large replica of Nova's, so I find the stairs in no time. As I reach the curve on the stairs, I spot the twins running up them. They stop when they see me, both dry from being in the pool.

I shift uncomfortably at how they are watching me. "You can't swim?" Ethan asks, like it's a foreign concept.

Feeling defensive, I glower at them. "This might be hard for you to believe, but not all of us were fed with a silver spoon or got swimming lessons. I come from nothing. I learned to ride a bike at the age of eleven when I found an old one left in a park. That was the only thing I ever learned to do—aside from school and skateboarding."

"Woah, woah, woah," Lucca remarks. "We weren't going to take the piss."

"Well, maybe a little," Ethan says, grinning with a shrug.

"Fuck you," I snap at him. I take a step down, but Lucca's arm on the banister blocks me. I groan. "Can I leave now, or do you all feel like you need to humiliate me more?"

He shrugs, not caring. "We could. But we don't want to."

Lucca steps closer to me, his expression tight now. Gone is the easy-going, boy-next-door look. "Watch out for Grant. He never goes against Kai like that. He's dangerous to be around as it is, but he's unravelling. Now he's plain crazy. Having you here is bringing back bad memories. Luckily for you, Kai is worse."

"I've never been here before," I accuse, throwing my hands up. "How do you guys walk in a straight line if you can't even talk straight?"

Ethan grins at his brother. "We live dangerously. Do you really not know—about your mum?"

"I don't even know who my mum was anymore. She's always been a drunk, a druggie and a slut, but since coming here, I don't know anymore," I admit out loud.

The look they share has the hair on the back on my neck standing on end. "Just... We'll tell everyone to back off."

I snort. "It's too fucking late for that. He stripped me bare out there," I say, pointing in the direction of the garden. "He did that for a reason, and I want to know why."

Lucca's eyes harden. "Don't go looking for things you don't want the answers to, Ivy. Your mum isn't painted in a pretty colour."

"Like I give a fuck," I snap back, leaning closer to him. "If there's something you guys didn't want me to know, you shouldn't have thrown it in my face every chance you got. Don't you think I deserve to know why I'm being targeted like this?"

"No, I don't," Kaiden's hard voice rumbles behind me. I jump away from Lucca, not realising how close I had gotten to him.

I take a step down, next to the twins, looking up at Kaiden. He's wearing a black T-shirt now with jeans and a pair of trainers. He looks good. Real good.

His eyes flash when they land on me, and my entire body flushes.

"I thought I told you to go home."

I don't answer, too scared to reply in case the twins pick up on the fact I'm very much aroused right now.

Why does Kaiden do this to me? He's a fucking jerk, and I don't even like him personally. That body though... completely different story. It's one I'd like to lick and suck.

Gah! Get your head in the game.

When I don't reply, the twins clear their throats. "Are you ready to go do that *thing*?"

He takes his gaze away from me to his brother. "Yeah. You get everything packed?"

They nod, still talking in codes. "Do you guys come with a code book?" I blurt out.

All eyes come to me, and I shrink back a little. The twins laugh, but Kaiden continues to burn holes into me.

"Let's go," Kaiden rumbles, passing by us. The twins follow, and I can do nothing but do the same.

When they head outside to Kaiden's car, I curse myself for following them. I could have used that chance to search their house.

I look back at it, the music still blaring and people still drinking and having a good time. A shiver of fear runs up my spine. There is no way I can go back inside there. For one, I don't know where Grant is or what he'd do now I don't have the twins to save me.

Car doors slamming has me jumping. None of them spare me a glance as they turn, speeding off down the hill.

Yep, I'm well and truly fucked. They're one great big mystery and it's bugging me to no end that I can't figure them out.

I head inside Nova's house, shutting the door quietly behind me so I don't wake anyone up.

"Back already, Miss Monroe?"

I scream, spinning to see Annette stepping out of the huge family room. "Annette, you scared me."

She smiles. "I'm sorry, dear. Did you have a good time?"

"They're a little much," I tell her.

She smiles in understanding. "They can be."

When she goes to move on, I quickly take a step forward. "How long have you worked here?"

She has to be in her fifties, I think, and seems to be well aware of everything in the house.

"It will be nineteen years this year."

Around the time my mum would have left. "Annette, did you know my mum?"

A guarded expression crosses her face, but she's honest when she answers. "She left three days before I started working here. I took over from the last lady who had to leave suddenly due to a death in the family."

"This place, these people... they are full of secrets, and I know it's because of my mum. Maybe something she did, was accused of, or something that happened to her, I don't know. But they all hate me."

"They don't hate you, Ivy," she tells me, stepping closer. She surveys the area before pulling me in closer, keeping her voice low. "Keep away from the secrets. No good can come of them."

She turns to leave, and I chase after her. "Wait, Annette, I need to know. No one is telling me anything, and Nova is as tight-lipped as a nun's vagina."

Annette gasps. "Do not say such crude things. I can't talk about this. I'll lose my job, and me and my husband love it here."

I don't want her to lose her job, not when she has it good here. She doesn't have to pay rent or household bills here. If she were fired, she'd have none of that.

"I'm sorry." Tears of frustration gather in my eyes. "I just want answers. I've grown up both hating and loving my mum. I always thought she was weak and a waste of space, but something inside of me is telling me she was that way for a reason." Deflated, my shoulders sag. "Or maybe it's wishful thinking."

A cold hand clasps mine when I go to walk away. Annette blinks, watching me for a moment, deciding what she wants to say. "Why don't you pick a nice book from the library tomorrow and sit outside."

The bizarre order comes out more like a question. However, it's the fearful look in her eyes that has me mutely nodding. I stand in the foyer, wondering what world I've been thrown in to.

chapter seven

I STARE OUTSIDE THE WINDOW, FEELING MY eyes slowly droop from two sleepless nights.

The night of the twins' party did something to me. Not just the pool incident, but also what happened with Kaiden. It's played over and over in my mind.

I had heard them arrive back at around four in the morning, but I didn't bother going to the window to check who it was. I felt emotionally drained, and I didn't want them to see me that way. I couldn't let them see me vulnerable, because like the pack of wolves they are, they would pounce.

Nova was busy with work, but she did send Annette up to my room to bring me food when I refused to go down. I lied and told them I wasn't feeling very well, but Annette knew the truth.

I just need a plan, something to help me figure this shit out.

I scream when my door flies open with a bang. I sit up in bed, clutching the thin bedsheet to my chest.

For a moment, my mind went to Grant, thinking he had come to finish the job he started in that pool, but my eyebrows draw together when a slim figure with bright red hair steps through the door.

"Cousin!" the loud girl yells.

I look around, wondering if this is another prank. "Um..."

"I'm Selina. Nova's my aunt—kind of aunt. My uncle was married to her, until—you know..."

Wait, Nova was married? She never mentioned that, but then again, I never asked. Hold on...

"Does Nova have kids?" I ask, wishing I had asked Nova this when we first decided I was coming here.

Selina's eyebrows arch before she giggles, throwing herself across the bottom of my bed. "No, silly. I'm like a daughter to her. My dad is always away for work, and I think my mum forgot she had a child."

I know how that feels.

"How can she forget she had a child?" More importantly, someone as bubbly as her.

She rolls her eyes at me. "I know, right? She loves to shop though."

"Not to be rude or anything, but what are you doing in here?"

"I'm staying here. School starts soon and usually I spend time with Dad, but the jerk went and booked flight tickets to go somewhere with his mistress. I didn't want to stay in London for four weeks on my own, so I came here early."

"That doesn't explain why you're in here."

"You really are closed off, huh? Nova did warn me."

I can't help but grin. "Not really. But Nova didn't even mention she had a niece."

Her mouth gapes open. "She didn't mention me? But I'm the light of her life." Exhaling, she drops down onto her back. "I guess I'm nothing now she has the real deal."

"Wouldn't call me that. We don't really know each other."

Rolling back over, she tucks her hands under her chin, blinking up at me. "Yeah, I heard about your mum. I'm sorry."

"Don't be. It was the best thing to ever happen to her." And it was. She was clearly suffering with her illness. It was cold and harsh, but it was the truth.

Selina's lips turn up in a pout. "Well, that's dark. Nova said you're working for Mrs White. Did you meet the husband?"

I blink, trying to catch up with the change of subject. "Yes. He's lovely."

Her eyes widen for a moment before she drops her face onto my blanket and begins to roar with laughter. "No way. There's no way you can associate 'lovely' with Mr White. He's an old, grumpy grouch. I asked Mrs White if I could ride my horse on her field, and he told me to go take a run and jump my happy off a cliff."

I begin to cough on my sudden laughter when she says that last part. That really does sound like Mr White.

When I sober up, I ask her, "So you stay here and go to school?"

"I'm starting Kingsley Academy this year. I can't wait. I went to school here for my last year of high school, and boy are the lads fit. It's like they spike the water around here."

"Looks don't mean anything if they're arseholes," I murmur, my mind drifting to Kaiden.

Selina grins. "You met Kai, I take it?"

"You know Kaiden?"

She shrugs. "Not personally. He'd never speak to someone like me, not even to get a blowjob. I talk to the twins, and if they weren't like little, annoying brothers to me, I'd totally do the tag team with them. Every girl around here has fantasised about it."

"What does that mean?"

She claps her hands twice. "I'd say the rumour is… but, it's not a rumour. They always fuck the same girl. One right after the other. Not sure if they both tap it at the same time," she says, her lips twisted in thought. "Although, even that sounds sexy as hell."

"They always sleep with one girl at the same time?" I ask, surprised and kind of grossed out. Yet, I'm kind of intrigued. Who wouldn't be? They're extremely hot and there's two of them.

"Not sure if it's true. I didn't ask them outright, even though I wanted to, but apparently, they like doing everything the same. If one does something, the other follows. It's the same with their women. If they like someone, the other has dibs too. Neither has had a girlfriend, and the few girls that have tried soon learned where their place was."

"That can't be healthy."

"It's Lucca and Ethan; they can do what they want. Their dad and granddad pretty much own everything around here. Well, except for what the Monroe's have. I think they own the other half."

"What if one likes a girl but the other doesn't?" I'm more interested in the twins' sex life than I am about who owns what. I should be telling this stranger to get out of my room, my personal space, but I find I like having someone to talk to.

"It's never happened. Not that I know of. But if it does, I wouldn't mind being a fly on that wall."

"And you're friends with them?"

"The twins?" I nod and she continues. "Yes. We're as close as they let me be. Not as close as they are to their brother and Grant, but no one will ever get that close. People have tried and failed."

"Why do people act like they're gods?"

"Because they are," she says in all seriousness.

"You can't be for real."

"I am. Kaiden is like the king around here—fitting with his last name and all. People follow him, even Grant and the twins. People who go against him have been known to disappear, but that's all hearsay. I've not known anyone personally who has disappeared."

"This world is fucking crazy. I swear, sometimes I feel like I've swallowed too many pills and I'm in a coma right now. All this is in my mind." She pinches my leg hard, and I cry out. "What the fuck was that for, you psycho? Do you like your face?"

"Woah there, tiger. Just proving you aren't in a coma," she tells me sweetly. I rub at my thigh, wincing when I can feel a bruise already forming. "I guess they haven't been welcoming to you."

"Who?" I ask, distracted.

"All of them; the Kingsley's, Grant."

That has my attention. "What makes you say that?"

She looks at me like I've got a third head. "Apparently they hate you. I don't know why; my friend didn't know either. She just said she heard them talking about you at the party."

"What were they saying?" Did she know about what happened in the pool?

"That they hated you and vowed to do anything to get rid of you. You can't let them win though. I know your mum caused loads of shit before she left. People in my family still talk about it. I don't know details, just that she's the reason people led different lives to the ones they were heading for."

I scrub a hand down my face. "They do hate me. I don't know why, either, but yeah, from what I can figure out, it's about my mum. I want to know though," I admit, trusting her a little. If my instincts are right, and they usually are, she'll be a good friend, not a fake one.

"Have you asked Aunt Nova?"

I arch my eyebrow at her. "I know you've had happy pills this morning, but you can't be serious. Every time I broach the subject, she deflects and talks about something else."

"They were twins," she murmurs, deep in thought.

"I didn't even know my mum had family, let alone a twin sister. You'd think someone would give me a break."

"I'm sorry. It must suck."

Seeing the sincerity, I don't snap at her pity. Plus, she's like an excited puppy. I don't want to make the puppy sad.

"It's fine. No one seems to want to talk about her directly, yet they don't mind talking in riddles."

"All I know is that they were all best friends, really close."

"Who?"

"Your mum, Nova, my uncle, Kai and the twins' parents, and Grant's parents. The men all own a business together too."

"They do?" I ask.

"Yeah. My uncle owns majority of the oil company now though. Mr. Kingsley sold some shares to him years back when he ran for mayor here in Cheshire Grove. He went on to London to become an MP, but he had to resign for unknown reasons. To the public anyway. I heard he had an affair with an eighteen-year-old." She laughs when I scrunch my face up. He might look good for his age, but he's still old as shit. "I know. Anyway, I do know he tried to buy back more shares in the company, but Grant's dad had also sold him shares. Not as many as Mr Kingsley though. It's been tense because Dad also helps my uncle. He doesn't have shares, but he is partner. He also has someone manage his own business."

"So, you're saying your uncle is more loaded than the other two?"

She shrugs. "I don't think so. Kingsley is seriously loaded, but it's his wife's money."

"What does that mean?" I ask, interested in her answer. All this is new to me, and the more I get to know about them, the more of a chance I have of finding out what happened to my mum. Selina doesn't seem to mind spilling all their secrets either.

"It's actually Nina Kingsley who is rich. His family was wealthy, all into politics, but nowhere near as rich as Nina's family. They founded this land and most of the buildings in this town. They own shops, schools, colleges, universities, and a boarding school not too far away. They have companies overseas and dabble in everything and anything. When her parents died, it was all left to her, but Mr Kingsley took over it all until it's ready to be passed down to her firstborn."

"Wait, he took her last name?" I ask disbelievingly. Royce doesn't seem like the type to be unmanned like that.

"He was happy about it, probably wanted the connections the name gave him."

"Where is their mum? I've not seen her, but I did meet Royce briefly the day after I arrived."

She looks away for a minute, seeming troubled. "No one really sees her."

"But she's here?" I ask, to be sure.

She shrugs. "She's not really with it. Whenever I asked my dad, he would avoid answering. Just said it was none of our business." She scoffs, rolling her eyes at me. "He never has a problem gossiping about anyone else. Anyway, rumour is she's away at a spa. Everyone around here knows that means she's probably in a rehab centre."

"Really?" I breathe out, flabbergasted by the news. I also feel sorry for Kaiden and the twins. My mum might have been neglectful and just a shit mum, but she never left me.

Probably too lazy to.

"Anyway, I came in to tell you we're going to a party tonight."

I groan. "No. I've had my fair share of parties."

She grins. "Don't worry. I heard you made an appearance at Lucca's and Ethan's," she says, waggling her eyebrows at my chest.

I hold the blanket higher, feeling my blood boil. "Bet they forgot to mention how Grant ripped my top off me when I was trying to get away."

She pales, scanning my face for any signs I'm joking. I harden my jaw, looking at her dead on. "I'm so fucking sorry. You need to tell Nova."

I grab her hand, afraid the puppy will bounce off to find Nova. She can't know. No one can. "Please don't say anything."

"Why the hell not?" she screeches, looking at me wide-eyed.

"One, she might not even believe me—the woman did see where I lived. Two, because I'm not a grass. I plan to get even, not to have him told off."

"How do you plan to get even? I didn't even know Grant was like that. I mean, yeah, he's a mean son of a bitch, but this really is surprising."

I laugh. "I might be closed off, but you really do live in a bubble. They're all mean. Don't mistake it for anything else."

"All right," she says, sighing. "But you are coming to the party. And it's perfect. It's in the next town over. No one from Kingsley Academy will be there except us."

"Why?"

She rubs her hands together after sitting up. "Because for years and years, Remington Academy and Kingsley Academy have had an ongoing feud."

"Of course, they have," I mutter, rolling my eyes.

"It was over the land. The Remington family is just as rich as the Kingsley's, yet years ago when the Academies were in the works, the Remington's accused the Kingsley's of stealing the land out from under them. The people who it was bought from promised the Remington's the estate, but the Kingsley's apparently blackmailed the owner into selling to them." She inhales, taking one deep breath before continuing. "The Kingsley's, however, say that the Remington's made up the story so that no one knew they didn't have enough money and went for the small piece of land. Which is true, I don't know. It was so many years ago, I think even the two families don't know what is true, just what is passed down. Now they have to prove who is bigger and better and all that crap. I heard that Kai, his brothers and Grant blew up Carter's car."

"Carter?"

I really must be in a coma. I pinch the skin in the crease of my elbow, wincing. Yep, this is completely real.

"Carter Remington. He's so hot I talk stupid around him. But I went to school there for a while before I got my place in the high school here. I made friends and we still hang out. None of them know. The twins would kill me if they found out, and the school would probably hate me."

I grin at her. She's like a terrified little mouse now. "All right. Do we have to dress up though?" My lips turn up in a snarl at the thought.

She laughs. "The people might be rich around here, but there's only a handful of them who are snobs and think their shit smells like strawberries."

I laugh, remembering some of the girls I met at the party last night. "Yeah, I can see that."

"But for real, everyone is pretty much down to earth. There might be a few girls who dress up like they're going to the Oscars, but for the most part, everyone dresses casually. It's at Remington's house tonight, so you'll get to meet your neighbours' rival."

"Looking forward to it," I mutter.

"Miss Selina, your car is here," Annette announces at the door.

Selina's wild red hair flies everywhere when she swings around to Annette. "Coming," she tells her, before looking at me. "I'll be back later for dinner, then we can get ready. I need to go visit my nanna and go shopping for a new outfit."

"All right," I tell her and watch her bounce off. Annette is still inside the door, watching me warily. "She's full of energy."

Her lips tip up in a small smile. "She's a good girl is Selina."

When she stays quiet and doesn't leave, I question her. "Is everything okay, Annette?"

She keeps twisting the bracelet on her wrist, her eyes darting anywhere but at me. "Did you pick a book from the library?"

Random. "Um, no. I'll go tomorrow. Selina's taking me to a party later, so I'm going to try and get some sleep in. I'll get one tomorrow for sure."

She nods sharply. "That is good. Make sure you go once you are up. Reading is good for the soul."

I watch her leave, feeling weird. It's the second time she's ordered me to go to the library. If I didn't want to go in there, I'd be worried there was a hidden dungeon where they tortured orphaned nieces.

Noises from next door grab my attention, and I race to the window when I hear a car slam into something.

I look out, my eyes widening when I see Lucca—or Ethan—shove Kaiden away, before curling over a little, clutching his stomach. When he stands to say something to Kaiden, a startled gasp escapes me. He's covered in bruises.

Like he can hear me or sense me, Kaiden looks up to my window, staring directly at me. His jaw his clenched, his eyes hard and on me. If looks could kill, I'd be sleeping next to my mum.

I step away from the window, deciding to watch Netflix instead of going to sleep. There are so many secrets around here, so much mystery, and those boys next door are a huge one.

Selina had her driver take us over to the Remington estate. Unlike the gated community I'm staying in, this one is at the end of a private road filled with luxurious houses that could rival the manors.

The house at the end is bigger, the one the car pulls up outside. The driver turns around, addressing Selina.

"Are you sure you don't want me to stick around, Selina?"

She seems to be close with her driver, something I thought was beneath rich people. He's an older gentleman and watches her the way I imagine a father looks at his daughter. I wouldn't know. My mum told me I didn't have a dad and never once answered my questions about him. She just yelled and screamed about her not being enough.

Selina leans forward and kisses him on the cheek. "Curt, we'll be fine. I have money in my purse to get a taxi back. If, somehow, I misplace my bag, I have another twenty tucked away in my bra. And if, by some miracle, I lose that baby, I promise to call you."

He grimaces at the mention of her bra, and I chuckle. "Okay. Have fun."

"I will. See ya," she sings, then pulls me out of the car behind her. She claps her hands, looking at the intimidating house with glee. "Tonight is going to be so much fun."

"Yeah," I murmur, not sounding so convinced.

She bumps her shoulder against mine. "Come on, Ivy. A party is just what you need. You've been through a lot and this is the best way to forget about it all."

The car pulls off when something occurs to me. "Wait, I didn't bring any cash. Mrs White gave me some money, but I've left it at home."

She looks confused for a moment. "Hasn't Nova given you money?"

I nod. I still have ninety something quid tucked away in my drawer, but something occurred to me that day I spent helping Mrs White: I need to work to get what I want. It felt good, great even, when Ellie handed me that money. She was right, it wasn't a lot, but it was the first lot of money I had earned. And some part of me hoped that if I earned my own money, people might give me a break and treat me better. I'm not so naïve to think it will be that easy. Their issues run deeper than where my cash flow is coming from. But I knew where it came from and that's what counted.

And I want to use as little of Nova's money as possible. I don't trust her enough not to throw it in my face down the road, so until I can be sure she won't use it against me, I'm not going to spend more than I can afford.

And thanks to Elle, I might have some extra work with her son, who now runs their land. They breed horses. I jumped at the offer and said I'd do anything.

"Yes, but I don't want to use it unless it's an emergency. I want to make my own money," I finish explaining.

She shrugs, waving me off. "Well, I've got it covered."

"And what if I lose you?"

"Here, pass me your phone," she orders, and I pull it out of my back pocket and hand it to her. I decided on jeans today, and a red flowy top that actually looks and feels good on me. I was used to T-shirts and tank tops. This is between a tank top and a blouse. I found I liked it. "Now you have Curt's number programmed into your phone. I'm surprised Nova hasn't hired him before now. He's always there when I need him. A few times he comes to London, depending on what we're doing."

"Thanks," I say, forcing a smile. I still don't feel comfortable. I have no idea where we are, only whose house it is. I have no means to get home and calling Nova in the middle of the night when she isn't even home, sucks. I found out when I showed up for dinner and she wasn't there. She had to go out of town for the night and won't be back till morning.

"Let's get a drink and I'll introduce you to my friends."

I follow her inside, amazed by how many people are here and how no one has called the police. We only had to make a bit of noise in a park back where I lived, and someone would call the police to get us moved on. I guess the rich really do live by different rules.

The place is filled with smoke and weed fumes. I wave it out of my face as we walk through a lavish hallway, oil paintings of different landscapes hanging on the wall. Something like that wouldn't last five minutes where I'm from. A stick man standing in the middle would have been drawn on with permanent marker by now.

It's hot in here. Really hot. And sweat is already clinging to my skin.

I can't help but compare the house to Nova's. Where Nova's house is all white and creams, this place is dark and mahogany. I'm intrigued to find out who lives here.

Selina waves at a few people as we shove our way through the crowd, and none of them give me a second glance. I'm grateful and begin to feel a little easier about coming.

When we make it into a large kitchen, I feel a cooler breeze coming in from the patio doors. I sigh, wanting to get out there so I can breathe. She walks over to some clear plastic cups and pours a heavy amount of vodka into them. I glance away, taking in everyone standing around. There's a couple up against the fridge, making out, a game of cards going on at the huge glass, rectangular table, and a few people munching on the food lying around in bowls.

When she hands me the clear drink, I just force a smile. She doesn't know I don't drink alcohol, so I can't berate her for handing it to me. She'll figure it out eventually when I don't drink any, but until she's drunk herself,

I'll hide it. She seems like someone who won't give up until I start drinking with her. It just doesn't excite me the way it does these people. I tried it once to see why my mum loved it so much and never did it again. It was horrible.

My mum didn't even notice I was close to going to hospital because I was violently sick. She never noticed much of anything when it came to me. She tolerated me at the best of times, so for her to pay attention, she'd have to care. And I don't think she did. Sometimes it felt like she couldn't even look at me. It freaked me out, like I reminded her of someone.

Selina shakes me out of my thoughts when she nudges me with her hip. She looks up from her phone after taking a swig of her drink.

"My friends are outside," she yells over the music, nodding towards the patio doors. I nod, following her out into a wide, long garden. Again, there is a pool, and I grimace.

Why they have spent money to get one, I don't know. More times than not, it's cold and raining here in Britain. It's a waste of money if you ask me, and utterly pointless.

One thing is for sure, however: no one here is staring at me in revulsion. No one is giving me the side eye or glaring holes into my head.

They don't know me.

The tension in my body eases a bit as we step up to a small group of people. "Guys, this is my cousin, Ivy. Ivy, these are my friends, Chrissy, Bee, Dawson and Si."

"Hey," I wave, and the girl called Bee grins over her cup at me.

"Don't mind her. She's checking you out. Bee, no," Selina warns, and I feel my eyes trying to pop out of my head.

She's flirting with me?

When I look at Bee again, she winks. "Sorry, but I had to try," she drawls before narrowing her eyes at Selina. "Stop pussy blocking me. Not all girls are as strait-laced as you, Selina. Some like a bit of both."

"I like boys," I add in quickly.

She laughs, not caring in the slightest. "Ever want to try it, give me a call. You're seriously fucking hot. That hair reminds me of a raven's feather. It's sexy."

Hearing her mention my hair is just another reminder of Kaiden and how he was drawn to it, running his fingers through it.

I hate that my thoughts are going to an arsehole like him, and, distracted with the beratement I'm giving myself, I accidently lift the cup to my lips, taking a sip. I choke and look to Selina, glaring. "Seriously, did you want some lemonade with your vodka?"

"It's not that strong," she dismisses, taking a sip.

Chrissy, who seems like a hot IT nerd, snatches the cup out of my hand, bringing the cup to her lips. She grimaces, dropping the drink to the floor. "Seriously, Selina, where's the lemonade?" Her voice is smoky and rich.

Selina snorts, taking another sip, and Dawson snatches the cup from her hand, tipping the contents on the floor. "You are not throwing up tonight. I'll go make you another drink."

From the way he watches her, I can't tell if he likes her or not. Not in a friend's way, but romantically.

He's not bad looking if you ignore his long hair that fall across his forehead and down behind his ears. He's slim, but not in a way that says he missed puberty, not like his friend, Si, who looks like he did miss that part. He's scrawny, covered in acne, yet has this uptight air to him.

Selina beams up at him, already a glazed look in her eye. When Dawson reaches for her arm, linking it through his, they step away, forgetting all about it.

Or so I thought. Selina's hair swings through the air as she spins to look over her shoulder at me, making me smile.

"You okay here?"

I hide my grin when Dawson, eyes wide, silently pleads for me to say yes.

I nod, watching them go. I feel a little uncomfortable, so I slowly turn around to make boring small talk with her friends. At least the Bee chick seems cool.

But they're gone. I look around for them, seeing Bee first, chatting up some girl. Chrissy and Si seem to be in a heated argument with another couple not far away from her, and there is no way I'm going to look like a lemon just standing there next to them.

Selina is already out of sight by the time I turn back. I sigh, heading into the crowd to take a look around while I wait for her.

It's refreshing that no one knows me here. It gives me more of a chance to really look at the scene without being worried someone is going to chew my head off.

I'm a big girl. I'm used to taking care of myself, and I've had to be strong for as long as I can remember. A few times I've got into scraps because of jealous bitches. I might have come from nothing, but it didn't put anyone off from hitting on me. The girls at school hated it, especially when they found out where I came from and who my mum was. They didn't get why they weren't chosen over the town's tramp.

I got it, I did, but I still had to stick up for myself. I didn't have anyone else, not even a best friend who was truly on my side.

Being here is different though. They're vultures and clearly money hungry. I don't think they'd know what to do if they didn't have any cash to blow on shit they don't need.

That said, they still make me feel small. I might be able to fight with the best of them, even talk smack back when it's given, but these guys have a whole different power play. They have the upper hand. They could crush me in a second and no one would blink. I need to face the fact that I'll be spending my time here deflecting all their insults.

I sigh, shifting my depressing thoughts aside, and move closer to the side of the property. Seeing the pool near terrifies me, so I skirt around it, heading towards a long picnic bench. I take a seat on the table, putting my legs on the seat, and begin to watch those around me, dancing and having fun.

I can still smell weed and it makes my stomach heave. When I scan the crowd to see who's smoking it, I spot three people doing coke on a table near the pool.

"Who do we have here," a deep, masculine voice rumbles from beside me. My mouth gapes a little at how fucking gorgeous he is. Selina was right earlier in saying they put something in the water, because this guy is dangerously hot; dark blonde hair with a slight curl to it, the most piercing blue eyes I've ever seen, with dark eyelashes that make them pop out more. If his 'come to bed' eyes aren't enough, then the wicked smile he gives me is. My knees lock together when I see those deep dimples.

"Um..." I mumble, looking around for Selina. I don't know who this guy is.

"What's the name, sweetheart?"

I turn around and glare at him. He might have all those pretty looks, but he ruined them by calling me 'sweetheart'. My mum's boyfriends called me that, and I hated it.

"None of your business."

"You're in my house, so I think it is," he says, still easy-going. He doesn't seem pissed at being snapped at.

Wait.

"You're Carter Remington?"

Jesus, Selina was right, he is fucking hot. No wonder she talks stupid around him. I swear I can feel my brain cells dying off just being in his presence. It's a pretty, boy-next-door kind of hot though. Not the dangerous, smouldering and intense look Kaiden holds. `

He grins, flashing those straight, white teeth at me. "The one and only."

Maybe he can give me the answers I need about the Kingsley's. I lean forward, flashing him my best smile.

"Is that right?"

His grin only spreads. Clearly, he thinks he's scored. Boy does he have it wrong though. He steps between my legs, his arms caging me in on either side.

"Want to go somewhere private, baby?"

His breath causes shivers to run down spine, and as I look over his shoulder, feeling a little dizzy, my eyes land on Selina. She looks deflated and so sad it makes my body tense.

And she's looking right at me.

No, at us.

Oh my God, she *likes* Carter Remington.

I'm about to push him away, but then I watch as her eyes go round. The cup she's holding slips from her hand as she takes a step forward. I open my mouth to call out to her, but the sound of glass shattering, has me turning towards the house.

I lift my hands up to push Carter away, when someone beats me to it, dragging him off me. I'm relieved to have him away, but that relief is diminished when I lock eyes with Kaiden, his gazing burning into me.

The punch he lands on Carter throws him onto the grass, just in time for the commotion inside to settle down. I don't know where to look—there's too much go on. However, I gravitate towards the house where Lucca—or Ethan—steps out with Grant. There's a few more guys with them, some I think I saw at the twins' birthday.

My attention moves back to Kaiden, who stares impassively at me for a moment longer before leaning against a tree. He makes it look so casual, like he didn't just gate crash a party and knock the host to the floor with one punch.

Our eyes meet again, and I'm not surprised to see hatred and betrayal shining back at me.

"Are you okay?" Selina asks breathlessly, her eyes glazed over.

"What is going on?" I whisper.

"A clusterfuck is what is going on. They're so going to kill me," she whines.

I jump off the bench when more lads step out of the house. A shiver runs up my spine because they aren't friends of Kaiden and his group.

No.

This is bad.

"We should go," I whisper in her ear.

"Yes. It's going to kick off big time," she squeaks, just as one of the twins pushes his way through the crowd, coming towards us.

Carter is standing up now, wiping blood off his lip. He glares up at Kaiden, taking a step towards him.

"A sucker punch, really?" Carter quips.

Kaiden arches his eyebrow, not speaking.

"You mean like the sucker punch you gave my brother when you and your friends ganged up on him?"

"We really need to go," Selina squeaks, sounding more panicked now.

I pull her back when she goes to leave. Call me crazy, but I really want to see how this pans out.

"How is Ethan?" Carter mocks, just as a group of his friends gather to stand beside him. They try to make it look casual, but you can tell they're there to support him.

It's also good to know it was Ethan who was hurt. Now I'll be able to tell them apart for a while.

Briefly, I look to Kaiden. He's still leaning against the tree, his expression completely blank.

What I would do to make him feel.

No! Do not think like that, Ivy. It's that bloody sip of vodka making you think it.

"You think you're a big man? Too scared to take him on, one on one?" Lucca snaps, pushing at Carter's chest. He goes back an inch, bumping into his friends.

Carter smirks, straightening his shirt. "It was one on one."

Not the right thing to say, because Lucca's face goes an angry red. "Yeah, and when he beat you, another one went at him. Still a fucking coward, I see."

Lucca swings and chaos erupts around us. There are more of Carter and his friends. A lot more.

Even so, Lucca and the guys he walked in with start to get in on the fight, swinging at anyone close to them.

I watch in horror as someone tries to come up behind Lucca. He might have been a jerk that first day, but he doesn't deserve that. Without thinking, I pick up the bottle Carter was drinking from and move forward. I smack the bottle around the guy's head, and he falls in a lump to the floor, glass raining down on him. Lucca's eyes meet mine, stunned, but then he grins, winking at me, and carries on punching whoever he can get his hands on.

People push and shove into me. A cold hand grips my arm and I startle.

I spin around with the broken bottle raised. When I see Selina, I drop it to the floor, my heart racing.

"We need to go."

I nod, stepping over an unconscious body, and take her hand. We run towards the gate Kaiden must have walked through to get into the garden. On the way, I see him still standing next to the tree, fighting four huge guys. He doesn't even seem to be out of breath.

He looks up through a sea of moving limbs and stares at me until goose bumps form on my arms. I shake myself out of it, taking a look around. Spotting a hose pipe wound up on a reel, I pull back on Selina's arm. She falls back a step, looking at me like I've grown two heads.

"What are you doing?" she hisses yet follows me over.

"Turn that on," I order, pulling the hose. Once I have enough, I move over to Kaiden and notice another two guys there. He's still standing, still fighting them off, but I can see he's taken some shots. A red mark is beginning to swell on his right cheekbone.

I keep pulling the hose for more length, and just as I get close enough, Selina has the tap running. It's not strong enough to break them apart—I'm not stupid—but it surprises them enough to give Kaiden a chance to get the upper hand.

He knocks one clean out, and I shouldn't, but I begin to feel turned on.

"Now can we go?" Selina hisses, dragging me by the arm.

"Yeah," I tell her, nodding. Then find myself smiling. It felt good to let off some steam. When we're down the street, I begin to laugh. "Thanks for bringing me. This is exactly what I needed."

She looks at me for a moment like I've grown two heads, but then begins to laugh herself. "We can call Curt to come get us. Let's just move further away from the house. People will begin to leave now, and we don't want to be caught up if another fight breaks out."

chapter nine

I BLINK AWAKE WHEN A *CREAK* IN THE floorboards sounds close. I still on the bed, my cheek to the pillow and my gaze away from the door as I train my ears to hear another sound.

Any kind of sound.

I can't hear anything, but it doesn't mean something or some*one* isn't there.

I can feel it. Chills break out over my body and cools parts of my skin that are damp with sweat.

I had come back from the party with Selina and headed straight for my room, deciding I would wait until tomorrow to explain what she saw with Carter. She might deny it, but there was no mistaking the fact that she liked him. It was written all over her face.

I inhale when no other sound is made. I slide my fingers through the back of my black knickers, which are firmly wedged between my arse cheeks, and pull them out.

I literally only had energy to pull on the tank top I had on earlier when I got back. The adrenaline that was pumping through my body had completely worn off before we even hit the gated community. I was out before I could even conjure up images of Kaiden and what he looked like fighting. He was lethal.

I roll over, pulling the hair out of my face, and stare up at the ceiling. A shadow at the end of the bed catches my attention, and a small, startled scream bubbles up my throat.

No sound has chance to escape as the dark, looming body jumps over me and a hand clamps down over my mouth so hard my teeth dig into my bottom lip.

"Wha—" My yell of outrage is muffled when the hand presses down harder.

They lean down, and I get my first glimpse of Kaiden. He surges forward, his face a breath away from mine.

"Shut the fuck up!" he snaps.

One hand goes around my neck, tightening, and a cold shiver of fear runs down my spine. His weight settles down on me, and a different kind of shiver runs through me.

What the fuck is he doing?

His hand at my mouth moves, yet he keeps his other hand at my throat, his fingers digging in with a warning, to remind me he's there.

"Get off me," I hiss quietly, placing my hands on his chest to push him. His hand tightens, and I stop, pulling back to glare up at him.

"What game are you playing now?" I tense slightly at the predatory tone in his voice.

"I'm not the one playing games," I snap, closer to his face.

"You were at a Remington Academy party."

I can't work out if he's pissed I was at the party because they have this rival shit going on or because I went to a party. It's hard to get a read on him any other time, but in the dark, I can only go by the tone of his voice.

"Get off me," I try again, not bothering to hide the annoyance.

"Don't push me, Monroe. You won't like the consequences," he growls, the weight of his body feeling heavier. "Now tell me, why were you at that party?"

Does he have… is that… No, surely not. I'd love to ask if that's a gun in his pocket, but I'm almost too scared that the answer is yes.

My core tightens, and I hate my betraying body for it. He shouldn't turn me on. His dick, even though covered in rough denim, shouldn't turn me on. But it does. And every time he slightly moves, rubbing that rough material across my clit that is barely covered in the thin cotton material, there's no mistaking the pleasure running through my system.

I'm sick.

There's no other excuse for it. I'm a sick, sick person.

I almost want to disobey, to see exactly what he would do. He might look relaxed, but there's no mistaking he's a wolf ready to pounce on his prey.

I also don't want to get Selina into shit, so I lie. "I heard about a party and I went."

His body tenses above me and the room grows silent. He doesn't move, doesn't speak, but I can feel angry waves coming from him.

"You lied," he whispers, and a sense of foreboding spreads through me.

"Why should I tell you anything? Why are you even here—in my room, Kaiden? For someone who doesn't like me so much, you sure want to spend time with me."

For the first time, I see his face clearly. He looks and smells freshly showered, which is probably what took him so long to seek me out. His bottom lip is torn, and so is the edge of his eyebrow, close to his hairline.

It's unfair that even beaten he looks like a god. A dangerous, sexy god.

He smirks, resting on his elbows so he's barely hovering above me. "You think I want you?"

On a shaky whisper, I reply, "Yes." I don't believe it. I think he just loves toying with me. He likes getting a reaction out of me.

I hate that I like it.

And now I feel like I'm playing a part in the Rihanna and Eminem song, 'Love the Way You Lie'.

He runs the tip of his finger down my throat, across my chest, where I'm not wearing a bra. I can see my nipples through the white, thin material, but in my defence, I didn't know the psycho would break into my room.

"Did you wear this for me?" he murmurs, his voice low and seductive.

My body trembles until I'm visibly shaking. "Yes, because everything I do revolves around you."

He chuckles darkly, his fingers circling my breast. "Yes, it really does."

"Why are you being like this?" I demand, trying to wriggle away from his touch. It just causes me to rub up against him, creating friction I really don't need stimulating me right now.

I try to swallow the moan, but it's no use. He hears, his eyes darkening with a heat I've not seen before.

He doesn't speak, continuing his torture on my nipple for a moment longer. And I let him. Because my head and heart might hate him, but my body has other plans with him.

"Please stop," I plead, but it falls out half-arsed. It doesn't even sound convincing to me. I groan when his fingers continue a trail down my body, skimming across my hip bones to the top of my knickers.

"Why are you doing this?" I try again, attempting to wriggle free. He's half onto me now, weighing me down so I can't do shit. The other half is lying on the bed so he can watch what he is doing to me.

He looks away from what his fingers are doing, and I try to concentrate when he leans down closer.

"Because you're Ivy Monroe. I hate everything about you; what you represent, where you come from, and who you come from. While you are here, I own you."

"Nobody owns me," I whisper, moaning when his fingers slide into my knickers.

His smirk spreads. "I do."

"What, you want me to be your girlfriend?"

Is he crazy?

He laughs, and it's the first time I've heard a genuine one from him. He looks different, relaxed, and his eyes shine with a light I've not seen from him. But it's gone in a second, and for a moment, I'm sure I imagined it.

"You are nothing to me," he warns.

His fingers begin to circle my clit in a smooth, circular motion. My toes curl, and I arch a little off the bed. I should scream for Selina, for Annette, for him to stop.

Nothing comes out but the sound of a moan.

He chuckles again. "Because, you see, I have you right where I want you."

My body tenses as he begins to move faster, sliding his fingers through my wetness, and fuck am I wet. I can feel it dripping between my arse cheeks.

His thumb rubs at my clit now, and I cry out when he shoves two fingers inside me, not slow and steady, but rough and hard.

"Oh God!"

"Your mum ruined lives when she was here. She fucked with the wrong families."

I want to question him, to tell him I'm not my mother, but his fingers work faster, harder, and I feel my lower stomach tensing, an orgasm cresting.

"Figuratively and literally speaking."

His voice is hoarse, low, but the warning and hatred is still there, heightening my arousal. Why it feels good when he's being cruel, I don't know, but the juxtaposition makes a tear slide out from the corner of my eye.

"Kaiden!" I moan; a plea, a curse.

He makes a noise at the back of his throat, shoving another finger roughly inside of me. I cry out, turning my head away from him.

He removes his hand, and my body relaxes against the mattress. But then his fingers, coated in my arousal, grip my chin, forcing me to look at him. He leans forward, licking away my tear.

"Suck."

"W-what?"

He shoves his fingers in my mouth, and I gag, but do as he demands. I feel him tense when I swirl my tongue around the tips, sucking off my juices.

He's hard against my thigh. I can feel it. The crazy part of me wants to reach for him, beg him to fuck me so hard I black out. The other is weeping in the corner of my mind, begging him to stop degrading me this way.

"Good girl." He removes his fingers, yanking down my tank top and baring my breasts. He reaches down, taking one in his mouth, and I cry out. He bites down hard, but my clit pulses all the same.

With pleasure comes pain.

With pain comes pleasure.

It's a fucked-up cycle I can't make sense of in my mind.

Another tear slides down the side of my face when he shifts to his knees, between my spread legs.

I try to close them on him, but his hands wedge them apart, pulling at my hamstrings.

"Kaiden," I whisper, feeling the burn everywhere.

He reaches a hand down between my legs, rubbing my wetness over my clit, my slit, before shoving two fingers back inside me.

I moan, my hips thrashing side to side. "No."

His slides his fingers out before adding a third one once again, ramming them so hard inside me my back arches off the bed and I can't mute the sound coming from my throat. He grins, placing his free hand at my breast, squeezing.

When he runs my wetness over my clit again, I nearly shoot off the bed. He circles my virgin arse, and the glint in his eyes tells me he knows that.

And he's enjoying my discomfort.

"You like being played with," he rasps, looking down at me.

"Please, not there," I beg when he presses his finger there. The pressure feels foreign, uncomfortable but pleasurable. I'm surprised when he obeys, instead sliding his fingers through my sex.

"Maybe I should fuck you."

"No," I tell him, shaking my head, yet my body tells another story when it rocks against his hand.

He chuckles. "I'm going to break you."

"I hate you!"

He shoves his fingers back inside of my sex, his thumb at my clit. He hits a spot inside me that sends every nerve ending wild.

"You're going to wish you never came to Cheshire Grove."

His breathing is laboured now, his fingers twisting inside me, making that spot come alive again. I can feel it everywhere.

He hovers above me, his lips close to mine as he continues to play. Sweat is beading at the back of my neck and my breasts bounce with each rough thrust of his fingers.

"I don't believe you came here for no reason. I don't trust that you have no idea what is going on. You want to play games? Game on. But I'll win. Every single time. I won't have you fucking up their lives."

Who are they? His brothers? Grant? Nova? Who?

"I don't—" I pause, crying out as my orgasm builds and builds, to the point I can no longer hold it at bay.

"I'm going to have fun breaking you—just like your mum broke them."

I come apart, my entire body lighting up, and before a sound can escape past my lips, Kaiden surprises me by kissing me.

I grip his shoulders, kissing him back. It's demanding, controlling and filled with passion and fire.

Then he's gone.

I'm breathing heavily when I open my eyes. His fingers leave my body and my sex pulses with aftershocks.

I lean up on my elbows, watching him clench his fists at the end of the bed, staring down at me.

"Kaiden?" I call out hesitantly, unsure about what all of this means. Did he finger fuck me into submission, or was it a way to say he can control me? Or for his sick pleasure…

"Tonight, I saw what you did. You hit that guy who was going to take Lucca out from behind. Then with me."

"I was trying to help," I snap defensively. The way he says it… accusingly, like I'm the one who orchestrated the whole thing.

He presses his fists into the mattress, leaning towards me. "You're lying. I don't fucking trust you." He scoffs, looking at me in disgust. "You drop your knickers at a sneeze in your direction. I saw you."

"Saw me?"

I'm so fucking confused. A headache forms, and I grab the thin blanket and cover my body. He snickers, his lip curling.

"Carter. I saw him over you. You wanted it."

"No, I—" I start, but he growls low in the back of his throat.

"So whatever game you think you are playing, don't. Because I'm warning you, I can make your life hell for however long you've got left. You leave and I'll follow. I'll make sure you never get a job, not even sucking dick for a living like your mum."

My heart drops when he says it. "Tell me what she did that was so wrong you would treat her daughter like this. A daughter she didn't look after. One I don't think she loved. Tell me!"

He stands, his eyes still cast down. When he speaks, his voice is quiet, deadly and filled with vengeance. "She destroyed the people who tried to save her."

"Wait, what?" I say when he moves to the door.

With his hand on the doorknob, he pauses, looking over his shoulder. "The difference between you and her—the *only* fucking difference," he states, before delivering the blow, "is that she had people who wanted to save her. There's no one in this world who can save you from me."

The door slowly clicks shut behind him. I curl into a ball on my side, a single tear sliding down my face and onto my pillow.

I can't believe I let him do that to me. I'm revolted with myself for letting it happen. He didn't force me. I could have screamed at any time, told him to stop, but I didn't. It made me feel alive. It made me feel *something*.

I'd slept with one person, one time, and that took me months and months to let happen. But he was right. He didn't have to work for anything before I dropped my knickers.

You aren't this person, Monroe.

I sigh, sitting up. I'm not this person. I don't let people get to me.

Fuck him. Fuck Kaiden Kingsley. I'm not my mother. I'm not a slag. I'm Ivy fucking Monroe, and I take shit from no one.

He thinks he can break me.

But what he doesn't seem to realise, is you can't break something that's already broken.

CHAPTER TEN

chapter ten

My mind wouldn't shut off. I couldn't stop thinking about Kaiden. How he could make me want him one second and hate him the next. It was driving me insane, and I couldn't shut my mind off long enough to find sleep again. I could still feel him, feel what he did to me, the rush of emotions and self-hatred. He made me feel weak, and it's the one thing I'm not. I've lived through tougher things.

After what seemed to be hours of tossing and turning, I finally got up to change into some fresh underwear and put on a pair of sleep shorts and tank top. I didn't think he'd come back, but I also wasn't taking chances.

Stepping back into my room, my gaze drifts over to next door. There's a lamp on, the room lit in a dim glow, but I don't see any sign of Kaiden.

Why am I still thinking about him? I want to smack my head against a wall. This is just crazy.

Sighing, I head out of my room and go downstairs, needing a glass of water. The house is eerily quiet during the night. I'm thankful for Selina staying here while Nova's gone until tomorrow. Still, the place gives me the creeps at night.

I grab a glass from the top cupboard before taking the orange juice out of the fridge and pouring myself a glass. I down half the glass, then refill it before putting the juice away.

Taking the glass with me, I move to the door.

The house is so big, too big for Nova. I've learned over the past few days that it's her childhood home. I knew it belonged in her family, but I presumed she'd inherited it from her granddad or something.

She was raised in this house with Mum, her brother and their parents. Their granddad moved to America not long after his wife died. The family history went on and on, and it was hard to keep up with Nova when I hadn't met any of them. Or seen pictures—except the one in her office.

Even the room I'm staying in once belonged to my mum. It had clearly been decorated and refurnished since, but still, it's surreal. Nothing in this house screams the mum I knew. Not one thing.

The deeds are now in Nova's name as her brother—my uncle—lives in America, where he oversees the family business there with their granddad.

It's all too much to process. I thought my family died with my mum. I had made peace with the fact I was going to be on my own in the world, and then Nova knocked on my door and shocked the hell out of me. I'll never forget the feeling of the blood draining from my face when I saw her. I thought she was my mum. I was seconds away from fainting when she rushed out and explained who she was.

And now here we are.

I head towards the cinema room but pause before I make it to the door. Nova or Annette hadn't taught me how to set it up, and I don't fancy spending half the night figuring it out.

Walking back through the kitchen, I head to the other side of the house, seeking out the stairs I noticed on my tour of the manor. If I can't watch a movie to pass the time, then maybe a book will do.

I walk up the winding staircase, coming to Nova's side of the house. She said she liked the view from her window so chose to move to this side of the house. She'd shared with my mum up until they turned thirteen and both needed their own space. It was weird hearing her talk about her. It was like she was talking about another family member I hadn't met yet. And I guess I hadn't.

The library is the first door I come to. I hadn't been inside yet, but she had one downstairs that was bigger than the public library back where I come from, and I made sure to take a good look around when I was in there.

Stepping in, I see it's a quarter of the size of the one downstairs. It has a half moon platform where it rises a few steps off the ground and houses shelves of books.

God, I love the smell of books.

It was the only thing I could do back home that didn't cost money and kept me out of the cold and away from my mum when she had people around in the day. The night was another matter.

On the bottom floor, a long, semi-circle, dark grey sofa runs alongside the banister and a black crystal table is set in the centre of the floor with black suede chairs around it.

A lone book on the table beckons me. It's just there, so out of place when everything else in the room is spick and span.

Weird.

It's like someone strategically placed it there.

I walk over, running my finger along the surface of the black crystal before reaching it.

It's crinkled, thick from the used pages, and clearly old by the colouring. On the front are doodles of hearts, stars and inspirational quotes. 'Live today like tomorrow will never come'. I smile, wondering what famous poet came up with that. It symbolises my entire life. It's how I've lived it.

The men in my mum's life were dangerous. There were a few here and there that respected me, but for the most part, they were dangerous, cunning and untrustworthy. Given the chance, they would have hurt me—some even came close before I managed to escape. So, I knew I had been living on borrowed time; it wouldn't have taken long for one of them to succeed. I knew staying with her would get me hurt or killed, especially if she owed them money.

Opening the cover, the air rushes from my lungs when I see, 'This diary belongs to Cara Monroe. Nova, KEEP OUT!' written in bold letters.

I stagger to the side, gripping the book in my hand.

She kept a diary?

This is my mum's.

The book isn't filled; it was probably one of the last ones she wrote by the looks of it. Needing some insight into who my mother was, I move over to the long, dark grey sofa and take a seat.

I swallow past the lump in my throat, staring down at the worn, pink book. For some reason, I feel like I'm invading her privacy. Not my mum's—she didn't know how to keep anything private—but the girl's, the one who wrote inside this diary.

But I need to know who this girl was.

I need to know why everyone hated her so much. Why Kaiden, his friend and brothers have a problem with her. I need to understand, because from what Nova said, Mum left before she even knew she was pregnant with me, and Kaiden and Grant would have been far too young to remember her.

Giving in, I skip to the last entry, needing to see what made her stop. At least that much. Did she just grow out of keeping a diary? Does it explain why she left?

My heart beats wildly in my chest as I read her words.

July 20th, 1995

I hate my life.

I wish I was dead.

I hate them.

I really hate them, and I wish they'd all burn in hell for what they did to me.

They took my innocence.

They stripped parts of my soul away from me, bit by bit, while they pinned me down and defiled me.

They fucking destroyed me.

They didn't care how much I begged, how much I pleaded. They didn't care. Now I don't care about anything.

I hope they all drop dead.

I wish they'd drop dead.

My stomach twists in knots at her angry, scrawled words. I swallow back the bile rising in my throat when the words finally sink in.

She was raped.

By more than one person, if I'm reading this correctly. The way the letters are indented into the page tells me how angry she was, as well as how rough the lettering is. She *could* have worded it wrong in her haste though.

Even as I try to make an excuse, I know she meant every single word she wrote on this page.

This is where it all began. This is what changed my mum. It doesn't excuse my upbringing, nor my mum's behaviour, but this was the root of it all. I can feel it in my bones. If this hadn't happened, maybe my life would have been different.

Or maybe I wouldn't have been born?

Taking a deep breath, I turn the page and continue reading.

I wish for a lot of things. I wish I never went to that party. I wish I could forget. Forget what they did.

The drugs TJ is providing are helping. They dull the pain, the memories I've had to live with for the past seven weeks. It helps me forget, forget what they did. But even they aren't as effective anymore. Nothing can erase what they did to me. No matter what I do to try and numb the pain, to feel like the girl I once was, I remember. I remember it all.

It's always there. Every time I see their faces, hear their voices or have to listen to people talk about how great they are.

And now I've got a demon growing inside of me. I want to take a knife to my stomach, to get it out any way possible. I don't even care if it kills me, as long as I get it out of me. It's a part of them and it's inside of me. I feel like I did that night all over again.

The few times I've thought about my future, I've pictured the perfect family, where my children have everything they need and love me unconditionally. I can never love this baby. I hate it. I hate it, I hate it, I hate it. And every moment it lives on inside of me is another day I loathe who I am, who they are. My skin is crawling, and my stomach is red raw from where I've clawed at my skin. I don't care. I feel sick to my stomach knowing it's inside of me.

That night, they didn't just rape me, they impregnated me. And I want it gone.

I flick back to the previous page, my breathing heavy. This can't be happening. It can't be. I feel sick to my stomach, and it threatens to come up when my hands shake and the page floats back down.

When I finally manage to get the page to turn, I look at the date again, my shoulders sagging with relief.

I'm not a product of rape.

It would have explained why my mum couldn't stand the sight of me. It would have explained a lot of things in my life.

This was six years before I was born though.

The relief I feel that it isn't me is short-lived, and a moment of self-loathing penetrates. There's still a child out there. Or maybe she lost it. Or worse… No. I can't think about any of that. I can't. She was young, too young to be going through this.

What happened?

Did Nova know? Did any of the family know? And why didn't any of them get her help? I have so many questions and my mum isn't here to answer any of them. I wish she had told me this, made me understand her. I could have gotten her help, the treatment she needed.

And her words on how she pictured raising a child, her family… a pang hits my chest, and I don't know what to think about her anymore.

I hate whoever did this to her, who ruined the girl she was and made her into the woman she was when she died. I hate them. I hate them for everything.

I flick through the pages, nearly tearing them in the process. My feelings are a mixture of anger and sadness. I want to cry for my mum, for the baby she carried who was innocent, no matter how they were conceived, and for the life she left behind. The night she was raped, Cara Monroe died. The person left behind was just a shell; she was barely human. And that breaks my heart a little bit more.

I look down at the pages, blinking my tears away as I carry on reading. I won't cry. I won't.

And what's worse is I don't have anyone I can turn to, no one that will believe me anyway. I can't tell Nova. She's distracted, in love, and doesn't have time for me. I tried. I tried so many times after that night when it became apparent I couldn't forget. I needed her and she wasn't there.

I hate her too. I hate that it happened to me and not her. And I can't live with myself for thinking that. I'd never wish this upon anyone.

I can't tell my parents either.

They think I don't know, but I do. I know why they raped me. It was all for the fame and fortune they'd get from being with me. And I know why they didn't pick Nova. I know it all. It wasn't hard to work out.

And my granddad won't stand for a scandal getting out into the papers. No. He'll make me marry the monster whose baby I'm carrying. He'll make me stand up and tell people I'm lying.

They all will.

And I'd rather die than live a life where that is my future. One way or another, I will get this thing out of me. I will make them pay for what they did to me, make them feel what I felt.

I sit back against the chair, reading the last page once more before closing the book.

My mum was raped.

If I hadn't read the book, seen and felt every word she wrote, I wouldn't have believed her. My mum never cared who she had sex with. Didn't care where or when either. If it got her what she wanted, she did it, and unfortunately, growing up, I was a witness to it.

I want to know if Nova knew, but I'm afraid if I mention it, she'll shut down and take measures into making sure I never find out what happened. I can't trust her. How can I? Her twin sister was suffering, and she didn't even take notice, didn't add anything up.

A part of me wants to leave, to take as much as I can carry and get the hell out of here.

My biggest question right now, is who the hell is she talking about? She doesn't mention names. The only names she's written are Nova's and T.J's, and that is either his name or his initials.

I open the book back up, going to the entry before her last, and my eyebrows draw together.

June 1st, 1995

Dear Diary,

I can't wait to go to the party this weekend. Mum and Dad don't know Nova and I are planning on sneaking out. We're going to meet the others beyond the gate in case one of us gets caught sneaking out. That way, the rest of us get to party.

Life is so good right now. Mum asked me what I want to do when I finish school. Of course, I'm going to the Academy once I've finished my A-Levels. They've opened a new wing that will specialise in medicine. I'm going be a surgeon. I want to heal people.

And I won't have to do any lessons during the holidays. Today, I hacked into the school emails and found out I passed my exams. I can't wait for my future.

'Be kind, even when those around you aren't.'

Cara

P.S. They were acting even weirder today. I don't know what's going on, but I don't have a good feeling. It's like they're planning something. I swear, if they push us in a pool again, I'm going to be so annoyed with them.

P.S.S. S.F. is being clingy too. I think Nova likes it though. He doesn't even let her out of his sight if she leaves the house. It's weird as hell because he never acted like that before.

It's like someone spiked their drinks at school and made everyone act weird.

Maybe T.J. spiked the water. He's always known for raiding his dad's practice. I'm pretty sure he sells more than pharmaceuticals though.

Anyway, until tomorrow. <3

The difference in the writing has my eyes watering. In this entry, she's happy, easy going and fun, and excited about her future. In the last entry, she just wants it all to end. She doesn't want tomorrow to happen.

She wanted to be a surgeon? My mum couldn't even put dinner together. This is all too much.

All of it.

I don't even know how to feel about her anymore.

One thing is for sure, whoever hurt her was definitely the reason she changed. There's no mistaking Mum was meant for great things.

And S.F.? Who was that?

Why couldn't she have left a decoding sheet?

"Hey, there you are," Selina greets, popping her head around the door.

Feeling the blood rush from my face, I hide the diary under the pillow behind me and stand up. She's staring down at her phone but looks up when I knock into the table.

"I went down to get a drink and passed your room. When I saw your door open and light on and you weren't there, I thought you were sick like me, but then I remembered you didn't drink. You didn't drink, right?"

I force out a dry laugh as I shake my head. "Hangover?"

She nods, looking a little green, her red hair shoved in a bun at the top of her head. "Yeah. I really didn't think those couple of drinks would affect me," she explains, before looking around the room, her lip curling. "What are you doing in here?"

"I couldn't sleep. I was going to get a book to read."

She looks at me with round eyes. "Yeah, you can borrow my kindle. I'm pretty sure the books in here are as old as this house."

I nod and follow her out, but I can't help but take one last look at the diary. I want to get it, but I can't risk Selina seeing it.

I can't risk anyone seeing it. It's basically evidence.

And my earlier thoughts of keeping it from Nova go out of the window. I want answers. I need them. She was my mum, and if I feel like Nova is lying to me, I'll go searching for answers myself.

I GROAN AS BRIGHT SUNLIGHT STREAMS INTO my room, piercing my eyelids. God, my mouth is as dry as a desert, my eyes are stinging, and I feel like I've been hit by a truck.

Selina dragged me into her room last night, after finding me in the library, and spent fifteen minutes showing me how to use her kindle. She then proceeded to go through each of her favourite books, explaining in detail why she loved them so much. I had to sit for an hour listening to her rave about lads she was in love with who weren't even real. It was kind of torture, but a welcome distraction from the turmoil going through my head.

By the time I got back to my room, I was completely knackered. I crawled back into bed and fell straight to sleep, face first on my pillow. I didn't think of the diary once I was utterly exhausted.

I rub sleep from my eyes, still stunned I managed to get to sleep after last night.

What happened with Kaiden seems like a lifetime ago after reading Mum's diary.

The whole situation regarding my mum is fucked up. I don't know what to believe anymore.

Some part of me has always questioned what made my mum the way she was. She wasn't a good person, and an even worse parent, but people aren't born like that; they are made, whether it's self-destruction or a traumatic event.

The little girl inside me, who desperately sought her mother's love, wants it to be the latter, no matter how morbid that sounds. But I don't want to go looking for excuses if there aren't any.

Those words in her diary haunt me, even awake. They're such a contradiction to the woman I knew. My heart breaks a little for both of them. I don't want to care—she never cared about me—but I do, because at the end of the day, she was still the woman who birthed me. And I never want to become the person she was. I might not give two fucks about stuff, but I still have a heart.

I pick up my phone to check the time, groaning when I see it's eleven. Rolling out of bed, I quickly take care of business in the bathroom before grabbing a long cardigan from my wardrobe. I'm still tired, and today, I want to chill.

My stomach rumbles, reminding me I haven't eaten. I make my way out of my room, intending to head downstairs, but then pause, remembering the diary I shoved behind the cushion last night.

I rush past Selina's closed door as quietly as I can, in case she's still in there, and head towards the other side of the house.

I'm out of breath by the time I reach the library, closing the door before rushing over to the sofa. I rip away the cushion I'd used to hide the diary last night. But there's no sign of those doodled hearts or inspirational quotes.

Panicking, I pull off the next one. Then the next. And the next.

It's not here.

There's no other place it could have gone. I check again, feeling my heart race. *It's not here.*

I run my fingers through my hair, looking around the room—for what, I have no idea; maybe some clue as to where it's gone?

Fuck!

I sit back on my arse, hugging my knees to my chest, when the realisation someone moved it hits me. What if I never find it? I should have come back for it last night, after Selina went back to bed. Now it's gone. I'd wanted to read it from the beginning, to see if any of the other entries gave a clue as to what happened. Maybe someone was bothering her before or had tried to hurt her before. I need answers, if for nothing else than my own peace of mind.

I need to get out of this room, away from the temptation to smash the room up until I find it.

Slowly, I get to my feet and make my way out of the library, my shoulders sagging when I give the sofa one final look.

Someone knew that diary was there. Someone who put the book there in the first place.

As I make my way down the side stairs, I hear voices from somewhere inside the house. As I head towards the kitchen, the voices get louder, and I identify Selina and Annette straight away.

I'm surprised when I hear Nova's voice carry along the hallway. I didn't think she'd be back until later this evening at the earliest. I had hoped to have the day to get my head straight.

My blood boils the minute I step inside the kitchen and see her happy face. How could she not know her twin needed her? Aren't they supposed to have some kind of psychic connection? I just can't believe someone who is a lawyer didn't see her twin was in pain and needed her. She's meant to be good at reading people.

"That will teach you not to drink," Nova tells Selina, chuckling.

"Please don't remind me," Selina groans.

"You're awake," Nova states, smiling wide at me. My stomach twists into knots.

I grunt, looking away from her and taking a seat next to Selina at the breakfast bar. My lips twitch when she raises her hand in greeting, her head shoved into her arms, which are folded under her on the table. Other than that, she doesn't verbally greet me.

"Would you like some eggs, Ivy?" Annette asks softly, and I look up, taken aback by her scrutinising gaze.

I shake it off, nodding. "That'd be awesome," I mutter.

Nova pours me a glass of orange juice before leaning against the counter opposite me. "I thought we could spend the day shopping, go out of town for the day, just us three girls. What do you think, Ivy?"

I stare at her for a moment, wondering if she knows about my mum. Did she care either way? Has she thought about any of it while I've been here?

I hate that I have all this turmoil going on inside of me while she's happy planning shopping trips and joking around.

"Ivy?" she pushes when I don't answer.

I can't hold back any longer.

Looking at her dead on, I ask her outright. "Did you know my mother was raped?"

I don't turn my attention away from her, not even when I hear someone walk in from the side entrance attached to the kitchen. Nor when Selina gasps from beside me.

"W-what?"

"You heard me," I tell her, my voice steady.

Annette quickly turns to the stove, but I don't miss how pale she looks. Does she know? Was it her who left that diary out for me to find?

"Maybe we should talk about this in private." She focuses on something behind me, shifting on her feet. "And don't think I won't be asking about those bruises later." I look over my shoulder, finding the twins and Kaiden standing in the doorway. Ethan really does look worse for wear.

A snarky retort is on the tip of my tongue, but the look in Kaiden's eyes stops me. He's not giving much away, but I can tell from the tightness around his lips and the muscles in his jaw clenching that he's angry. He looks two seconds away from saying something. My attention flicks to the twins, who look uncomfortable with being in the room.

I don't care.

I don't care about any of them. They've given me nothing but shit since I moved here.

"Um, I'll leave you to it," Selina murmurs, grabbing her plate of food.

I let her go without a word, meeting Nova's gaze once again. I arch my eyebrows, waiting for her to answer. Because goddammit, I deserve those answers.

"Boys, why don't you take these plates and go eat with Selina for me," Annette says. I don't bother to see if they listen. Instead, I stare at Nova, silently imploring her to answer me.

"Kaiden?" Nova calls, twisting her hands together. She hides it quickly, but there's no mistaking it with the quiver in her voice. "Could you leave?"

"No!"

"Please, Kaiden. This is between me and Ivy," she tells him, her voice stronger now.

I hear footsteps, and although I don't see him leave, I feel him leave, his looming presence no longer in the room.

I didn't realise how tense I was from him being in the room until he's gone, my shoulders sagging somewhat.

"Tell me!"

"Where did you hear your mother was raped?" Nova asks gently.

"I read her diary," I tell her honestly.

"Her diary?" Nova asks, surprised. "Where did you find her diary?"

I open my mouth to tell her, but something inside of me screams at me not to. "It doesn't matter where I found it. I want to know the truth, Nova, or I'm leaving here for good."

She sighs, placing her cup of coffee down on the side. "It's a lie."

My lip curls. "I read her diary, Nova. That wasn't a fucking lie."

"Language," she calls sharply, before pinching the bridge of her nose. "Your mum got drunk at a party. *Really* drunk. She was a wild child, always looking for a good time. One thing led to another, but she wasn't raped."

That sounds like the mum I knew, but not the girl I read about in that diary. The two entries I read were too different, even the style of writing.

"I don't believe you."

"Believe me. She slept with her best friend's boyfriends."

"Boyfriends?" I ask, now in two minds.

She did write it like it was more than one person. She kept saying 'they', but until now, I was unsure whether or not to believe it.

She nods, sadness clouding her features. "Yes. She regretted it terribly the next day. She was scared her friends would find out so she told people they forced her."

"That wasn't the version I read," I tell her, feeling conflicted. Either Mum twisted the truth or Nova is twisting it; either protecting herself or the people who raped my mum.

"I'm sure she filled her diary with a version of the lie. She carried the secret for weeks and weeks, Ivy. You have to understand—your mum… she was sick. She drank and did a lot of drugs."

Her words ring true, but something doesn't seem to be adding up.

"She was pregnant," I tell her, reading her reaction.

She pales further, grabbing the counter for support. "What?"

I nod. "Yes. She was pregnant with one of their babies. She wanted it out of her, even admitted to drug abuse to help her forget what they did. That doesn't sound like someone who was lying. It would be one hell of a story to keep up if she was."

"A baby?"

"You didn't know?"

"No," she whispers, no longer paying attention to me but focussing on the counter, seeming lost in thought.

"Are you lying to me? I need to know. I want to know if that was the reason my mum was the way she was."

"Have you got this diary?" she asks, suddenly looking up at me.

"No," I tell her, raising my eyebrow.

She grips my arm. "Please. I want to see that diary. Did it say what happened to the baby?"

Confused, I rip my arm from her trembling grasp. "I don't know where it is. It was gone this morning," I tell her. "You really didn't know?"

"Please—if you have it, I need to see it," she tells me, more urgent now.

"I'm not the one fucking lying," I yell at her. "I need to know the truth, Nova. No more fucking lying."

"I've told you the truth. Please, I implore you to let the past stay where it belongs: in the past. Don't dredge up old memories that won't help anyone involved. It will cause more harm than good."

I pull my hair out of my face and tie it into a bobble. "I just want answers, Nova. I've had my mum thrown in my face more than once since being here. I'm not her. I'll never be her. But I won't sit back and be lied to. Something happened to her, something so traumatic that she ran away from all of this and decided to raise a child she didn't want."

"That can't be true," she whispers, looking pale.

I force out a laugh. "She didn't love me. She didn't hate me either. She just didn't care. And I was raised all my life in that environment. Sometimes I wonder how I survived being a baby, got through infancy. She had no moral compass. I want to know if what she wrote is true. I'm not asking for anything else. I need to know there was a goddamn reason she chose to bring me up like that."

"I'm sure that's not true," she tells me. "If I could have helped, I would have."

"Would you though? Because like I said, I've had her thrown in my face more than once since being here, people acting like they have a right to judge me."

"Who said something about your mum?"

I let out a heavy sigh. "It doesn't matter. I just feel like there's a lot you aren't telling me and I'm sick of it."

"Your mum made some seriously bad choices that affected a lot of lives. She caused a lot of damage before she left, Ivy. Lives were ruined."

"*Mine* was ruined," I scream at her, losing my patience. "Mine was fucking ruined. And I want to fucking know why. I can handle it."

She holds her hand out to me, and I want to smack it away. "Please, calm down. It's all in the past. I can't make excuses for your mum. Only she knows the reasons why she did what she did. All I can say is that I'm sorry. It's all in the past now. You can have a good life here, Ivy."

I stand up, shoving the stool to the floor in the process as I laugh bitterly. "No, it's fucking not! I didn't even know her, and I lived with her. Everyone here acts like they knew her better than me. I don't know *anything*. Why did she leave here? Why? Why did we live on scraps when she had all of this? Why would she say she was raped if she wasn't? You aren't telling me the truth," I scream, slamming my fists down on the table. "Tell me! Fucking tell me!"

"She slept with my husband," Nova yells, her expression horrified. She places her hand over her mouth, falling back a few steps, the clacking of her heels on the tiled floor in sync with my racing heart.

"What?" I ask, quieter this time, stunned by her answer.

"I'm so, so, *so* sorry, Ivy," she says, her eyes watering. "I didn't want to tell you this yet. I wanted you to have time to settle in, to get to know me and decide to stay of your own accord. The night your mum left… I-I found her in bed with my husband. I had been with him for as long as I could remember, and I walked in on them in bed together." She takes a deep breath, calming herself. "I hated her. I hated her so much that I told her I wished she was dead," she admits as the first tear flows down her cheek. She swipes it away quickly. "She left that night before anyone could calm down, and for three months our parents searched for her. When they finally found her, they discovered her pregnant with you."

"What are you trying to tell me?" I ask, my stomach sinking.

"Sam, my ex-husband, is your father. You have his hair, his eyes… My dad managed to get a DNA test done to confirm it, but before the results were back, your mum was gone again. We couldn't find her. After a time, I think everyone just gave up."

I begin to sway, feeling my world tilt once again. This can't be happening. My mum told me my dad didn't want me.

A dad.

"I-I… this can't be happening," I whisper.

"I'm sorry. I really wanted to tell you when the time was right. I wasn't sure how much your mum had told you, but by your reaction, she told you nothing."

"Why didn't he come for me?" I ask, my heart hardening.

"I tracked your mum down when you were one. We thought it would be better for me to go since I was the reason she left. But she didn't want to see me. She caused a massive scene, so I left to give her time to calm down. When I went back the next day, she was gone. You were both gone. I didn't find you until I got the phone call that your mother died."

"This is too much," I tell her.

"Just take a moment," she tells me. "It's a lot to process."

I laugh without humour. "Process? My mum slept with her twin sister's husband and got pregnant—and then neglected me my whole life."

"Ivy, where are you going?" she calls when I turn to leave, my gaze finding Kaiden's in the doorway. I narrow my eyes at him before turning around.

"Anywhere but fucking here," I tell her, heading towards the backdoor. I notice a tray on a small bar area, with bottles of alcohol sat atop it, and grab the nearest one.

"Ivy," she calls, but I ignore her, slamming the door shut behind me. The glass rattles from the force.

I don't care.

Maybe Mum had the right idea when she drank her troubles away, because as of right now, all I want to do is forget. I want to forget I read that fucking diary, and everything Nova just told me.

How dare she keep something like that from me. Who the fuck does she think she is? And why isn't he here? Why hasn't he come to see me?

Fuck him.

Fuck her.

Fuck all of them.

I've never needed anyone, and I won't start now.

I storm towards the tree I sat under the second day I arrived here, opening the bottle on the way. The vodka burns my throat as I take a hefty swig. I hiss through my teeth, placing the top of my hand against my mouth.

I take another as I reach the tree, already feeling the effects as I drop my arse to the ground.

A quarter of the bottle is gone by the time I hear people approaching. I look up, finding the twins and Selina coming over. Selina looks reluctant to be there, yet the twins are grinning, holding their own bottle of something.

Great, more alcohol for me to drink after I finish this one, I think sourly as I take another swig.

My eyes catch some movement behind Selina, and leaning against the entryway to Nova's garden, is Kaiden, his sunglass covering those eyes of his. Doesn't matter, I can still feel them on me.

The twins block the sun when they step in front of me.

Lucca drops to the ground, grinning smugly at me, even with that cut on his lip. I guess he didn't get hit as much as I thought in the fight, because the bruising is minimal. "So, is this a private party, or can anyone join?"

I SNEER AT LUCCA. "GO THE FUCK AWAY."

Ethan winces as he sits down next to his brother, and I grimace at the sight of him. His bruises look worse than they did in the kitchen. I shrug, not giving a shit. It's kind of revenge for groping me the first time we met.

My gaze drifts over his shoulder, eyeing Kaiden with disgust as I gulp down more of the bottle. My tongue feels numb, but it doesn't stop my spite lashing out when I get the urge to get shit off my chest. "Come to see the great Ivy Monroe fall down on her arse? Are you here to deliver the punchline or the killer blow? Going to tell me how worthless I am, big man?"

"Ivy," Selina whispers, trying to take the bottle away from me.

"No! This is mine. You know my mum drank to forget, don't you? She had it figured out."

She shakes her head, her lips tipped down. "I didn't know your mother, Ivy."

I laugh in her face. "Me neither." After taking another swig, I turn to the twins. "Why the fuck are you two here?"

Ethan looks up from his phone. "Hey, I had the life beat out of me. I deserve a drink, don't you think?"

I shrug, not bothering to answer.

"Are you sure this is a good idea?" Selina asks gently, looking at my bottle.

I snort, laughing harder at the sound.

"This is a *great* fucking idea," Lucca chuckles, drinking from his own bottle.

I roll my eyes, snatching the blue liquid from his hands, causing some to spill down his shirt. "*You* weren't invited."

"Hey, that's mine," he snaps. I shove the vodka in his lap, and he grabs it before the contents completely soak his shorts.

"So... mummy and daddy issues, huh?" Ethan asks, smirking.

"Ethan!" Selina snaps.

"What? It's not like we all don't have them," he mutters back.

"Yeah, join the club," Lucca salutes, holding his bottle up in the air.

A lightbulb goes off, and my head spins when I face Selina too fast. "Wait, didn't you say your uncle was married to Nova?"

Selina bites her bottom lip, nodding slowly. "I didn't know, if that's what you're asking."

"Of course, you didn't. We know fuck all, remember? But that would mean we're cousins, right?"

Her entire face brightens. I'm glad someone is happy. "Oh, yes—that is so cool."

"So, no foursome then?" Lucca asks, and both Selina and I roll our eyes at him. "That's a no then."

"*Anyway*... So, if we're cousins, that means you have to drink with me," I tell her, handing her the bottle. I have no idea what it is, but it tastes better than vodka.

She takes the bottle, looking unsure. "Are you sure you don't want to talk about it? We only heard the last bit. We heard you yelling and came to see if you were okay."

"See if Nova was okay you mean," I snap sarcastically. Because let's face it, none of them know me enough to care.

No one cares about me.

Not my mum.

Not my dad.

And I couldn't give a flying fuck anymore.

They can all go to hell, for all I care.

"That's not true," she tells me, almost looking sincere.

Lucca laughs. "We were checking on Nova. She's done a lot for our mum over the years."

"More than she did for mine."

"Your mum was a slag and a drunk," Ethan comments, not harshly, but not nicely either.

I glare at him, sitting up from my slouched position. "Yeah? Was it you she flaunted it in front of? Was it you she ignored or forgot about? No, so shut the fuck up, Ethan. If she did something that affected you, then pipe in. Until then, simmer down and keep ya mouth shut, yeah?"

He chuckles, holding his hands up. "All right. All right."

"I still think you should talk about it. Was your mum really raped?" Selina asks, and my stomach sinks.

"She was pregnant. I don't even know if she had that baby or not. I could have a sibling out there and she never even told me. They're better off though," I tell her, snatching the bottle back.

Her eyes hold pity, and I look away. When she goes to reach for me, I pull away, standing up.

"I don't want to talk about this. I don't give a fuck. My mum lied to me my whole life, so why should I expect anything different from other people?"

"Where's the party?" is yelled, and I look towards the Kingsley's garden, seeing a bunch of people piling through the gate.

I look down at the twins with hardened eyes. "What did you do?" I bite out.

Lucca grins. "You picked up a bottle of vodka. That's a call for a party. We invited everyone and anyone to come out to the lake. Think of it like a welcome to Cheshire Grove party."

Someone sets up speakers while another trails behind him with an extension lead. I groan, bringing the bottle to my lips, and drink a hefty amount.

When I'm done, I wipe my mouth with the back of my hand and let out a heavy sigh. "Then let's fucking party."

I LAUGH UPROARIOUSLY as Selina and I decorate the face of a stranger with permanent marker. I have no idea where she even got them, but before I knew it, the guy who passed out not long ago was covered in our artwork.

Mature? No. But it was funny. And I wish I could see his face when he realises he looks like a desk from my old school with graffiti all over it.

"Shh," she hisses, nearly toppling me over when she bumps her shoulder into me.

I stand up, dusting off my pyjama shorts. I still hadn't bothered to get dressed. The evening was upon us, and I had no plans for that to change. I hadn't spoken to anyone else at the party. Instead, I stayed to myself, unless the twins or Selina spoke to me. I was happy with that.

"Uh-oh," Selina hisses, and I look in the direction that's grabbed her attention, my lip curling when I see two Nova's walking towards us.

"Are there two of her?" I ask from the side of my mouth to Selina. She giggles, sobering when Nova sends her a cautioning gaze. I tighten the cardigan I wrapped around my waist, waiting for her to approach.

"Ivy, can you please come inside?" she calls, her voice firm and calm.

I sway on my feet as I try to take a step towards her. "No!"

"Are you drunk?"

I clap my hands, laughing. "And the genius award goes to—"

"Ivy," she whispers harshly. "It's time for you to come inside. You haven't eaten all day and we need to talk."

"The time for talking is long gone. How can I trust anything you have to say to me?"

"I explained why I kept information from you. I did not lie to you, Ivy. I had every intention of telling you."

I snort, looking around. "I'm bored. Want to go swimming?" I ask Selina.

Selina looks up from the ground, swaying herself. "I thought you couldn't swim?"

"No better time to start than with liquid courage," I tell her, laughing when her eyes widen and her nose crinkles. I whip the tank from my body, eyeing Nova, who doesn't even blink at me in my underwear.

"Ivy, please, stop this nonsense and come inside."

I walk backwards. Well, I try the best I can in my current state. When she takes a step towards me, a glare at her.

I want to forget about everything, just five minutes where I'm not angry at everyone. And Nova, coming out here and acting like she has control over me… I snort, shaking my head at her.

She really hasn't learned anything about me in the short amount of time we've known each other.

Without a thought, I spin around and run towards the lake.

The crowd begins to hoot and laugh. When I reach the small wooden pier, I jump as high as I can and plunge into the dark depths of the lake. Even with the temperature being high all day, the water still has a bite to it as I sink into darkness.

The water wakes me up, and my brain begins working again. That's when the panic of what I've done sets in. I didn't think this through.

I open my mouth to scream, coughing and spluttering under the water. I kick my feet with all my might, getting no closer to the surface. Instead, I sink further down.

I'm so stupid.

Why did I let them get to me? I'm made of stronger stuff than this.

Arms grip me from under my armpits, lifting me up. The second we reach the surface, I begin to choke, fighting to take in more air.

"Ivy!" I hear screamed.

I keep coughing, hiding my face against the chest of the person carrying me up the bank, clinging to their warmth.

"Is she okay?" Nova asks, and I feel another set of hands touching me.

"Don't touch me," I croak out.

"Ivy, why would you do that if you knew you couldn't swim?"

"Why do you care? You're just like Mum. A liar."

"Ivy," she whispers, and I close my eyes, blocking out the pain in her voice.

"I hate you," I mumble, my words slurring.

"I've got her, Nova."

Kaiden.

I should have known it would be him. Messing with my mind once again.

"I hate you too," I tell him, clinging to him tighter.

The light breeze disappears when he steps inside. "I don't get you at all. One minute you act like you hate me, the next... I don't even know what. For all I know, you could have saved me because you want to kill me yourself."

I hear him chuckle as he gently puts me back on my feet. I didn't even know he could be kind. I wobble forward, my forehead smacking into his chest.

I really shouldn't have drunk alcohol today.

"We need to get you out of these wet clothes."

"Why? So you can have your way with me again?"

He lifts my chin until I'm staring into his eyes. "I never took advantage of you the first time. And I don't sleep with drunk girls." He expression is stern. "What you did tonight was reckless."

I snort as he slides my shorts and knickers down, keeping his gaze locked on mine. I grip his shoulders when I become unsteady again.

He's a breath away when he stands, and I become mesmerised by his emerald green eyes staring back at me.

"I'm not her, you know," I tell him.

I feel my bra loosen before he slides the straps off my arms. "I'm getting that."

"Then why do you hate me? Why did you come here last night?"

He steps back, and I nearly topple over from the loss. I don't care I'm stark naked in front of him. He grabs his T-shirt at the back of his neck and pulls it over his head. His abs flex, and I think I drool a little, even let out a sigh.

He pushes it over my head, engulfing me in warmth as the soft material falls down my body. Letting out a sigh, he grips my shoulders, pushing me back until the backs of my legs hit the bed. I drop down immediately, my head feeling heavier.

I lie back on my pillows, watching Kaiden carefully. He could still secretly be planning on attacking me.

"Ivy, your mum didn't just ruin your aunt Nova's life."

"I know, she ruined her own," I tell him, yawning. "God, the room is still fucking spinning."

"You don't get it. My mum drinks and takes pain pills to forget what she did. Grant's mum died because of her."

That has my attention, and I blink up at him. "My mum killed his mum?" I whisper, my stomach sinking.

He scrubs his hand down his face. "No. But she was the reason she was driving in a state. She crashed her car."

"But *I* didn't do all of those things," I tell him, struggling to keep my eyes open. "I'm not here to cause trouble. I'm here because I had nowhere else to go, and you'll never know how that feels."

"I'm starting to get that."

"And you and your brothers sexually assaulted me. Who does that?"

I open my eyes when I feel him move. I blink, lost for words when he runs his finger over my jaw.

"They did that to scare you."

"Why?" I whisper.

"Because they knew I was going to ruin you," he tells me hoarsely. "They wanted to scare you, to make you run, to see if you were strong enough to handle what I was going to throw at you. They would never have taken it any further than they did. My brothers can be dickheads, but they aren't monsters."

"What does this mean? Is this an olive branch?" My eyes flutter shut, missing his expression.

"I don't fucking know anymore."

I STIR AWAKE at the sound of two people whispering. Fuck, my head is pounding and my eyes sting with tiredness. They droop, and I fight to stay awake, to hear what they are saying.

I'm curled into a ball under the blanket, facing away from the door. I can't remember how I got to bed, and I don't have enough energy to care.

"Is she okay?" my aunt Nova whispers.

"She'll be hungover tomorrow, that's for sure." I'm surprised to find it's Kaiden in the room. He pauses, and I hear movement, like someone is leaning forward in a chair. "Does she really not know anything, Nova?"

"She didn't know a thing until this morning, Kaiden. Anything else there is to know is better left forgotten. No child should hear bad things about their mum, whether they had Ivy's upbringing or not."

"How? Why? Why is she here, really?"

I hear my aunt sigh. "I don't know. Cara clearly washed us completely out of her life. The poor girl grew up with nothing, Kaiden. The flat she lived in wasn't even the size of this room, and she barely had the minimum essentials. I don't know how she survived. And she's my niece. She isn't here under another agenda. If she had a different upbringing, I don't think she would be here at all. She's really closed off."

Kaiden clears his throat. "What she said about the diary—is it true?"

"Kaiden, I don't feel comfortable speaking about this with you."

"I deserve to know if she's going to start accusing people, like her mum did. Look what happened to Grant's mum. Whatever her mum said that night, it was the catalyst for what happened."

"Kaiden," she says sharply. "Drop it. She doesn't know anything."

"Fuck!"

"Why don't you go home and get some rest. I think I saw Lucca and a few friends carrying Ethan inside."

A sigh from Kaiden this time. "I'll stay here, if that's okay with you. I just want to make sure she's not going to be sick."

"You're a good boy," she tells him.

Someone moves further into the room, and I close my eyes, trying to even out my breathing when I feel them come around the bed.

A cold finger moves a strand of hair out of my face. My heart beats rapidly when I feel her breath fan across my cheek, right before she presses her lips to my head.

I relax somewhat when I feel her step away.

"She's going to need protecting. This is a new world for her. Don't... Please make sure she doesn't follow the same path as her mum."

My mind begins to fog, and I don't hear Kaiden's reply. Instead, I fall into a deep slumber, my heart feeling heavy.

chapter thirteen

I WAKE UP FEELING LIKE I SHOULD BE REMEMBERING something, but everything is foggy as I stare at the wall next to my bedroom window.

I don't even know how I got to bed. The last thing I remember is betting one of the twins to take a shot of something and then spin around twenty times really fast. Everything after that is a blur.

My eyes widen when I realise I don't have any knickers on. I gasp, sitting up in bed, my fingers running through my hair. A startled yelp escapes when I find Kaiden sitting in the armchair in the corner of my room, his head resting back, his eyes closed, bare chested. Again.

Please, not again.

I get a good look at his fabulous body before glancing down at the T-shirt I'm wearing. I bring it to my nose, breathing in his woodsy scent.

God, his shirt smells hot.

I shake the inappropriate thoughts from my mind and once again look at Kaiden. I freeze when I see his eyes are open, staring at me, his expression blank.

"W-What—" I pause, clearing my dry throat. "What are you doing here?"

He sits forward, spreading his legs, and rests his forearms on his thighs, clasping his hands together.

Jesus Christ.

He's sinfully sexy, even sitting.

He opens his mouth, but the bedroom door flies open to reveal Selina standing in the doorway.

"We're going on a boat trip," she squeals.

I clutch my head, glaring at her. "Will you go be loud somewhere else? Anywhere else?"

She beams, shaking her head at me in a way that says she thinks I'm teasing. I don't think she realises I could throat punch her right now. I just need some energy.

"Silly," she gushes, then jumps a little when she sees Kaiden, her eyebrows scrunching together. "That's not creepy at all."

I'd laugh, but I really don't have the energy. "Why are you here?"

"Boat trip, remember. It will only be on the lake, but how cool is it going to be. Get ready, we're leaving soon," she tells me in a high-pitched fashion. She looks to Kaiden, raising an eyebrow. "The twins are looking for you."

He stands up and her eyes immediately go to his chest. When she licks her lips, I jump in, clearing my throat.

"I'm not going on a boat trip," I tell her. "I'd rather die in bed."

Her smile drops. "Ah, you and Nova *do* have a lot to talk about."

That hits me like a truck, and I remember everything that happened yesterday. *Fuck.* "I'll get in the shower in a second."

When she doesn't leave, I continue to stare until she gets the point. She bounces on her feet, smiling. "I'll leave you two to it then."

Once she leaves, I turn to Kaiden. "Why are you in here?"

He keeps his expression blank as he shoves his hands into his front pockets. "How much do you remember about last night?"

I groan, covering my face with the blanket for a moment. Dropping it to my lap, I open one eye, then two, grimacing. "What did I do?"

His lips twitch into a smirk, and for a second, I get excited, believing he's going to smile.

"You jumped into the lake," he reminds me, and I close my eyes, thinking back. Why don't I remember?

"I didn't?" I ask, shocked, too stunned over that to believe we're having a civilised conversation right now.

He nods. "Yeah, I pulled you out. You shouldn't be so immature. If you can't handle your drink, then don't drink it," he warns me.

And there's the ray of sunshine I've come to know.

"Fuck you. It's not like I drink every day. That was my second time drinking, and trust me, it reminded me of why I don't," I reply snottily. "It still doesn't explain why you're here."

"I brought you up here after that and put you to bed."

For some stupid reason, my gaze goes to my bed. Shaking my head, I ask him again, "And you're here because?"

He mutters something under his breath. "It doesn't matter. Just don't do stupid shit again."

"Wait," I call out when he walks to the door. He pauses, looking back at me. "Thank you."

He gives me a chin lift. "You should start getting ready," he says, before leaving.

Well, fuck a duck.

What the hell is going on? Why did he stay? I was clearly safe in bed. I close my eyes, clutching my head as I try to remember something.

For some reason, I can hear Nova's voice, but the words are a jumbled mess.

My door flies open, Selina leaning in. "Chop, chop! We need to get going. Annette is making us some lunch to take with us."

Guess I'm going on a boat trip. Great. Just what a girl who can't swim needs to do.

When they said boat trip, I'd pictured a low, long, small wooden shack boat. Not this. The gleaming white boat is huge. Not the biggest here, but still big enough to stand out.

I thought it would be outside the back of our house, but when Selina piled me and the twins into the car, we travelled thirty minutes before pulling into a private marina.

"What's all that?" the twins ask as Selina takes the bags from her driver.

"Annette wanted to make sure we had drinks and food."

Their eyes light up. "Cool. Kaiden has bags of shit, too, from Lenore."

Wait, what?

"Kaiden is here?"

The twins grin at me, each taking a step to the side of me before wrapping their arms around my shoulders. "Aw, someone regretting last night?"

"What?" I squeak, glaring at the two when they begin to chuckle.

Selina giggles. "You did keep telling us how hot his body was."

"I didn't," I whisper, horrified.

"You did. Among other stuff," Ethan informs me. I try to shrug him off, but he pulls me tighter against him.

"And he stayed out last night. He won't tell us where, the dirty dog," Lucca says.

Selina opens her mouth. "Well, he was—"

"Probably getting space from these overbearing babies," I finish for her, giving her a warning look.

She nods, looking slightly confused before leading the way onto the boat. I follow her up the small path, grateful when the twins pull away from me. I feel hotter than normal, even though it's only half ten in the morning.

I step onto the luxurious boat. My muscles tighten when I see a group of girls I don't recognise sitting on the cream, leather seats at the back of the boat. Right next to my worst nightmare.

Grant.

All the girls squeal when they see the twins, but the minute their eyes fall on me, I can feel the hostility.

Grant, on the other hand, looks ready to murder me, and I wonder if being on a secluded boat, dead in the water, when I can't swim and don't really have anyone I fully trust yet, is a wise idea. I mean, who's to say Selina would have my back if a fight broke out?

"Grant, my man, brought us a treat?" Ethan asks, sitting next to a pretty blonde.

"That's Emma Lexington," Selina whispers.

Grant laughs, his arm around a brunette, who eyes me with distain. "Always."

"And that's Sophia Morton. Her daddy invented some gadget," Selina continues as another lad steps out from below deck, a goofy grin on his face.

"Ethan, Lucca, my boys," he yells, doing that weird hand clasp thing before lounging in his own seat.

I don't look away from the group as they continue to greet each other, but I lean in closer to Selina, keeping my voice low. "Who's the other three?"

"The lad is Kyle Hansen. His dad owns a bunch of ships," she starts. "The redhead is Krysten Cambell, and the last one is Jenny Fields."

"And here's the dirty stop out," Lucca hoots.

Grant looks sharply to Lucca. "What do you mean?"

"Shut the fuck up," I hear Kaiden rumble from behind me, sending shivers up my spine.

His voice.

"What's he talking about?" Grant asks, directly to Kaiden now.

"Jealous?" Ethan asks, laughing when Grant leans over to punch him in the shoulder.

"Where were you, if you weren't with them?" a high-pitched voice asks, and my entire body tenses as I turn to the grating sound.

Clad in short shorts and a bikini top, which is covered with a see-through top that falls off the shoulder, is Barbie's replica. In fact, Barbie's tits look more real.

She gives me a side eye as she presses her body against Kaiden's side, running her finger over his bare chest.

I meet his gaze, narrowing mine. I can't see if he's looking at me, but I do see his jaw clench.

What the fuck?

He has a girlfriend. After everything, he has a girlfriend. Why am I not surprised? Does she know what he's like?

"No one told me we were doing charitable work today," the girl says.

"Danielle," Kaiden warns, before pushing away from her to take a seat on another sofa. He spreads his legs, looking out at the view.

"We aren't," Jenny says, twisting her lips together.

"You sure?" Danielle asks, shoving her shoulder into me. I take a step towards her, ready to teach her some respect, but Selina grabs my hand and pulls me away from the group.

"Why don't we go and get a drink before we set off?" she asks.

"Five minutes, sir," a loud, booming voice shouts from above us.

I look over my shoulder in time to see Kaiden give whoever spoke a chin lift. My stomach twists when Danielle drapes herself over him.

Ridiculous.

And why the fuck do I care? I don't even fucking like him.

"Phew! For a minute there, I thought you were going to throttle her," Selina says as she walks over to the bar. The boat is just as plush inside as it is outside. Jesus, did they not bargain buy at all?

I help myself to a glass of orange juice. "I was."

Her head twists to me so fast, I'm surprised it didn't spin off. "You were?"

I arch an eyebrow at her. "Yes. I'm not going to let some Barbie bitch talk down to me like that."

She bites her lip worriedly. "I don't think that's a great idea. The Kingsley's are kings around here. Since the Monroe's didn't have children—" She stops midsentence, her eyes widening. "I mean, until we found out about you. She's the next thing to queen."

I wave her off, finishing off my drink. "It's fine. I know what you meant. I'm just a nobody, even if I am related to the Monroe's."

Her expression saddens. "No, I didn't mean it like that. And you do matter, even if you weren't related to the Monroe's."

Whatever.

"What is her deal, anyway?" I ask, busying myself with my glass.

When she doesn't answer, I glance at her from the corner of my eye to find her smirking. "You like him," she teases.

I narrow my eyes at her. "I do fucking not. Do you not remember the shit I told you? I can't even stand him, and I'm pretty sure I'm only on this trip so they can dump my body in the middle of the ocean."

Her eyes widen a fraction. "They wouldn't. They can be jerks at times, but they never really bully people. We all went to school together, so I've known them a long time. I'm surprised they've acted like this. I would have thought being related to their godmother meant they'd be protective of you."

I snort. "So, are you going to answer me?"

She sighs, like she's frustrated with my lack of sharing. "Danielle Holden. Her dad is some bigwig in London. He's really high up in the *political world*," she tells me, using air quotes. "Her mum also owns her own fashion line and is always working away in Paris or Rome."

"What's her problem with me, then?"

"Kaiden," she tells me on a resigned sigh. "She thinks she has some magical hold over him because of who their families are. Half the time I don't think he can stand her."

"Then why is he with her?" I ask, trying not to sound too interested.

"Because believe it or not, she doesn't sleep around when she's back at school. I heard he even makes her get tested."

"I'm so confused. Are they together or not?"

She chuckles. "No. He's always straight with her. Like at the winter ball last year, she was telling everyone she felt like Kaiden was going to propose, so he put a stop to the rumours. Publicly. I felt embarrassed for her. He yelled at her, saying she was just some pussy he fucked from time to time."

"Pig," I grunt in disgust.

"Yes, but an honest one. I've never actually seen him with many girls. If he does, he keeps them quiet, but he doesn't really sleep around. That's the twins."

"Gah! This place is crazy. It's like you have your own set of rules."

She looks at me dead serious. "That's 'cause we do. It's shameful to admit, but the people here… they get away with everything. Money talks. You'd be surprised what people are willing to do, willing to lie about, just for some cash. Kaiden and his brothers might be dicks, but they don't act entitled. They don't throw their money around."

"They don't?" I ask, feeling my eyes bug out, because that's not how it seems to me. Although, they've never screamed, I have more money than you.

She gives me a pitying look, which I hate. "You'll find out soon enough. The Kingsley's don't do it. They don't need to; they're the richest people in Cheshire Grove. Third in the UK. They don't need to brag about it."

"I'm still not following."

"When you get back to school, just don't get in anyone's faces. Danielle up there has the means to make your life hell—and the money to get away with it," she rushes out, taking a deep breath. "Is that easier to follow?"

I pat her on the shoulder, grinning. "Yes, but there's a difference between me and everyone else: I don't give a fuck. I have nothing to lose. I don't have a career I want to peruse, where my reputation could jeopardize that. You're underestimating me, Selina."

"Ivy," she warns, following me back out.

"Relax, I'll try to behave."

She groans, loudly. "Oh God."

chapter fourteen

It's coming up to midday and the sun is belting down on us. I'm glad I listened to Selina and wore a bikini top under my tank top. Even with a slight breeze, I have droplets of sweat running down my back and between my tits. I feel like my body has swelled to twice its size. Even my shorts are feeling a little tight.

And when I'm this hot, I get bitchy. And Danielle is getting on my last nerve. Her snarky remarks are grating on me, and I am seconds away from punching her perfect nose.

It's not like she can't afford another nose job.

"Did you see that picture of Katrina online? Her parents are going, like, crazy over it," Jenny mentions.

Jenny is the definition of bimbo, even though she isn't blonde. She takes everything at face value and is pretty clueless to the snide remarks thrown at her. I can understand them though. She thought there was different types of ice and asked for diet. I kind of snorted in her face, as she was standing next to me at the outside bar. It didn't go over well with her friends.

"Her mum is threatening to send her to her aunt, who lives in the Hamptons. I mean, what is she going to do in America? She won't know anyone."

"She shouldn't have been cheating on Grant," Sophia adds, rubbing herself up against him.

Yeah, I'm not even going to go there with him. He's clearly not happy with me being here, but any time he has said something, a look from Kaiden has stopped him. But I know it's killing him to stay silent.

"And that's what she gets for going against our group," Danielle snidely remarks. When I turn her way, she's giving me a pointed look.

Yeah, I really want to punch the bitch.

"I, for one, can't wait for school," Selina states, changing the subject.

Danielle laughs, but her face is twisted in disgust. "You would. It's not like you have a social life."

Seeing Selina's face flush with embarrassment, I grip my glass tighter. "It's better than the alternative," I start, and all eyes come to me. "I mean, she's going to have a career. She won't be some washed up whore with a husband that will most likely have his casket already picked out." I force a wide, fake smile and turn back to Selina, who ducks her head, smirking.

The twins and Kyle laugh, high fiving each other.

"What is that supposed to mean?" Danielle hisses, getting off Kaiden's lap. I'm surprised she's moved. She's like a lost little puppy following him around. I'm pretty sure she's scared I'll take him away.

I blink my lashes innocently. "Most likely what you thought I meant. But then, you are a little slow," I snark.

"You bitch," she hisses, throwing her sparkling water over me.

"Dude, nipples," Ethan hoots.

I go to grab the bitch when hands wrap around my waist, lifting me off the floor. "Let me fucking go," I growl.

I know it's not Kaiden because I see him grab Danielle by the bicep, pushing her down in the chair.

"Keep causing shit. I can't wait to see what they do to you," Grant whispers in my ear.

"Were you born a bastard?" I bite out when he puts me down.

His expression hardens, his face like thunder. "No. But I was raised motherless thanks to your bitch of a mum."

That makes me pause. "What?" I whisper, wondering if I heard that right.

His lips curl into an angry snarl. "My mum died in a car crash because of your mum."

"My mum has never driven," I murmur, but then it's clear already that I know nothing about my mum. My stomach twists into knots and I can't help but wonder what the hell she did to everyone.

"She wasn't even in the car. She told my mum something that caused her to drive upset. There was a massive storm, and she crashed her car into a tree on a bend."

Does he not hear himself? My body tightens when I step forward, tilting my head. "So, my mum tells your mum something she didn't like. Your mum, a grown adult, runs off to her car and drives in the middle of a storm, probably going too fast, and crashes? Dickhead, she could have been going five miles an hour in that condition and still crashed. Don't fucking blame my mum for your mum's choices. Where the fuck do you get off?"

I scoff, going to walk away.

"I lost my whole fucking life that night. Your mum took that away from me. And I'll do everything in my power to make sure you pay."

I push him away. "And I thought I had mummy issues. Seriously, grow the fuck up. I'm sorry your mum died. I truly am. But don't fucking take it out on me when I was still in my dad's ballbag. And from where I'm standing, your life didn't really change that much. I'm pretty positive you'd still be an insensitive jerk."

"I don't want you here," he growls low, so the others don't hear him.

"And I don't care," I snap back.

"You're going to regret this you know. Big time."

"And for someone who doesn't shit money, I'm still not the slightest bit scared," I tell him, shrugging.

He pushes past me, nearly knocking me over, and I shake my head. Rich people really are fucking sensitive arseholes. They pretty much have everything and it's still not good enough.

Rubbing my chest, I frown when I find it sticky. I head downstairs, where Selina showed me the bathroom was. Following the directions, I come down another hallway. A large bed made up with cream sheets is in the room ahead. To the side is a bathroom, with a small glass shower, toilet and sink.

They really don't do things small. Even the boat is bigger than the flat I shared with Mum.

I step into the bathroom, grabbing a white towel off the rack, and walk over to the sink. Looking up into the mirror, a startled scream escapes me.

Kaiden is standing in the doorway, all creepy like. Our eyes meet for a split second before he steps in and slides the door closed.

"What are you doing?" I ask, turning the hot water on.

"You need to be careful."

I drop the towel on the edge of the sink and turn to face him. "I'm actually fed up of all these warnings. In fact, I'm getting fucking sick of it. If she wants to come at me, go ahead. I've dealt with worse people than petty bitches like her. And you?" I say, raising my voice. "You can do one. I'm sick of you blowing hot and cold. One minute you're—" I pause, unable to say what I need to. I mean, telling him he's fingering me and giving me an amazing orgasm one minute isn't something he needs to hear. I wave my hand at him, gesturing to his body, which is looking mighty fine, glistening from the sea air and summer heat. "*You*, and the next you look ready to murder me. And don't even get me started on last night. What was all that about?"

I stop myself before the entire boat can hear me.

He steps closer, pushing me back against the sink. "Are you finished?"

I want to scream *no*, to tell him to fuck off. My body, however, has other plans, overwhelmed by his proximity.

How does he do this to me? I want to hate him. Desperately. But I want him more than I want to kill him.

"Maybe," I whisper, wishing I could step back to put some space between us.

"I didn't mean to be cryptic. I'm calling a truce."

"Why?" I ask, not trusting this 'truce' is real.

"Because I think I was wrong about you. I think there's more to the story than what our parents told us."

"What story?" I ask, still in the dark about pretty much everything. And there he is. A veil appears over his expression and his jaw tightens. "You know what, forget about it. I don't even know why I care. Whatever issues you have, I don't want to know. If they are anything like Grant's, they aren't worth knowing. You can all just—"

He kisses me.

He fucking kisses me.

In my head, I reach out to push him away, to hell with this crap of cat and mouse, but in reality, I don't. No. Instead, I place my hands on his hips, my traitorous body betraying me when I pull him flush against me.

His fingers dig into my hips as he lifts me onto the counter, next to the sink. I moan, sliding my hands up his warm, hard body, lightly skimming over his shoulders before grabbing onto the back of his neck, kissing him harder.

Holy fuck, he can kiss.

I'm certain I'm having an out-of-body experience, because I'm pretty sure every time his lips partially close over mine, I'm having a mini orgasm. A lot of them.

I try to fight my body's instinct, I really do, but the longer he kisses me, the hotter I get.

But I'm not my mum. I don't do this.

I pull back, breathing hard, and look up at him, feeling dazed. "I'm not a slag. I've only slept with one person."

His fingers dance over the buttons of my shorts. "Never really thought you were," he tells me, leaning in to kiss me once more.

I pull back again, needing to see him.

All I see is the truth behind those words. He's not telling me what I want to hear. Not that I think he would anyway. He's had a way from day one to make me bend to his bidding.

His palm presses down on my clit, and a long, guttural moan escapes me. His eyes darken, and before I know it, I'm helping him take my shorts off.

Resting my hands on his shoulders, I lift my arse off the counter so he can pull them down.

I want him.

I don't care that I don't like him. That he hates me. I'm so turned on I could probably hump the side of the boat.

The second my shorts are off, I grab hold of his waistband and push his shorts down over his arse. I grip him, squeezing his cheeks in the palms of my hands as I bring him closer.

His lips press kisses down the side of my neck, causing me to have another mini orgasm. I'm almost afraid of what a real one by him will do to me.

My tits spring free when he loosens the strings tying my bikini around my back. His moves seem so practiced, like he's done this before, especially when he bends down, taking my nipple into his mouth whilst opening the drawer to the side of us.

I struggle to keep my eyes open, yet I manage to get a glimpse of a foiled packet.

"This is crazy," I pant when he pulls back from my nipple. "I don't even like you."

"I'm not forcing you," he snarls, a bite to his tone. "You want this."

I give him a sly smile, wiggling my fingers in front of him. "Does this look like I'm complaining?"

"You're infuriating," he growls.

"You need to stop talking before I change my mind," I sass back.

A small grin tugs at his lips. "Like that's going to happen."

He runs his dick through my wetness, teasing me, taunting me. Yeah, that isn't going to cut it. When he slides against my entrance, I take him by surprise by grabbing his arse in my hands and pulling, guiding him inside me with a roughness that steals my breath.

The groan that erupts from his throat has wetness seeping between my legs. I feel powerful in this moment, knowing I can make him lose control just as much as he can me.

He pulls back, keeping his gaze on me as he thrusts inside of me, punishingly. My arse slides back on the counter from the force, knocking a few bottles over in the process.

Game on.

He can fuck me like he hates me. I'll be doing the same thing.

Every time he hits the right spot, my stomach tightens, yet my orgasm is just out of reach, frustrating me.

"Fuck me harder," I bite out, digging my nails into his shoulders.

His eyes widen a fraction. "If I fuck you any harder, you'll put a hole through the side of the boat."

I throw my head back, my hair tumbling down my back as I moan, my body shaking with the need to come.

"Scared?" I rasp out.

His fingers slide to the back of my neck as he pulls me towards him. His lips slam against mine, our teeth knocking together in our frantic need.

With one hand around the back of my neck, the other at my hips, his thrusts become harder, deeper, sending delicious waves of pleasure through me.

And yet… I need him to go harder, deeper.

The sound of skin slapping together and our panting mingling together fills the small space.

Nothing has ever felt this good.

"Fuck! You're so fucking tight," he groans, his arse clenching in my hands with each thrust.

"Yes!" I moan, my orgasm building. "Yes!"

His lips slam back down on mine when my movements become frantic, my nails breaking the skin of his arse cheeks as I try to get him to go faster.

Then it happens.

For one moment, one blissful moment, nothing else matters. Not the person who is buried deep inside of me, not my mum, not Nova. Nothing.

My back arches as I slam myself down on him one last time, before I lose control of my body and my orgasm rips through me.

"Fuck," Kaiden grunts, slamming into me, one, two, three times before burying himself to the hilt. He shoves his face into the crook of my neck, breathing hard.

Voices nearby break up whatever this was between us.

"I'm just going to check if she's okay," Selina whispers harshly.

"I don't think she's going to appreciate you babysitting her," Lucca chuckles, before Selina squeals.

"Put me down this instant!"

"I will—over the side of the boat," he replies, his voice sounder further away.

I pull back from Kaiden, pushing him away a little. I'm unable to look him in the eye, afraid of what he will say to me. It was sex. It doesn't make me a slut. It doesn't make me like my mother. And I certainly don't need him to make me feel that way.

Before he can open his mouth, I jump off the counter, grab my shorts and knickers from the floor, and pull them on. Next, I grab my bikini top, still not giving him any attention. I can hear him pulling his own shorts on, but I'm too afraid to look, too afraid of what I'll do when I see his perfectly sculptured body.

He shouldn't be able to make me feel like this. He shouldn't be able to control me the way he does.

"Ivy," he starts.

I close my eyes, pained as I wait for his harsh words. "It was sex. Let's just pretend it never happened." I step past him, ready to go outside, but he grabs my arm, stopping me.

"Don't act fucking cold."

An undignified snort escapes me as I turn to face him. "Me? I'm acting cold? Turn around, dickhead, and take one long, hard look in the mirror. *That* is cold."

"You've just been fucked, come so hard I thought you were trying to squeeze the life out of my dick... Aren't you supposed to be in a good mood or something? You know, mellow?"

I arch my eyebrow at him. "Maybe you didn't do a good job. Maybe I faked it."

He grins, stepping forward. "You can't fake that shit. If you did, you're one hell of an actress. But I don't mind proving you wrong."

My cheeks heat a little as I look away from his smouldering gaze. "Just go before someone else comes looking. Maybe your girlfriend."

"She's not my girlfriend."

I know that, but I don't tell him. "Does she know that?"

He eyes me for a moment, making me feel uncomfortable. "This isn't over."

I look him dead in the eye, my body tensing. "It never is with you."

He shakes his head once more before turning and leaving the small bathroom. The minute he's gone, I lean back against the counter, letting out a puff of air.

And I thought my hangover was the worst that could happen to me today.

Maybe I was wrong.

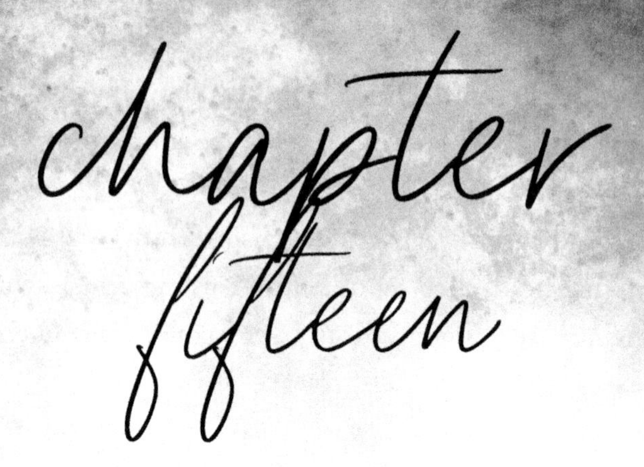

I DON'T RECOGNISE THE GIRL STARING BACK at me in the mirror. How did I become this person, someone who let a guy control her and manipulate her body in a way no one else can? It's frustrating. Infuriating. I want to hate him more because of it. But staring into the mirror, it dawns on me that it's me I hate.

I've gone from a girl who went days without food, who was scared to fall asleep in case one of Mum's 'boyfriends' thought they could keep it in the family, to a girl I barely recognise. I knew what to expect in life back home. I knew who not to push, who to avoid and how to take care of myself.

Cheshire Grove is a whole new world, a whole new crowd. It's filled with lies, secrets and deceit. With wealth, beauty and power.

And in the middle of all that, there's me.

A girl from a town that had prostitutes on street corners, and gangs and drug dealers living in the same block of flats. A girl who had to pinch shoes from a clothes bin because even the price at a charity shop was too steep.

To add to the confusion of all that, I went and slept with one of the wealthiest guys in Great Britain, a guy who clearly hates me because of who birthed me.

But I didn't just survive back where I came from. I fought.

Being in Cheshire Grove is either going to make me or break me. I knew that from the start. It's high time I stopped letting their words get to me, stopped the past from defining me.

I agreed to move in with Nova because I didn't want to live like I was anymore. I wanted more.

And if I let him, Kaiden could potentially take all that away from me, all the while living freely, without a care in the world.

With a deep sigh, I take a step back and wobble on my feet, my legs still like jelly. If I hide out any longer, it will be too obvious that something happened.

Looking at the door in the mirror's reflection, I shake my head. "Come on, Ivy. You've got this," I mutter quietly.

With one last deep breath, I head out, making my way through the hallway to the stairs leading to the back deck.

The minute Ethan sees me, he winks, walking backwards to the ledge before doing a backflip off it.

"What took you so long? Ethan said you were on an important phone call," Danielle hisses.

"Like he said, I was on the phone," Kaiden deadpans.

"To who?" I hear Danielle ask, her voice whiney.

My stomach sinks. She might be a bitch, but she's clearly claimed him. And I just fucked him with her close by.

And Ethan clearly knew what we were doing, if his efforts to keep her away are anything to go by.

The minute I step further onto the decking, Danielle spins to face me, her expression hard and deadly. Her gaze goes from me to Kaiden, a knowing look in her eye.

Did her mother never tell her that her face will stick like that?

"Enjoying yourself?" she bites out. "I bet you've never even seen a boat before."

I pointedly look to Kaiden when I say, "Immensely." The heated look we share makes my stomach swirl, and I want him all over again.

I look away before I'm caught staring too long.

Danielle flips her hair over her shoulder, cocking her hip to the side as she runs her finger down Kaiden's chest.

Her gaze flicks to me briefly before she turns back to him. "Want me to spend the night tonight?"

I watch as his jaw tightens and he takes a step back, enough so her finger is touching air. Her gaze narrows on him.

I feel out of place standing here watching him, but everyone is in the water, splashing around and having fun. It's just us three on the boat.

"No. You know I'd never let you stay."

"Kaiden," she whines.

"Danielle, come in the water. It's really cool," Krysten shouts, squealing when Kyle lifts her out of the water and throws her.

Danielle turns to the water, her lip curled. "I'm not getting into that water. I dread to think what is in there."

"Come on," Sophia yells, laughing at one of the twins.

I stand awkwardly, watching the scene play out, not knowing what to do. The bar grabs my attention, and even though I promised myself I wouldn't drink this morning, I don't care.

I need that drink if I'm going to put up with Danielle all over Kaiden.

"No. I've just had my hair done. I'm not getting it wet."

And it happens. The moment that will define my time at Kingsley Academy.

An undignified snort escapes me, and Danielle's ugly snarl turns my way.

"Do you have something to say?" she asks harshly.

I press a finger to my chest, arching my eyebrow at her. "Me?"

"Yes, you."

"Why don't we grab something to eat?" Selina asks, climbing up the ladder.

"No. I want to know what the charity trash has to say," Danielle interrupts.

I chuckle, staring at her. Could she be any more pathetic? "Is that supposed to hurt my feelings? I'd rather be trash than some plastic Barbie who can't tell her left from her right."

"Are you going to let her talk to me like this?" she asks, her attention on Kaiden. He's watching me intently, a look I can't decipher.

"Danielle, why don't you calm down. I'm sure Ivy doesn't have anything to say," Selina says, wrapping her towel around her.

"Please don't talk for me," I tell her, forcing my tone to be gentle.

Danielle laughs. "Oh, Farley, did you really just talk back to me?"

Selina cowers a little, and it pisses me off. Danielle doesn't get to bully me, or bully Selina.

"And what are you going to do if she is?" I ask Danielle.

She looks like a Pit bull chewing a wasp when she turns to me. "You have no idea who you're talking to."

"I don't care to."

"You should. I'm going to make your life hell."

"Like it isn't already," I reply sharply.

"Want to bet?" she asks snidely.

"No. Because I don't care either way."

"You will."

"Danielle, why don't you just come in for a swim?" Lucca yells from the water.

"Grab me my water, please, Ivy," Ethan calls, and I know they're trying to diffuse the situation, but it's not going to help. I grab the water bottle anyway and walk over to the edge of the boat to pass it down to him.

"Why doesn't the charity case go into the water?" she asks, smiling brightly at me.

Bitch.

"Danielle," Kaiden calls sharply.

"What?" she asks innocently, before she points her finger at me. "Oh, that's right, you can't swim. Because Mummy Dearest couldn't afford to pay for lessons."

"Actually, she didn't love me enough to take me," I tell her, stepping towards her. "But I mean, you wouldn't know anything about that, right? I bet your parents love you unconditionally. Feed you with a silver spoon, still wipe your arse because, you know, their precious daughter doesn't do minor tasks."

"You bitch!" she hisses, coming towards me.

"Bitch I may be, but at least I'm real. *All* real. I don't need surgery to try and hide who I really am," I snap back.

"Why don't we teach you to swim," she bites out, and reaches for me, trying to push me over the edge.

I struggle with my footing, nearly slipping off the side as I grab her hands and, using her forward momentum, sling her off the side of the boat.

"Oh my God," Selina whispers, as the guys laugh.

I step back from the edge as she screams in anger, splashing the water as she glares up me, wet hair covering her face.

"You are going to regret this. I'm going to make life with your mum seem like heaven by the time I'm done with you."

Her friends whisper to each other, all shooting daggers at me. I don't give a fuck. She has no idea what I went through, what my life was like. There is nothing she could do to me that I wouldn't survive.

It's going to be fun to see her face when she realises that.

"Here, I'll help you up," Sophia offers.

"I can do it," Danielle yells at her, wiping the wet hair from her face. She steps up the ladder, never taking her gaze from me. "I'm going to fucking ruin you in ways you've never imagined."

"Yada, yada, yada," I reply. "Do you ever tire of hearing your own voice?"

"Did you tire from hearing your mum fuck every man? Did you fuck them too? I bet you loved it."

I lunge forward when she steps into my space and grab a handful of her hair, causing her to scream out. I bend down, getting in her face, ignoring the biting pain of her nails clawing at my skin.

"I'm going to tell you this once, and once only, don't ever, and I mean *ever*, talk about me like you know me. Don't presume that I won't react if you talk shit about me. If you want to keep this pretty hair, I suggest you listen to me."

I push her away, and she falls into the arms of her friends who have stepped out of the water.

"Don't touch her," Krysten yells.

"Why? You were going to stand by and watch her push me into the water, knowing I can't swim. I'm not one of those weak girls you bully. You push and I'll push back. Harder."

"Are you going to let that piece of *filth* speak to us like that?" When Kaiden doesn't speak, she looks over her shoulder. "Baby?"

"We're done."

"Kaiden," Grant says with a warning in his tone, getting out of the water too.

She looks confused when she answers. "What?"

"You heard me," he says shortly, before whistling. The bloke driving the boat looks over the side and down at us.

"Yes, sir?"

"Take us to the dock. We'd like to go home."

He nods before disappearing, and I stand, shocked. Is he actually sticking up for me? Or are we going so he can drop me back home?

"For *her?*"

"I don't need to explain myself to you, Danielle. We were never an item."

"This is because of that slut."

"No, this is because of you. I suggest you and your friends go downstairs and get dressed."

"And call someone to pick you up," Ethan adds, trying and failing to hide his grin.

"Watch your back," she hisses at me as she storms past.

"I think I peed my pants a little," Selina whispers.

Feeling uncomfortable with the intensity of Kaiden's stare, I move over to the bench and take a seat, staring into the dark, murky water.

♡

We dropped the girls off a few docks back. A group of people were waiting for them in their cars. It was awkward to say the least, and tension on the boat still hadn't dropped. Grant was still glaring at me; not happy his fuck piece was kicked offboard.

I was kind of hoping the people driving the boats back would take him with them. He was getting on my last nerve.

The manors come into view, and even seeing my escape doesn't relax me. It's getting dark, though it's still too early for me to hide away in my room and go to sleep.

I was so tired this morning, but I'm too pumped up to go to sleep right now.

"Uh oh," Selina whispers, and I look over at the dock, groaning when I see Nova standing there with Annette.

I don't want to have a conversation with her right now. I'm not ready. I'm angry. Angry at her, angry at my mum, angry at everything.

"I really don't want to deal with her right now."

"I don't think you have a choice," Selina adds.

Grabbing my bag, I head to the bridge leading off the boat, not waiting for anyone else. They've already seen me make a fool of myself too many times.

"Ivy, we need to talk," Nova calls.

I roll my eyes childishly. "I—"

"If you're about to make an excuse, I don't want to hear it. I'll see you in the kitchen," she orders, giving me a sharp look. I swallow, finally seeing the lawyer in her. "Boys."

"Nova," they all greet.

I sigh when she starts to walk away, Annette following behind her. "I'm going to see if Elle needs help with anything."

"Elle?"

"Mrs White," I explain to Selina.

"But Aunt Nova said—"

"I don't care," I tell her sharply. "I need time and some space. I need to get out of here."

I start to walk away, ignoring her when she calls my name. I probably won't go to Elle's house. The sun is setting, and she's most likely getting ready for bed. She did mention she liked going to bed early so she can wake up earlier.

As soon as I hit the driveway, I begin to run, before Nova finds out I don't plan on going inside. I'm not sure how she'll react. Will she come after me? Wait until I get home?

Slowing down to a walk, I look around at the houses. Two couples are sitting outside their home, drinking wine and chatting. They stop when they see me, so I put my head down and walk faster, needing to get out of here.

A car approaching from behind grabs my attention, and I begin to walk faster, hoping it's not Nova.

The car slows beside me, and I groan when I see the shiny red sports car. "Miss me already?" I ask dryly.

"Get in," Kaiden orders.

I arch an eyebrow. "Does that work with everyone?"

"Just get in."

"Are you fucking serious, Kai? She can't come," Grant states angrily from the passenger side.

I bend down, winking at him. "Oh, I already have today."

"Really, Kai?" he asks, his face scrunched up in disgust. It brings me great pleasure.

Kaiden turns to him and says something too low for me to hear. Grant sits back in his seat, throwing something on the dashboard. "This is a bad idea."

Kaiden turns to me, opening his door. He gets out, pulling his chair forward. "Get in."

I sigh, because right now, I don't really have much of an option, and walking around the countryside where they don't like streetlights isn't my cup of tea.

"All right, but only because Grant's misery delights me."

"Bitch!"

I laugh as I bend down to get in the car, ignoring the pained groan coming from Kaiden. "And you're a tosser, but you don't hear me whining like a little girl."

"Really, Kai?" he asks when he gets in the car.

"Oh, like he can stop me."

Kaiden looks at me through the rear-view mirror, his expression always so serious. "Can I trust you to keep your mouth shut?"

Oh shit. Where the fuck are we going?

"Like she won't tell. This is a bad idea."

"What's a bad idea?" I ask, ignoring Grant's moaning.

"You," Grant snaps.

"Will you keep what happens tonight quiet? You can't tell anyone."

I shrug. "I've got no one to tell anyway, but sure. Anything beats going back to listen to Nova."

"This is a mistake," Grant warns as Kaiden begins to drive. He stops at the gate and shares a look with Grant when they don't open.

"What the fuck?" Grant whispers.

"Get down."

"Who?" Grant asks, but I'm one step ahead, lying down on the seats and covering my body with the hoody I found next to me. Hopefully he can't see through the open window, and it's lucky the rest are tinted.

The security guard nervously steps up to the driver's side. "I'm sorry, Mr Kingsley, but Miss Monroe called down and said not to let her niece out."

"Do you see her here?" Kaiden asks, his tone lethal.

"Um, n-no. I'll, u-um, let you go on with your evening."

"Good," Kaiden barks. "And if you ever stop me from leaving again, I'll have you fired."

"Y-yes, sir."

When we drive off, I sit back up, watching Kaiden's jaw harden.

"You really want to punch something right now, don't you?"

"Yes," Kaiden answers Grant.

Grant sighs. "Then let's go."

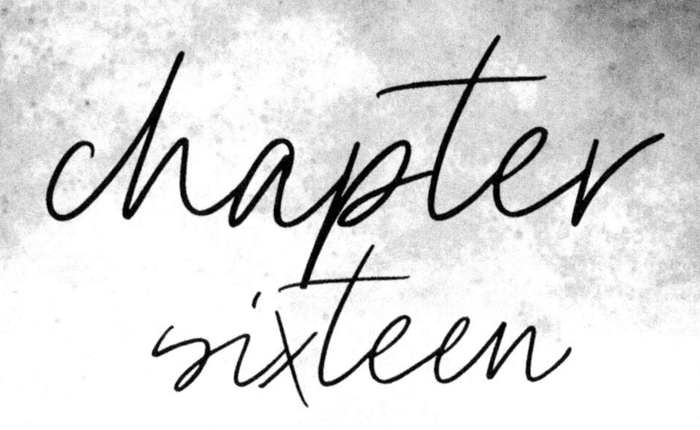

chapter sixteen

We pull up outside an old warehouse after an hour of driving, the gravel road crunching under the tyres. I peek out the window, in awe at the scenery. There are cars everywhere, all of them looking like they cost a mint, all kitted out to the nines.

Holy shit!

What is this place?

"Where are we?" I ask, not caring which of the two answer. There's an old rusty sign hanging from a chain, words missing; still, it's clear it used to be a carpet factory.

"It used to be a carpet factory. It closed down years ago when the foundations collapsed on the outbuilding," Kaiden answers, driving past all the cars parked out the front.

I'm confused when he keeps going, away from the building and up a long, spiral dirt road.

"Yeah, I can see that from the worn-out sign back there, but what is it now? Why are we here?"

"You'll see," he replies, pulling the car over to the side.

All right then. We're back to being cryptic.

He holds the seat forward so I can get out, and I run my hands down my arms at the chill brushing against them.

He eyes me for a moment before bending down into the backseat, then wordlessly handing me a zip up jacket.

"Thanks," I tell him quietly.

He doesn't say anything, just goes to meet Grant at the back of the car. "Are you sure about this?"

"Grant," Kaiden warns.

"If you get caught again, your granddad is going to disown you, man. You'll lose everything you've worked hard to get. Your dad—"

"Grant!" Kaiden barks. "Not now."

I blink innocently when they both turn around to face me. "Don't mind me. I don't understand all this cryptic shit anyway."

Grant scoffs. "Bringing her is a big mistake."

"I need the release," Kaiden replies.

"I thought you got that earlier," Grant bites out.

It takes us ten minutes to get to the building, and instead of going through the main door, they move around the side, heading towards the back.

The noise is booming; people yelling and cheering fill the air. The smell of blood hits me, and it doesn't take long to realise why. A guy younger than me walks past us, his face busted up and covered in blood.

When we step into the back, I inhale a lungful of air, taken aback by how many people are here. There are more cars, more people, and a ditch dug into the dirt where a crowd has congregated.

Through the sea of bodies, I see a guy land a knockout blow to his opponent, and wince. Fucking hell. These guys are savage. Lads where I lived fought all the time, but it was nothing like this, nothing organised. I don't know whether to be impressed or sick.

"Kai, my man, you racing tonight?" a guy with long, wavy blonde hair asks, clasping his hand with Kaiden's before bumping his shoulder against his.

"Not tonight, Dane."

Dane scans Kaiden's expression before giving him a single nod. "You're in luck. Remington is fighting tonight."

Carter Remington?

Grant chuckles, happy about the news, and Kaiden's lips twitch, like he's happy about it too.

"When's the race start?" Grant asks.

"Main race starts at eleven. We've had to change course since the fucking pigs keep trying to break us up."

"You need to find a new location," Kaiden tells him, his voice a warning.

Dane shrugs. "We know. We're trying to find someone who wants to buy the land. Police can't come on then, unless they have a warrant."

Grant and Kaiden share a look. "We'll talk about it."

Dane grins. "Knew I could count on you two fuckers," he says, before losing his smile. "Please tell me the twins aren't here."

Grant laughs. "No. We left them at home tonight."

Dane visibly relaxes. "Thank fuck. Grey is here, and I think he's looking for them."

Kaiden's jaw hardens. "If his girlfriend dropped her knickers for my brothers, that's on her. They're single. Is he fighting tonight?"

Dane grins. "Sure is. Want me to put you with him?"

Kaiden nods. "Yeah, save Carter for last."

"All right," he tells them, then his gaze comes to me, and a flirtatious grin spreads across his face. "Newbie?"

"Hands off," Kaiden warns, something else in his tone now, something more lethal.

It takes Dane by surprise, and he nods, audibly swallowing. "Got it. See you later."

The minute Dane walks away, Grant spins to face Kaiden. "Man, I'm not trying to be a nagging wife, but you heard him. The cops are onto him."

"Go find a pussy to fuck and let me worry about the cops."

Grant scrubs a hand through his hair. "All right."

When he's gone, I stand a little closer to Kaiden, pulling his jacket tighter around me. "You do this a lot?"

He looks down at me, his smoky green eyes watching me. "Fighting? No. But every now and then, I need the release." I feel like he's blaming me for that need. "Racing, however, I do every fortnight."

"You seem popular," I murmur, noticing the curious glances.

He ignores their stares. "They're interested in my family's money."

"You mean *your* money?"

He clenches his jaw. "No. It's not mine. I didn't earn it."

I nod, because I can understand that. "Can I ask you something?"

"Yeah, but it doesn't mean I'll answer."

I shrug. "That's fair," I tell him, taking a deep breath. "Earlier, on the boat..."

"It was what it was."

I roll my eyes at him. "That's good to know, but that isn't what I'm talking about. I meant Grant. He said my mum said something to his mum that caused her to drive in a storm. What did she say?"

He sighs, closing his eyes briefly. "We don't know, but he's spent all his life hearing how your mum killed his. He grew up to hate you."

I think about that for a minute. "And you?"

"My mum isn't the mum I remember. She has good days and bad days, but she's spent most her adult life popping prescription pills and staying at spas because of something your mum did to her. I resented you."

"Because I took your mum away?"

"Yes. No. Fuck!" he says, running his hand over his face. "It's fucking ridiculous when said like that, but it's been hard for us."

I snort. "You don't know the meaning of hard. It sucks. It really does suck that he lost his mum, that you lost yours to drugs. But I never had a mum. I had a roommate that brought back men so she could get her next fix or get some money to get her next fix. I had to constantly sleep with one eye open, sometimes not at all because I was scared one of her boyfriends would try to get into bed with me again. No one at school wanted to be friends with me once they found out who my mum was. We didn't have food. And until I moved into Nova's, I had never owned anything new. I lived in a mouldy flat with no carpets, wallpaper peeling off the walls, and where everyone inside was a drug addict or a prostitute. I'm not making anyone's life hell for her choices. So please don't tell me it was hard. Ever."

I storm off, angry all over again. A hand grips my arm, pulling me back. I don't struggle, not wanting to draw attention to us.

I let him drag me towards the building. We walk into a darkened alley, heading to the end, which is blocked off. There's no light, no people, just us.

"Why are we down here?"

He doesn't speak. Instead, he grabs my face and kisses me.

Damn him and his fucking kisses.

I kiss him back, because that seems to be what I do now. Give in to him. He slowly pulls back, breathing hard.

"You weren't meant to be you," he whispers.

"Me?" I whisper back, in a haze.

"You represented everything that was wrong with our families. When we heard you were coming, we couldn't let you stay. My mum's broken. I don't know how she'd react if she found out you're here. And you've seen Grant's reaction." He slams his fist against the wall. "Our dads… They aren't good men. My dad is an even worse husband. He uses my mum. He uses her for her name and her fortune, even though he comes from wealth himself. My grandfather is old-fashioned. He doesn't care that his daughter is broken, that he's using him. He never had a son, so Royce is that son. My granddad on my dad's side is just as bad; money hungry, even though they have plenty. I'm all my brothers have. I couldn't let you jeopardise that."

"I didn't ask for any of this. I didn't ask for my mum to die. I didn't force her to do whatever it was she did back then to cause everyone to hate her. But I'm sorry, she isn't entirely to blame. She can't be the only one guilty. Your mum, Grant's mum… they both got upset, enough to believe whatever she told them. Have you ever thought about that?"

"I know. I don't know what to believe anymore. But I'm sorry—I'm sorry I treated you like shit."

"You treated me like a whore. Your brothers groped me, made me believe they were going to rape me, and don't even get me started on what Grant did to me." I try to sound light, teasing, but the resentment is still there. I can forgive the twins; their goofiness made up for it, but Grant… I'll never be able to trust Grant, even if he gave me the chance to.

His phone begins to ring, breaking the moment. He sighs, pulling his phone out. "Yeah?"

"Where the fuck are you? Dane is looking for you. It's about to start."

"Coming," Kaiden answers Grant, ending the call without a goodbye.

I go to leave the darkened alley, but Kaiden stops me. I glance over my shoulder at him. "Stay with me."

"Where else am I going to go?" I ask dryly.

"No, I mean stay the night with me."

"What?" I ask, raising my eyebrows.

"After the fight, when we go back—stay at mine," he says, and my heart races. "You don't want Nova to corner you, do you?"

"Um, sure… okay. I mean, to avoid Nova."

"Let's go," he orders, squeezing past me.

I blink, wondering if that really just happened. "Wait!" I call out.

"Yeah?"

"Whatever this is between us, I need you to keep it quiet. People can't know."

He turns around before he reaches the exit. "You're serious?"

"Deadly."

He chuckles under his breath. "I'm good with that, but you have to be the first girl who doesn't want to announce to the world that she's been with me."

"I'm not most girls."

He eyes darken. "I'm getting that."

My stomach flutters at the husky tone in his voice. I want to grab him, kiss him, do *other* things with him, because his body was made to worship.

I shake the lustful thoughts from my mind when he turns around, heading out of the alley.

I take in a deep breath, following him out. I try to prepare myself for what I'm about to watch, but a face I recognise is standing in the crowd, looking back at me with a calculating expression, his hands shoved into his front pockets.

Carter Remington looks to where Kaiden is heading, before coming back to me, a grin spreading across his face. He winks, and all I can do is stick my middle finger up at him. He mouths something, but I look away, heading in the direction Kaiden walked.

I lick my lips when he rips his top off. Then he jumps into the pit, landing on his feet.

Fucking hell, that was sexy.

A guy bigger than Kaiden steps up to the edge, his ripped body already out on show.

Wow! Does he eat babies for breakfast?

He jumps into the pit just as Dane jumps inside, stepping between the two. I move closer, pushing my way through bodies so I can get a clear view. Kaiden's gaze meets mine, and he does something out of character. He winks.

"You know the rules. You don't leave the pit until one of you taps out or there's a knockout. No weapons," Dane yells. "Are you ready, Grey?"

Grey nods, and when Dane turns to Kaiden, he doesn't look away from Grey, his intense stare burning through him. He looks lethal, deadly.

Dane smacks them both on the shoulder, before stepping back and dropping the white flag in his hand to the floor. He climbs out of the pit, his blonde hair falling down his back.

I drift my attention back to Kaiden, and immediately I'm taken aback by what I'm seeing. I didn't think he had a chance. Grey's size and muscle is bigger than Kaiden's, but Kaiden has the upper hand, dodging Grey's fists as he attempts to grab him.

Kaiden ducks under his arm, landing a blow to his stomach and knocking the wind out of him. He uses the distraction to punch him repeatedly in the face, blood spraying from Grey's nose.

I grimace yet find the whole thing highly arousing. The way Kaiden's body moves, each blow he lands on his opponent… it's sexy.

Grey staggers backwards, holding his nose. He doesn't look good, and Kaiden doesn't have a mark on him. He brings his leg up, kicking Grey in the chest. He falls, dirt blowing around him as crashes into it.

I take another step forward, nearly falling into the pit. I'm used to seeing people fight—it happened on every corner—but this... this is something else entirely.

There's no remorse in Kaiden's expression when he looms over him, bending down on one knee and bringing his fist back, before punching Grey repeatedly in the face until he passes out.

The crowd goes wild, screaming and yelling.

"That's a fucking record for Kingsley. Did you see how quick he went down?" a guy beside me says.

"I heard he pulls back at the fights, that he can knock someone out with one punch," his friend says.

"Run! Pigs!"

Kaiden looks up from the pit, his gaze meeting mine, wide and panicked. He runs towards me, jumping up and grabbing my hand.

"We need to get out of here!" he shouts.

"What's going on?"

Grant pushes through the crowd. "We need to go. I can't afford to get caught and neither can you," he yells at Kaiden. "Police are everywhere."

"Fuck!" Kaiden hisses.

I grip his hand tightly and look around as we run through the sea of people. Carter once again falls into sight, a smug grin on his face as he waves his phone at me.

He didn't? He called the police!

"Fuck," Grant whispers, suddenly stopping. We bump into him, nearly falling to the floor.

"What?" Kaiden asks, looking around him. "Shit."

I look too, seeing a group of officers walking towards Kaiden's car. It's barely visible, but a few more steps and they will see it.

A plan forms in my mind, and I let go of Kaiden's hand. "Go!"

"What?" he bites out, looking at me in confusion.

"Go."

Grant rolls his eyes. "We don't have fucking time to deal with you."

"Fuck you," I snap. "I'm going to distract them. Call Nova if I get caught."

Kaiden and I share a moment, something passing through his eyes. My intent must hit him, because he reaches out to stop me. I sidestep him and run into the forest, away from the direction of the car. "Hide the drugs! Hide them," I yell at the top of my lungs, keeping an eye on the group of cops. They hear me, and all begin to run towards me. I knew I could trust using drugs to get them moving.

"We're the police. Stop right there!"

I snort, wondering if that actually works. I keep running until my foot gets caught in some roots.

"Shit!"

chapter seventeen

I LOOK UP FROM MY COT, PITYING THE COP in front of me. "You really need more funding. You live in a town full of rich people and you have beds like this?" I could have been sleeping in a king-size bed, either at Nova's, or at Kaiden's. I'm still not sure if I would have stayed with him or not, but I would rather have my bed back at Mum's than this cot. It's painful.

PC Sullivan shakes his head at me. "It's not a hotel," he states dryly. "Your aunt is here. You could have said that before, rather than telling us she's your mum."

I grin, jumping up from the cot I got hardly any sleep on. "I just wish I could have seen her face when you said, 'daughter.'"

"The two boys were sent home."

"Two boys?" I ask, grabbing Kaiden's jacket.

"A Mr Kingsley and a Mr Tucker. They said they were family and were here to collect you."

"Ah, so that's why my aunt wasn't called until now?"

I feel his eyes on me as we walk down the corridor. "Your aunt looks pissed. She has every right to be."

"Why?" I ask, stopping at the doors leading out into the waiting area. I can see Nova pacing the floor, and I inwardly groan. "She doesn't even know me. She hasn't really taken the time to."

"Kid, whatever your issues are, that woman isn't one of them. She cares for you."

"What do you know?" I mutter, before clearing my throat. "And I don't have issues. You have issues. Cots being number one on the list."

He chuckles deeply. "For starters, she started crying, thinking we were delivering bad news, repeating 'not again' over and over," he explains, taking a deep breath. "Secondly, I do know you aren't like the rest. You waited until this morning to complain about the cot. Usually, we have complaints through the night."

I continue to stare at Nova, grateful she hasn't seen me yet. "How mad is she?"

"She'll be glad that you're safe and sound, then she'll scream and shout before going back to being happy you're okay."

I tilt my head up to look him in the eye, arching my eyebrow. "You've been doing this job way too long."

"Twenty-two years," he tells me with pride. "You're a good kid. I don't want to have to see you again in here. You shouldn't be hanging around with that crowd."

He's dead serious. "So, you're saying the rich are the wrong crowd?"

"In this area? Yes. They fight dirtier than any gang or drug dealer. The middleman takes the fall, and I'd hate to see that happen to you. I read your file and made a few calls after I realised you lied about your aunt being your mum. You are easy pickings for these guys. Don't let it happen."

Nova finally turns in our direction, her gaze meeting mine and her shoulders sagging with relief. "Tick me off for being warned, but, Sullivan, I'm not the fall guy. I won't ever be the fall guy."

He chuckles, using his card to open the door. "Keep it that way."

"Has she signed out?" Nova asks when she reaches us.

"She needs to go to the front desk. They have her phone and keys."

She nods. "Thank you."

I grimace when she walks off. Mum never got mad like this. Ever. I turn to PC Sullivan, widening my eyes.

He chuckles, waving me on. "Good luck, Miss Monroe."

"No, help," I groan. I ignore his laughter as I stomp off to Nova, who has collected my belongings.

"Nova," I start when she faces me.

She holds her hand up. "I don't want to hear it," she snaps, storming off. I follow, wondering if Sullivan will keep me another night. When I turn back around, he's still laughing.

"How could you do this? What were you thinking? A fighting gang, really? How long have you been here?"

I stop just outside the building, becoming angry. When she sees I'm not following her, she turns back around.

"Don't! Don't act like a caring adult right now. Not now. You lied to me, Nova."

"Is that what this is about?" she asks incredulously.

Rolling my eyes, I take a step closer to her. "No. This isn't about that. This is about me needing to get away from you. I didn't even know where I was, or who they were. I just wasn't ready for you to push more lies onto me."

"You didn't even know them?" she asks quietly, her expression hard. "How did you get there? You couldn't have walked, and you don't drive."

Oh fuck!

"It doesn't matter," I yell, throwing my hands up. "You don't get to yell at me, Nova. You aren't my parent. You weren't there for me when I needed someone. You weren't there."

"Your mother didn't want me there," she screams back, shocking me. "She didn't want any of us there, Ivy. She was my twin sister, and I loved her. I loved her despite what she did to me, but she didn't want me in her life."

"Nova," I say, my voice gentler this time. I'm not this person. I'm not a bitch.

She puts her hand up, stopping me. "Don't. I don't want to hear it. But you're right. I'm not your parent. And I shouldn't have kept what I knew from you. I didn't want to, but you had just lost your mum and moved across the country. I didn't want to add anything else to your troubles."

"I need time to adjust, to process. That is all I need, and I need you to give it to me," I tell her. A look passes across her face, one I know all too well. It's the one Mum got every time she spent our money. "What?"

"Ivy, there's something else..."

My eyes bug out of their sockets. "Something else? What else could there possibly be?"

"Last night, when you didn't come home, I had to call Sam. Your dad."

"What?"

"I'm out of my depth here. You were gone. And he needed to know."

No, he didn't. He doesn't have the right to know anything. I can't believe she'd go behind my back like this.

"I want to go home."

I don't stick around to listen to another word. I walk towards the carpark, spotting her car right away.

THE CAR RIDE HOME is silent. I can feel her stewing, ready to blow up like PC Sullivan warned.

I like Nova. I don't know her all that well, but I do like her. I want it to work here. I'm grateful I don't have to go back to the life I lived, but I can't deal with the lies, the secrets.

And until I feel she's been honest, she won't get my trust or respect.

She doesn't get to tell me what to do, how to live my life, until she earns a place too. And right now, she went too far. I'm nearly eighteen. I get to make the choice of whether my *dad* gets to know.

When we pull up to the house, I see Kaiden and Grant are standing outside with the twins, talking to each other. When they hear the car, they all look in our direction.

As soon as the car stops, I undo my belt.

"We really need to talk, Ivy. You can't put this off forever," Nova warns me.

"I need sleep," I tell her, opening the car door and getting out.

"Jail bird, coming around for breakfast?" Ethan yells.

"Not today, Ethan," Nova answers.

"Don't answer for me," I warn her.

Her tight lips, squinting eyes and flushed cheeks give me pause. She lets out a exasperated sigh, not pleased at all. "Not right now, Ivy. You've spent the night at the police station, your mum has just died, and you've moved miles away from home. We are going to talk, and you are going to listen to me. You promised to try."

Taking a deep breath, I nod. "All right. There's no need to get prissy."

She growls. "You are an infuriating girl at times, Ivy."

I wink, turning to the guys. "I'll catch up with you later," I tell them, avoiding Kaiden and Grant.

"Ivy," Nova calls from the front door.

I close my eyes, groaning. "Please let this day end already."

I stomp up the stairs behind her and slam the door shut. Annette is there in seconds, taking my jacket from me.

"I'll get this in the wash, Ivy."

"No!" I yell, inwardly groaning. "Um, just stick it on my bed. If that's okay?"

Smiling, she nods. "As you wish."

I take a step into the foyer, when the doorbell rings. If that's Kaiden, I hope he knows what mood Nova is in.

I pull open the door, only to have the air sucked out of my lungs. I grab the doorframe for balance, staring at the man in front of me.

He has similar facial features to me. We have the same shaped ears, eyes and nose. He has raven black hair and dark brown eyes, just like me.

This is Sam.

This is my dad.

He's tall, lean and dressed impeccably in a navy-blue suit, his black hair swept back, nothing how I imagined when I was little.

I open my mouth—to say what, I don't know. It's there, on the tip of my tongue, but nothing comes out.

"Ivy," he drawls, his voice deep, controlled.

He stands on the top step, towering over me, and I flinch.

"Ivy, who's at the door?" Nova calls.

I can't move. I feel paralysed under his gaze, and I can't breathe or move a muscle. I can feel the blood rushing from my face, and he doesn't look too good either. He's pale, watching me like I'm a figment of his imagination.

Why can't I speak?

Why can't I move?

Do I call him Dad? Sam? At this point, I'll settle for 'Oi', but I'm frozen.

"Sam, what are you doing here? I said I'd call you," Nova says, sounding unsure and a little nervous.

"Nova," he greets. "You just told me my daughter was here, that Cara had died. Where else would I be?"

Nova clears her throat, and I can feel her gaze burning into me. "Ivy, have you said hello?"

I can't look away from Dad—Sam. Here's here. The man in front of me is my dad.

He's taller than I expected.

"I couldn't find you. Your mum kept you from me," he explains, his eyes boring into mine.

I snap out of it when I hear him mention my mum. "I've not been here long, but from what I've learned so far, the rich get what they want. If you wanted to find me, you would have. It wasn't exactly like she was hiding me. She didn't use a fake name. I didn't get a fake name. You could have found me."

It isn't until the words leave my mouth that I realise what's been upsetting me. They could have found me. All of them. They could have given me a better life, or supported Mum enough to let her give me a life.

They didn't. They just went about their lives like I didn't exist.

"I couldn't find you. She was never in one place long enough for us to find her. In the end, I gave up trying."

"Parents giving up is the story of my life," I mutter dryly.

"Nova said you are going to attend Kingsley Academy in a few weeks. That's quite the achievement."

My lip curls. "She paid for my acceptance. I didn't get in because of my grades."

"That's not true. Your grades were fine," Nova says, her voice soft.

"And I've just been collected from the police station," I inform him.

"What? What for? What did you do?" His eyes harden when they turn to Nova. "You said you were looking out for her, yet she's been arrested already?"

"Sam, I'll explain."

"Very well. But first, I'd like to get to know Ivy," he tells her, turning to me. "Would you care for some brunch?"

I'll never get used to the fact these people call it brunch.

"She'd love to. She hasn't eaten yet," Nova answers for me, and I narrow my eyes at her.

"Ivy doesn't want to go anywhere with a stranger," I snap.

"I'm your dad," he informs me.

I turn to him, arching my eyebrow. "No, you aren't. To me, you are just a man standing on a doorstep. I don't know you. I didn't know anything about you until two days ago."

"That's why we should go out."

"Go grab a jacket, Ivy. A walk around the estate won't hurt."

I roll my eyes but listen to what she says. I head up the stairs and smile thankfully when Annette brings back down Kaiden's jacket, handing it to me. "I thought you might like this, dear."

"Thank you, Annette."

"You're most welcome."

I head back downstairs, slower this time, and come to a halt when I hear them whispering.

"I'd still like another DNA test, one with me present this time. I'm not handing over any money until I receive it," he says, and my stomach bottoms out.

What?

"Oh, come on, Sam, she is you all over."

"That doesn't mean anything. She slept with everyone around that time. Ivy could be anyone's."

I clear my throat, drawing their attention, and force a smile. "Sorry, but I forgot I have plans. As for the DNA test, sure."

"Really?" he asks, his eyes widening in surprise.

I shrug, forcing down the hurt. "Sure. You've already had one set done, right?"

Nova's pitying look makes me grit my teeth together. "We did. It was a match."

"Then another won't hurt, right?"

"Great." He smiles, clapping his hands together. "I'll get it sorted."

"No rush. Because no matter the results, I never want to see you again. And I most certainly don't want your money. You've seen the first results. You've seen me. Even I can see the resemblance you're clearly too blind to see. Parents are meant to know. Yet you still want more proof, which just proves you don't really want me in your life," I tell him, letting out a deep breath before turning to Nova. "Can I please be excused from our chat? It looks like we don't need it."

She reaches out to comfort me, but I pull away, staring blankly at her. She sighs, nodding. "Of course. Please don't be gone long."

"You're going to let her out even though she's just been arrested?" Sam asks Nova as I push past him.

"Sam, shut up and come inside for a cup of tea. Then you can go to give her space."

I tune out his reply, heading over to Kingsley Manor. I ring the doorbell, waiting for them to answer.

Kaiden surprises me by opening the door. I thought for sure a butler or maid would do it.

The tension in my body eases somewhat. "My dad is over at Nova's and needs more proof that I'm his daughter before handing me his money. I don't even want his money."

Kaiden opens the door wider for me to step inside. Lucca is coming down the stairs when I walk in.

"You should tell your dad to buy you a pony or a horse to make up for all the birthdays he missed," Lucca announces, the eavesdropper.

"Wait, you had ponies for your birthdays?"

"I had a horse," Lucca admits.

I turn to Kaiden, who shrugs. "I had three horses growing up. I love riding."

"I didn't even get a card," I admit, still in awe.

"I'd play him for all he's worth if it was me," Lucca offers.

"Shut up, Luc," Kaiden groans.

I force a smile. "He doesn't have anything I want, Lucca. He might be rich, but that only means shit to rich people. I don't care."

"I'm getting that."

"You staying?" Kaiden asks when Lucca carries on down the hallway.

"That okay?"

"Fine by me. What you did last night—" he starts, but I hold my hand up, stopping him.

"It was stupid, I know, but I have nothing to lose." I force out a laugh, dropping my hands to my side. "Literally, *nothing*. From the sounds of it, you have a lot."

"All the same, thank you. I owe you."

I sag with relief, and his expression forms into one of disbelief, but I ignore it. "Does this mean I can crash somewhere? Those cots were terrible."

He chuckles, shaking his head. "They aren't bad. The police station in Littleton is worse."

I roll my eyes. "I'll take your word for it." My lips twitch when a thought occurs to me. "Maybe I should ask Sam to make a donation of new cots."

He laughs, his eyes crinkling in the corners. My stomach flutters at the sound, and his expression. He looks so hot right now I could kiss him.

Getting control of myself, I duck my head, following him into the kitchen before I do something drastic and permanently attach my mouth to his.

chapter eighteen

My eyes sting from looking at papers all day. Today was my last day of school, the last time I would see any exams, and I'm grateful. I want to get out of here, to make something of my life. I don't want to keep living like this. I just have to get Mum onboard. She needs to get her act together, otherwise I'm leaving her and not coming back.

She owes too much money to her drug dealer; not just some pimple-faced kid, but some hot shot drug dealer: Snake.

I'm shocked to find her dressed, looking ready to go out. She puts the phone down when she sees me, forcing that fake smile.

I know that smile.

I'm not going to like what she has to say, and she knows it. "Mum, are you coming with me to the soup kitchen today?"

She gets up, grabbing her long green coat I managed to snag at the clothes bank. It's roasting outside, but because of how thin and delicate she is, she's always cold.

"No. Got something big happening. Huge. We can finally get out of this shit hole."

I glance away so she doesn't see me roll my eyes. It will only make her mad.

"You need to eat, Mum," I tell her.

"Not hungry." She sniffs, looking jumpy, and I groan. She needs a fix. That's where she's going.

"Mum, if you have money, we need food. We need to pay Snake before he comes back."

She snorts. "What are they going to do? Take me to court? I don't have anything to give them. And I can give Snake what he really wants."

"Mum," I argue, gripping her bony bicep.

She shoves me off, still jittery. "No. I got the call, Ivy. It's happening."

I watch her walk out the door, and when it slams shut, I startle. There's no helping her anymore.

Snake won't wait much longer, and I'm scared he'll turn to me for payment once he can't get what he wants out of Mum.

I startle awake, breathing hard. That was the last time I saw my mum alive. She had gotten drugs from someone new, someone who didn't know she'd use their product instead of selling it.

Either that or Snake finally followed through on his promise to kill her.

I have a week until I turn eighteen, and she isn't here. Even if she were, I don't think she'd care.

That is the only reason I can think as to why I'm dreaming of her now. It has to be.

Time has passed quickly since I arrived. I've spent most of my time with Selina and the twins or sneaking into Kaiden's bed.

I'm not even going to question what we are, not yet. I like how we are right now, and I don't want to risk changing that. He's been my drug through all of this, a huge stress relief, and although a part of me wants to say I'm only using him, I can't. I've come to know him, and I like what I see.

I'll just never tell him that.

Nova, however, needs her own stress relief. Since the day Sam turned up, she's been trying to get me to sit down with him. I let him do his stupid test and should be getting the results back within the next week. My mind won't go there though. He's never been my dad. He doesn't get to walk in like he belongs here. Not now.

All the evidence was already there and yet he still refused to believe I was his daughter.

My phone beeps with a message. Groaning, I roll over and grab it from my bedside table.

KAIDEN: Pack a bag for two nights. We're going camping.

My door flies open, smacking against the wall. "We're going glamping!" Selina yells. "I never get invited. I'm friends with the twins, yeah, but I didn't really hang out like we have been the past few weeks until you turned up. You are awesome. I've always wanted to go."

"Slow down," I tell her, feeling dizzy.

She grins. "Sorry. I'm just so excited."

"Aren't you rich? You could have gone any time."

Her expression morphs into disbelief, her nose crinkled as she curls her lip. "You can't just go. Anyone who isn't invited gets their tyres slashed, or they're thrown in the lake, or egged. The guys don't really care about girls turning up—if they're hot—but the girls go crazy. I heard, one time, Danielle made a group of girls feel welcome. One had got with one the twins in the day, one with Grant during the night, and they all woke up with their hair cut off, eyebrows waxed, and their clothes thrown into the lake."

"Fucking bitches," I mutter, swinging my legs out of bed. "Has Nova approved us going?"

"Yeah. She's ordered a car for us and the twins, since they haven't passed their tests yet."

"That's it? No nagging about me going to see Sam?" I ask dubiously.

She grins, helping herself to my stacks of clothing. "Not today. She seemed distracted about something."

"I'm going to go downstairs and grab a drink. Did they say when to be ready?"

"Forty minutes."

ME: Selina's excited.

KAIDEN: Selina gets excited over everything.

I laugh, tucking my phone into my pyjama bottoms. He's right, she really does. Just the other day she found out there was going to be another season of *Veronica Mars* and started dancing around my room.

I nearly trip over my feet when I step into the kitchen, finding Royce Kingsley alone, leaning against the counter.

His dark, soulless eyes are like blades of ice, slicing into me. His jaw is firm, his lips tight.

Everything about him screams power, dominance, but there's something else that lingers under that ice-cold exterior, something I can't put my finger on.

I listen for any sounds that might indicate someone is close by, but the manor is silent. The only sound is the hum from the fridge.

He doesn't look happy, not at all, and I don't think its paranoia making me think it's aimed at me. I've had a feeling, from the very first moment I met him, that he doesn't like me. He looks through me, like I'm nobody. And I guess I am to him.

Then again, I don't think he's capable of a smile. His face would probably crack if he tried. This is my second time meeting him, and it seems this time will be just as hostile as the last.

I don't even care enough to want to know why he doesn't like me. His reasons are most likely as pathetic as everyone else's.

I don't like him, and it's clear he doesn't like me.

However, he is still a friend of Nova's.

"Would you like me to get Nova?" I ask, opening the fridge door.

"Do you just help yourself to food?" he accuses, like I'm some thief in the night.

I gently place the juice on the counter before grabbing a glass down from the shelf. "Doesn't everyone in their own home? Or is that a task rich people don't do?" I ask sarcastically, forcing a smile.

"Just reminding you where your place is. You wouldn't want to step out of place; bad things could happen."

"Step out of place? And what, spill juice on me?"

"Watch it, young lady. You have no idea who you are messing with."

"Are you threatening me?" I ask, appalled. Who does he think he is? I want to laugh, but I'm afraid it might piss him off more.

I want to slap the slimy smile off his face. "I hear you are, in fact, Sam Farley's biological daughter. Shocking. I guess you are the rightful heir to his empire. Such a large responsibility for someone like *you*."

I slam the glass down on the counter. "One, I don't know who hit your head hard enough to make you believe you have a right to know, but to save you putting your nose where it's not wanted again, he's still waiting on results. Two, his empire can burn to hell for all I care."

His gaze hardens. "Be careful. We all have stakes in that empire."

"Royce, what are you doing here?" Nova asks, looking from him to me, and I swear I see a flicker of fear.

His smile couldn't be any more fake. What the hell is he up to?

"Not to worry, now. I was just leaving. I forgot I have a business meeting soon."

"Was there a reason you were here?" she asks him, yet still watches me closely.

"I came to make sure no trouble would come of the boys this weekend. I heard that Ivy was attending, and after her arrest the other day, I had my worries."

I want to snort at the condescending dickhead. Has he met his sons? Within days of being here, I was groped, threatened, and had clothing torn from my body.

"I wasn't arrested, merely detained until morning," I bite out.

"Ivy wasn't charged. She happened to be in the wrong place at the wrong time," Nova explains. "She is still settling in."

"Still," he states calmly, making me want to punch him when his frosty gaze turns to me in disgust. "I'll be off. It was good talking to you, Ivy. You really should be careful where you step. Wouldn't want to get on anyone's toes."

I watch with a narrowed gaze as he strolls out of the kitchen, letting himself out. I finish my drink, ready to get out of here.

"What did he say to you?" Nova asks once we hear the door shut behind him.

I shrug. "Not a lot. He's a twat though."

She laughs and it's genuine. "He's a bit much. Always had a broom stuck up his arse."

It's my turn to laugh. "You did not just say that."

She shrugs back, sobering. "Ivy, I need you to stay away from Mr Kingsley."

"Why? I thought you were friends?"

She looks away, busying herself in the fridge. "We are, but he's notorious for his affairs. He likes younger girls."

I grab a banana from the fruit bowl. "Ew. I've just puked into my mouth."

She giggles, but it doesn't sound right. "Go have fun."

"Thank you."

"Oh, and Ivy?" she calls.

"Yeah?"

"Annette has put a card and pin number on your dressing table. Make sure you take it with you."

"Nova—"

"No," she interrupts, holding her hand up. "I know you don't feel comfortable taking my money, and I know you have the money Mrs White has been paying you, but I'd like to do this. It will give me peace of mind. I'd like you to have fun when you're there and not be worrying about buying stuff or feeling out of place when they do. Could you please, just take it?"

Feeling uncomfortable, I nod, not saying anything else as I walk off.

Since my arrest, I've tried to stay mad at her. I have. But it's like it hit her that I was really here, and she began to really get to know me. I still sense hidden secrets, but there's nothing I can do.

It will take me some time, but I am getting there to make it easier for her. Because whether I want to admit it or not, I need her. Not for her money, not for her home or schooling, but for who she is. I need to know I still have someone in this world I can call family, someone I can turn to, so I don't feel so alone. I've been alone all my life.

It's bloody Selina. She's made me soft. She's this ball of energy that likes to diffuse the tension.

I head back into my room, finding Selina throwing clothes off hangers. She sticks her head around the door.

"How come you get all the cool clothes? I'm getting Annette to go shopping for me."

I shrug while laughing, heading straight into the bathroom. Selina might love my clothes, but she wouldn't be her without her pink, girly ones.

Ankles crossed, my back against the boot of Nova's car, I wait for the twins and Kaiden. I'm kind of hoping Grant isn't coming this weekend. He's not a prick anymore, but he also hasn't warmed up to me. I made sure they didn't get arrested, and granted, I did that more for Kaiden, but still, you'd think he'd at least show some kind of gratitude.

"I'm feeling queasy," Selina groans.

I look over to the step she's sitting on. She does look a little pale. "You okay?"

"What if they do something to me?" she asks, her expression panicked.

"Then I'll punch them in their plastic noses," I tell her, shrugging.

She laughs, then groans, clutching her stomach. "Everything will be fine."

"It will. Have fun. I don't know why you are worried. They're just jealous, petty bitches."

She beams up at me. "You're right. They are. I'm not going to let them ruin my weekend."

"That'ta girl."

"I'm hoping I lose my virginity this weekend," she blurts out.

"Just don't pick the twins," I tease, winking.

She laughs. "My other friends would have talked me out of it."

"It's up to you, Selina. It's your life, your body. Don't listen to society. It doesn't need to be perfect if you don't want it to be. You want to wait until marriage, go for it. It's up to you. You don't need anyone's permission."

She stands up, dusting off her blue skirt that flows to her knees. "You're right. I don't. If it happens, it happens."

"Are you ready?" Ethan yells, jumping off the wall in front of his house.

A car pulls up, so I guess we are.

"Did you bring snacks?" Lucca yells from somewhere inside the house.

"On the stairs," Ethan shouts.

Selina rolls her eyes at me, taking her bag over to the car. A man opens the boot, taking the bag from Selina, so I follow, handing him mine.

Another car pulls up, Grant and a few others I recognise from their parties inside of it. I'm just grateful I don't have to sit in a car with him for two hours.

He beeps the horn. "Where's Kai? Let's get on the road."

"Here!" he rumbles, a rucksack thrown over his shoulder as he steps down.

Ethan pushes in front of me, diving into the back of the car. I don't think it's a limo, but it definitely has enough space in the back to be one.

Selina gets in after him, more refined and elegant than he did, which makes me smile.

"Ivy," Kaiden calls, and I spin around to face him. He crooks his finger at me, and I roll my eyes. Stepping away from the car, I head over to him, high-fiving Lucca on the way.

When the car door slams, I glance over my shoulder, my brows scrunching together. "What—why are they leaving me?"

"You're riding with me," Kaiden rumbles.

I struggle to hide my surprise. "I am?"

He smirks. "You are. Come on."

"So demanding," I mutter, surprised once more when he holds the door open.

chapter nineteen

THE DRIVE OVER WAS SILENT. We only did one stop and that was to meet up with a group of people from Kingsley Academy. Apart from that, Kaiden left me to my own devices.

We pull up to a gated lane, and 'Kingsley Retreat' is written in bold gold lettering above the gate.

"Do you own everything?" I ask, turning to Kaiden.

"You own ten hospitals in the UK alone," he sasses back.

"No, I don't," I screech. "Wait, Sam owns ten hospitals? Does he know anything about medicine?"

"No idea. They're private centres, run by the best surgeons in the UK. He has more in the US."

"Bloody hell. My mum had a TV big and thick enough that even a car going over it wouldn't crack it. No wonder he doesn't want to believe I'm his daughter."

I realise I'm talking about my personal issues, which is something Kaiden and I don't get into, not really. We fuck. He's seriously good at it, but together, it's phenomenal. I can never get enough.

I'm afraid to look at his reaction.

"I can't really talk about dads. Mine's the biggest prick you'll ever meet. I don't think he even wanted kids. Sam is different. He's made mistakes, yeah, but he's not like our dad."

"We can't pick our parents, right?"

He forces a laugh. "I love my mum. I'd die for her. But I wouldn't have chosen her for the twins. They needed love and support growing up and she gave them nothing. I had my nan until the day she died."

"I'm sorry."

"It's not your fault."

"No, it's my mums," I whisper quietly.

He pulls into a parking space, shutting the car off before turning to me. "No. It was our parents' fault. They made their own choices. I don't say sorry a lot, if ever, but I am for taking shit out on you."

"I get it," I tell him, taking a deep breath. "I've taken my mum's choices out on Nova. I've done it a lot, but I'm so angry at them all."

"Selina's on her way over," he states calmly. "Stay with me tonight."

He doesn't ask. He demands. "What about Selina? They'll know."

"She's staying next to the twins. We gave you both your own pods."

"Pods?"

He grins. "You'll see. I'm in number six."

I roll my eyes. "I'll find it when no one is looking."

"I know!"

A tap on the window grabs my attention, and I hold my finger up to Selina, who looks pale.

I open my mouth, a witty remark on the tip of my tongue, but he gets there first. "Don't be angry at Nova. She loves you, that much I can see."

He gets out of the car, leaving me to stew on his words. Selina begins to tap on the window again, impatient this time.

I push the car door open, glaring up at her. "Yes?"

She sags with relief. "You seem your normal happy self. They drove off before I could argue and said Kaiden wanted to talk to you alone. What did he want? Was it bad?"

I inwardly laugh. I dread to think what the twins said when they told the driver to drive off.

"He just wanted to ask how things were going with Nova," I lie.

She seems to relax more. "That's good. That's really good. After, you know, the things you told me, I was a little worried he was going to leave you on the side of the motorway. But you're here and in one piece."

"Yep, I am," I tell her, chuckling. I sober when I see Kaiden brush Danielle off, earning him a death glare in return. She looks around, searching, until her gaze finds mine and hardens. Her eyes narrow into slits.

Guess someone didn't eat her Cheerio's this morning.

"Come on. The guys are going to show us to our pod."

"What is with that?" I ask, letting her link her arm through mine. I've never done this shit, but Selina's like this excited puppy you don't want to say no to.

"They're beautiful. They looks like tree trunks laid down with the insides cut out and made into a room. Some have canopies outside the door, some don't. This isn't the main site, but it's been made specifically for parties like this."

We keep walking up a path, and my eyes widen at the sight in front of me. A circle of wooden 'pods' frames the area. All look exactly how Selina described, like someone had taken the thickest tree trunks and cut out the insides before laying them on the floor to make small homes. They're not made of trees, though they're clearly wood, the fronts carved into rounded triangles at the top. They have small decking areas and big double glass doors that are already open, the pristine white curtains blowing gently in the breeze.

Paths line the way to each pod, a string of fairy lights streaming along to light the way for when it gets dark.

We walk further down the path, passing pods as we go, and I'm in awe. Camping, to me, has always been a small tent you get cramped into. I've never been, but I remember a few homeless people on our estate sleeping in them.

These, to me, are a luxury. They're beautiful, and I'd happily live in one for the rest of my life, and I haven't even been inside.

"Which one's ours?" I whisper to Selina.

She leans in closer so the twins in front, who are flirting outrageously with a group of girls, don't overhear us.

"I think we're going to the tents," she explains, sounding almost disappointed. "I really wanted a pod."

The twins suddenly stop. "Selina, you're here next to us."

"Yay," she squeals, earning dirty looks from the girls. "Come on, roomie, let's go check our room."

Ethan steps forward from the group. "Um, Ivy is in one of the tents down the path."

Selina's excitement disappears, and her shoulders slump. "All right."

"Let's check out yours, then head down to mine," I tell her.

She nods, stepping up onto the porch. I follow her inside, my eyes widening a fraction as I pass two grey love seats on either side of the door.

A bed is set in the middle, and it's not a double, but it's not a single either. It's somewhere in between. The sheets are pristine, white, matching the curtains. The throw pillows are a light peachy colour, adding more light to the room.

Two small tables sit on either side of the bed, both holding peach lamps, a box of tissues, and complimentary chocolate.

The room is beautiful. There's even a dressing table with drawers to put clothes inside.

"Wow," I murmur, trying to take everything in.

The driver from earlier taps on the glass door, dropping a suitcase just inside. "Here's your bag, Miss Farley."

Shaking out of her daze, Selina smiles, grabbing her suitcase and throwing it on top of the covers.

"Thank you, Luke."

"Where would you like this one?"

"We've got it. We're just heading to Ivy's room now," Lucca says, taking my case off him—and nearly dropping it. "What the hell did you pack, Ivy? An arsenal?"

I scrunch my nose up. "I didn't pack."

Selina claps her hands. "Enough of all that. Let's go see your room."

Well, okay then.

Numbly, still a little stunned at the luxurious style, I follow. This is how the rich live. They can't just grab a tent and pitch it for the night. No. They need electric, comforts, a bed.

Selina talks my ear off as we follow the twins. I don't hear what she's saying, and I don't think she's noticed. I look to the middle of the circle, to the big fire pit in the centre, surrounded by logs for seats. Even that looks glamourous, and all they did was cut down a tree or two.

I'm so out of my element here.

When we walk past the hot tubs, I grimace a little. I wonder if that's why Selina packed me a swimsuit, even after knowing I don't swim?

There's only a few, a wide decking separating each of the five tubs. And there are huge barbeque areas set up with patio sets everywhere, some outside each pod or tent.

"Here you go," Ethan hollers. "It's a single, but you'll be okay."

I try not to look freaked out as I step around him, swallowing my gasp at the size of the room.

Selina made it sound like a tent would be sleeping out in the wild. This is huge. And I wouldn't call it a tent because I'm pretty sure tent parts aren't made of wood and metal. It even has windows, for Christ sakes.

And the bed… The bed could easily fit ten people inside.

I spin around, finding the twins gone, and their groupies. My eyes bug out at Selina. "This seriously can't be for just me?"

She scrunches her nose up. "The bed looks like heaven, but I dunno. If it rains, won't it come through?" she asks, looking up at the fabric that makes the tent.

I laugh, flopping down backwards on the bed, and let out a contented sigh. "It really is heaven."

"And you don't have electric like we do," she mutters, searching the room. I also have a lot more furniture. There's even a wardrobe inside, as well as two, two-seater sofas. "Wait, I think this device thingy is what you plug stuff into. I think. I don't see any plugs, but there's a wire."

I roll over, finding what she's found, and chuckle. "Lift the first flap." She does, chuckling to herself when she finds a plug. "This is too much."

She claps her hands once again, rushing over to my case by the door and pulling it over to the bed.

"Time to get this party started," she gushes, unzipping my case.

What could possibly be in there that could start a party? Balloons?

My eyes widen when she pulls out bottles of purple liquid, blue liquid, pink liquid and clear liquid. Wait, does that bottle have a unicorn on it?

"I am not drinking all that," I tell her, my voice high-pitched.

She waves me off. "Someone will drink it. But tonight, we party. Tomorrow, we can sunbathe by the lake while the lads fish."

"Fishing?" I ask, my ears perking up.

She snorts, rolling her eyes at me. "You can't seriously want to go fishing. I hear you have to touch maggots."

I grin at her. "Sorry, but if they'll let me, I'd rather fish. I've never been."

"Whatever. I'll have a book to keep me company, and a hangover."

"I'm still not drinking."

"Just one? Please?" she asks, batting those lashes at me.

"One. But nothing strong. I want the weakest shit you've got, and I want it diluted."

She rummages through my case, pulling out two bottles of lemonade. "Sorted."

"Did you pack me any clothes?" I ask, looking into the case. I sigh with relief when I see some clothes and pyjamas. "I am *not* wearing *that* swimsuit."

"Why not?" she asks absently, concentrating on opening the bottle of pink stuff. She pauses, looking around the room. "Shoot. We need cups."

"I'm not wearing it. Is it even my size?" I ask, my throat suddenly dry. There's nothing there. Like, nothing. The red bikini is barely a scrap of material.

"Of course, it is," she tells me, searching through one of the cupboards by the door. "Ah-ha."

Bringing the cups back over to the bed, she hands them to me. I mutely take them, still nervous about the bikini.

I'm not self-conscious about my body. I look how I look and I'm okay with it. I'm not one of those girls who stands in the mirror and thinks my nose is too pointy, my lips are too thin, my forehead is too wide. I don't think I'm fat, and honestly, I wouldn't care if I was. I don't care that I'm slim. I am who I am and I won't apologise for that.

But standing in a bikini, a see-through shirt over the top, my nerves are going haywire. I place a hand over my stomach, wishing it would calm down.

"Are you sure all the other girls will be wearing one?"

Selina's drink spills over edge of the cup, dripping down her arms. She hiccups, laughing. "No. They won't be wearing that over it," she tells me, her eyes glazed over.

I take the cup from her hand, leaving it on the dressing table. "Okay, cupcake, that's enough until later."

I let out a giggle at the cute pout she gives me. "Party pooper."

I shrug, not caring. "You'll thank me later when you only vomit two bottles up and not three."

"You are phenomenal, Ivy Monroe. Always helping me out. You're cool. You know that, right?"

I laugh, pulling her out the door, forgetting about this damn bikini that barely covers my tits. "And you're drunk, and here we are."

"I'm so glad you're here. I know we're technically cousins, but you're like a sister."

I wouldn't go that far, but she's right, we are close; as close as I've ever let anyone, anyway.

We head into the clearing where the fire pit is and see the barbeques are burning. My stomach rumbles, crying for a cheeseburger. Selina, however, has other plans and pulls us over to the hot tubs.

"Let's get in one before everyone fills them up. I'm not about to get in one with some skank who hasn't washed her lady parts." She pauses, her nose scrunching up. "Actually, I'd prefer that to a sweaty ball sack. They've been out in the sun all day."

"Maybe we shouldn't go in one then," I tell her, trying to persuade her not to.

"It will be fun. And I know you can drown in an inch of water, but I'll be here. I'll save you."

"No offence, but that doesn't reassure me."

We walk up the stairs, onto some decking, heading for the empty hot tub. There's a group of people in the one next to us.

Selina steps into the hot tub, looking saucily at the other hot tub beside us. It's going fine, completely fine, up until she slips, heading face first into the hot tub.

I reach forward to grab her, but hands behind me push me in, and panic seizes me. Luckily, it's not deep, and I manage to scramble to my feet without drowning.

I spin around, shoving wet hair out of my face and ignoring the howls of laughter around us. Selina's still coughing, unaware of what just happened.

"Are you for fucking real?" I yell, glaring up at Danielle.

Hand on hip, she looks down at me in the hot tub. Her gold, glitter half-suit clings to her body. I say half-suit because I'm pretty sure it's meant to be a full suit, but the entire centre of the swimsuit is missing, showing off her tits, stomach and pubic bone. A gold chain hangs down middle like a necklace.

She's going into chlorine water, not a photoshoot.

Danielle laughs with her friends. "You going to be okay in there, or would you like me to get you a paddling pool?"

I tilt my head to the side. "You're offering to lift a finger? Too much sun?" I pronounce slowly.

A few people chuckle, and she gets this stormy look on her face. "Whatever, tramp. They've got some food scraps if you're hungry."

I place my hand over my heart with a mock gasp. "You're still thinking of me. How will I ever repay you?"

"Ivy, I saved you a burger," Kaiden rumbles. I didn't see him walk up onto the decking, and I wonder how much he saw. Danielle's face is worth it. She looks ready to slit my throat.

"I could have eaten a burger," Selina whines under her breath, causing me to giggle.

"Thanks," I tell him, accepting the burger he offers and moving to sit on the side of the hot tub, before taking the largest bite I can, just to piss Danielle off. She looks ready to gag, making me smile around a mouthful. "Yum!"

Kaiden's lips twitch.

Danielle stands up taller, sticking her chest out, and pastes on a smile. "Want me to pop by your tent later, like old times?"

I look down at my burger, suddenly finding it interesting.

"No."

"But I could—" The twins cut her off when they jump into the hot tub, causing a huge wave of water to splash Danielle and her friends. She screeches, water dripping down her face.

Unable to hold it in, I begin to laugh at her wide-eyed, open-mouthed facial expression. She looks utterly distressed. She turns to me, her face like thunder. "You!"

I point to my chest, smiling. "Me?"

"You bitch!"

"It's called karma, look it up. Now ba-bye," I state dryly, waving my fingers at her.

She grabs Sophia, pulling her away from us.

Ethan grins at me. "And that's how you get rid of pests."

I shake my head at him. "I thought you two were busy with Legs?"

Lucca laughs. "Legs! Perfect."

Ethan grins at his brother. "She did have long legs."

"Looked better spread in the air while I fucked her from behind."

"Gross," I mutter.

"In the air?" Selina asks, looking dazed.

"Don't," I warn them, before they say anything remotely dirty.

They laugh, looking up at Kaiden. "You getting in?"

"Nah, maybe later," he rumbles, his intense gaze burning into me.

I try to not let him affect me, but he does, and I feel hot all over.

Once he's gone, the twins look to me and Selina, a calculating look on their face. "Let's get fucked up."

"I don't do drugs," Selina tells them, revolted by the idea.

Lucca laughs, shaking his head as he swims over to her. "My sweet Selina, we don't either. We are going to get pissed up."

Ethan leans over the side of the hot tub, looking down the stairs at a group of lads. "Yo, Grant, be a darlin' and grab us some beer."

Grant looks up from talking to Kaiden, his eyes narrowed into slits when they see me. "Ask Ivy. I'm sure for the right amount of money, she'll do it."

"Yeah, but you're the bitch. Ivy is high class. Not even all our trust funds could afford her."

Grant shakes his head, walking off. Ethan grimaces when he turns back around, looking dejected. "I'm not getting out now. Girls will faint when they see my wet abs."

He does have impressive abs.

Lucca snorts. "I see Lexi by the drinks table."

"Flexy Lexi?" Ethan asks, his ears perking up.

"Flexy Lexi?" Selina mutters in utter disgrace. Even I have to admit, I threw up in my mouth a little.

"She is flexible. I swear, she made up half of those sex positions," Lucca drawls, his eyes glazed over.

"Fuck off, you two, before I drown you," I snap in amusement.

They both fight to get out of the hot tub first, making me laugh. Once they're gone, it's peaceful, quiet.

"They aren't coming back with drinks, are they?" Selina asks.

I lean my head against the back of the hot tub, closing my eyes. "Not a chance in hell."

chapter twenty

I WRAP MY WHITE WOOL CARDIGAN AROUND me, wishing I was a little closer to the fire. It's warm out, but the wind has a chill to it, and it feels like a storm is brewing.

I'm in a daze, staring into the flames, but movement on the other side of the fire pit gains my attention.

Danielle swaggers slightly towards a group of guys, and I don't need the muscled back to turn around for me to figure out who the leech is trying to feed from. She wraps her arms around his neck, and I watch the muscles in his back tighten. He shrugs her off harshly, pulling away, and her face kicks up a storm.

"Someone's pissed," Selina slurs, falling against me.

I hold her up, watching as Danielle shoves Kaiden's chest. He doesn't move an inch, his body solid.

She storms off with a girl I don't recognise, her face like thunder, and when her gaze directs right at me… I smile.

She's been doing it all night—giving me death glares, that is. She even went as far as rallying her friends to cough pathetic insults at me, like I'd storm off and cry like a baby. They either gave me a wide berth, like I was infectious, or pushed into me. It was tiresome and kind of amusing at the same time.

Danielle's snide remarks are getting on my last nerve though. I don't like how close to the truth her insults are getting. It's clear she knows some bits about my past, and she's using them as ammunition, but the rest, I think she's guessing, hoping something might push me over the edge. It's not going to work though. I've been called a lot worse at school, treated horrifically because of the actions of my mum. They don't need to know that though. I didn't care then, and I don't care now.

Sticks and stones and all that.

Having a mum like mine will harden you. You need to be tough to survive. And I survived it all.

Danielle doesn't know her left from her right.

I don't like the feeling I get when she vies for Kaiden's attention. She went so far as to pretend her bikini top fell, giving him, and a few others, a flash of her tits.

And she called me a whore.

He'd shrug her off each time, either acting indifferent, walking away or like just now, shrugging her off like her touch burned him.

It gives me the warm fuzzies each time.

Selina snores, and I look down at her, grinning like an idiot when I find her asleep, her mouth hanging open.

I nudge her with my shoulder, laughing when she shoots up, looking around. "Where did Drogon go?"

"Drogon?"

"My dragon."

I laugh, wondering what she's going on about. "Come on, let's get you to bed."

She nods, letting me help her up with minimal effort. She looks around, her eyes barely open. "They'll bend the knee," she whispers.

"Well, okay then," I mutter, wrapping my arm around her, supporting her. I've got not one clue as to what she's going on about. It's funny, nonetheless.

We reach her pod with only two close calls. She's small, but she's dead weight when she's drunk. She's still muttering incoherent sentences.

We walk inside, and I place her down on the bed before slipping her pumps off. After, I grab the bin, a bottle of water, and place them next to her.

"Water is on the side," I tell her, shaking her a little.

"Jon doesn't know much," she mumbles, slapping her lips together before falling into a deep slumber. Snores fill the air, making me grateful I'm not sharing a room with her. It would drive me nuts.

And who the fuck is Jon?

I head out of the pod, deciding to go back to my tent. When I see the twins up ahead with the same flexible girl from earlier, I veer off to the side, to the edge of the forest.

A hand covers my mouth, another going around my neck, and I scream behind the hand, kicking my legs out.

"Shh, it's me," Kaiden whispers, letting me go.

Breathing hard, I spin around, smacking him in the chest. "You scared the fucking shit out of me." I take in a deep breath, glaring at him. "I've got Selina talking about her dragon and something about a Jon, and now you creeping up behind me—while I'm in a dark forest—to grab me."

He smirks, wrapping his arms around my waist. He doesn't speak, instead leaning down and capturing my lips. I sigh, placing my hands on his shoulders as I kiss him back. He picks me up, carrying me to the nearest pod and resting me against the side, kissing me harder.

"I've been dying to get you alone all night."

I grin, rubbing my hands over his smooth skin. "Yeah?"

"Yeah," he rasps, kissing me once again.

I lick his bottom lip before deepening the kiss, clinging to his hair. His kisses are deep, hot, and I can never get enough of them. He really knows how to use that mouth of his.

When we break apart, staring into each other's eyes, I can't help but feel something pass between us, something more than kissing, more than fucking.

"What?" I whisper, too afraid to talk louder.

"You want to go back to my tent?"

I sigh dreamily. "How romantic."

He shakes his head at me, his lips twitching in amusement. "That's a yes." He leans in, kissing down my neck, and I let out a low moan.

From the corner of my eye, I see a flash of white. Squinting, my eyes go round when Danielle comes into view, her hands on her hips, her lips pinched together.

My stomach bottoms out, panicked that someone has seen us. We've been keeping this between us, not wanting to rock the boat. Having other people knowing… it could ruin what we have.

The rage on her face sends a shiver up my spine.

I pull away from Kaiden, gripping his face. "We have an audience."

Thinking he'd tense up and drop me, I'm surprised when he doesn't. He slowly looks over his shoulder, scanning the area.

"Where?"

I look over, seeing she's gone. "Danielle."

He shakes his head. "You're probably seeing things. She'd kick off if she saw me kissing you."

"She's probably planning to kill you in your sleep," I tease.

He chuckles, slowly lowering me to my feet. "Let's go. I need to be inside you."

"You're the one holding us up."

His hot gaze sears into me, and I feel myself burning up.

Yeah, I'm getting fucked tonight, and it's going to be hot.

An extravagant tent hidden in the trees comes into view, and my lips part.

This is the size of a small modern home.

We step up onto the decking, my gaze wandering over the hot tub, lit up by a swirl of different coloured lights. There's a small patio set by the side of it, and I stare in wonderment.

His tent doors are already pulled open, so I have clear view of the open-spaced living area and kitchen.

This is three times the size of my tent, maybe more. It's huge. It has everything. It's a mix of fabric and wood.

Two, three-seater sofas with two armchairs surround a rectangular coffee table, all angled in a way so they are facing the television resting on a wooden TV stand. It also cuts it off from the other side of the room, which has a small kitchen and sink area, and a four-seater dining table.

The room isn't decorated with a lot of nick-knacks. They've kept it pretty simple with a few bowls of potpourri and some indoor shrub plants.

Fairy lights and a few low, dim lamps light up the room, giving it a soft glow. It looks homey, in an outdoor kind of way.

"Wow, it's tiny," I mutter dryly. It even has storage cupboards. He has everything.

Kaiden chuckles, grabbing me around the waist and lifting me up. I laugh, wrapping my arms around his neck.

"Did you have a good day?"

I tilt my head, letting my hair fall to the side. "You mean between Selina getting drunk and girls being immature and name-calling?"

"Who called you names?" he asks, and if I'm not mistaken, his jaw clenches, a frown creasing his forehead.

I run my finger over his crease line. "You sound like you care."

His expression turns wary. "We've been fucking, Ivy."

"That doesn't mean anything," I tell him as he drops me to my feet, our mood broken.

He runs his fingers through his hair. "I don't just fuck anyone!"

I arch my eyebrow at him. "Danielle ring a bell?"

His face twists up. "I've explained Danielle. We were never together."

"Neither are we," I fire back. "This is just sex."

"At first, yes, but you know it's not like that now."

"What?"

"We spend most nights together."

"Fucking," I finish for him.

He growls. "You're under my skin."

"I wish you were under me," I snap, not liking how intimate this conversation is becoming. We might have gotten to know each other sexually, but personally, we still hardly know each other.

I like what we have. I like that we aren't in each other's pockets, or all loved up like some sick couple.

And I'll never admit this, but I love that he wants more, that he thinks of me as more.

He smirks, stepping towards me and pulling me flush against him. "That can be arranged."

"No more sappy talk?"

He shakes his head. "You really are different."

I shrug, running my finger down his bare chest. It still amazes me how defined and muscular he is.

"Can we make some rules?"

I blink up at him, twisting my lips. "Rules?"

His eyes crinkle at the corners. "I don't share," he explains, his expression blank again. "While we're fucking, I don't want you to sleep with anyone else."

"I wasn't planning on it."

"And I want you to keep an open mind when it comes to us."

I pull away a little, frowning at him. "Where is this coming from? This isn't you. You're an arsehole who hates people."

Frustrated, he pulls at his hair. "Because I can't get enough of you, Ivy. I can't. I want to get to know you better."

I laugh, and his face reddens in anger. "You've got to be kidding me. Is this some sort of joke?"

I scan the room, looking for hidden cameras. Hope blossoms in my chest, and I hate it. I hate that I've let him get to me like this in just a few short weeks.

It wasn't meant to be like this.

"Do I look like I'm fucking kidding? I've never put myself on the line like this, Ivy. I'm being dead fucking serious."

I stare into his eyes. He is dead serious. He really wants more.

I sigh, ducking my head a little. "Baby steps?"

"Baby steps," he agrees.

"You never know, some chick might take your fancy and you'll forget how awesome I am in bed."

"Fucking hell. Get here!"

I giggle, stepping towards him, my movements slow, predatory. I let my cardigan fall to the floor, loving the way his eyes follow my movements. Next, I grab my tank top, glad I didn't put my bra back on as I lift it over my head.

His gaze darkens, and he licks his bottom lip. I swear he growls when I unbutton my shorts, causing me to grin.

I was sure he was going to let me give him a full strip tease, but the minute my finger runs down my stomach, he's on me, lifting me up his body.

I pant with desire, needing him inside of me. He never fails to turn me on.

I look around the room for the bed, my eyebrows pulling together. "Um, where's the bed?"

He plays with my nipple, twisting and pulling, rougher than normal, and it's driving me wild. He begins to walk across the room, tugging harder at my nipple when I go to protest. I moan, sticking my chest out, silently begging for more. He sucks and laps at my breasts like a starving man. I close my eyes when it becomes too much, my mind blank of images and thoughts. I can only feel. Feel what he's doing to me.

I hear fabric sigh, and something brushes against my bare shoulder. I open my eyes, finding the living area disappear as the flap opening falls closed behind us.

I'm thrown roughly onto a bed, and my eyes bug out of my head.

Holy fucking cow.

This is like two king-sized beds stuck together. It's fucking huge.

Do giants rent this place?

I quickly scan the room as I struggle to look away from Kaiden pulling his shorts down. There's an actual door to the side, not fabric.

Hands grip my ankles, pulling me roughly down the bed. My body shakes with anticipation at the predatory look in his eye. He drops the foiled packet down beside me.

He bends down, completely naked, and kisses the inside of my thigh. I push him away, giving him a pained look.

"As good as you are, I need you inside me. I'm afraid that if you touch me one more time, I'll come before the best bit happens," I tell him.

"Always greedy," he replies huskily, kissing my clit over my knickers. He snaps them off, throwing them across the room.

Taking the condom, he rolls it on, and I watch, feeling my sex pulse.

"Turn around," he demands.

"What?" I ask, surprised. I've learned Kaiden loves sex, and he's good at it, but so far, he prefers to be facing me when we're fucking.

He leans over me, bending down to kiss my lips, his voice low, raspy and filled with sex. "If I fuck you like this, I'm going to come from just watching you ride my dick. Your expression gets me hard every time. But I've watched you all day, strutting around in that red bikini, looking hot as fuck. Every guy here got a boner watching you get out of that hot tub. At one point, I was ready to lick the sweat and water running between your breasts."

To make a point, he licks between my breasts, causing me to shiver.

In a daze, I watch as he shuffles back down the bed, smirking. "Ready?"

"Ready?" I ask, trying to shake out of it.

I squeal when he spins me over. I land on my stomach, but seconds later, hands are on my hips, bringing me to my knees.

I moan, clenching my hands around the sheets, fists tight.

"Fuck me!" I call out, already feeling my walls tightening, ready for what's to come. I'm so turned on, I could come with one flick to my clit.

He aligns himself up behind me, groaning when his fingers feel how wet I am. "Fucking greedy."

He thrusts himself inside me so hard, my cry buzzes in my ears. His fingers dig into my hips as he pulls out slightly, before slamming himself back inside with a groan.

When I feel him start to pull out again, I get myself together, and when he thrusts back inside of me once more, hitting the right spot, I push back against him, feeling everything explode inside of me.

"Fuck! Yes!"

"Fucking hell, Ivy," he groans, picking up his pace.

"Harder," I plead, needing that bite of pain each time he hits the back of my cervix.

He growls low, spreading my knees wider apart and deepening his thrusts.

Fucking hell.

I lift a hand up, playing with my tit, and a guttural moan escapes him as he reaches round, smacking my hand away. He cups my tits, pulling me back against him. I bounce harder on his long, hard cock, squeezing the hell out of him while he twists and pulls at my nipples.

"Fucking Jesus, you're tight. Clench your arse again," he demands, and I do, feeling myself tighten around him. He moans, tilting me forward a little so he can fuck me harder.

I cry out, tightening around him.

One hand leaves my breast, reaching up to grab a handful of my hair. Pulling my head back, he kisses my neck, breathing heavily.

I need this release, almost weep for it as I cry out in pleasure.

"Wait. I'm nearly there," he pants.

"Kai, I can't," I tell him, feeling sweat bead at my temples.

Heat spreads through my veins, making everything more intense. I can't hold off, not with him so deep inside of me.

I'm almost afraid to let go, to give in before he's ready.

"Never forget you belong to me, Ivy, that this pussy belongs to me," he grunts, thrusting harder.

"Kai."

"Mine! Fucking perfect," he rasps.

"Kai!" I yell, needing to come so badly it hurts.

He leans forward, biting the side of my jaw. Not hard enough to leave a mark, but enough for me to feel it. "Let go!"

And I do, crying out as waves of ecstasy hit me. It's explosive, my entire body tensing as I ride my orgasm.

My eyes close, and I fall forward, my palms hitting the mattress, fingers spread to prevent me from collapsing completely.

Kaiden jackhammers in and out of me, and my walls tighten around him, another orgasm bursting through me.

Kaiden groans, slamming into me one last time, his dick pulsing inside of me as he rides out his own orgasm.

chapter twenty one

Groaning, I sit up in bed, pulling the sheet over my naked breasts. Kaiden isn't around, and a flash of disappointment hits me. After our amazing night last night, I thought he'd be here when I woke up.

After he showed me the shower room and made sure I knew how good shower sex was, we went into the living area and watched a movie together. It was nice; the silence, the intimacy of being held in his arms without fear he'd turn on me in a second.

After another round of great sex, he told me all about Kingsley Academy.

Sliding my legs out of bed, I grab my clothes from last night and quickly throw them on. It's still really early in the morning, but I have no doubt people are getting up, ready for a day on the lake, fishing, and I want to get back before anyone notices me in last night's clothes.

Popping my head out of the flap, I see the coast is clear. I quickly run down the path, my head ducked so no one can see me.

I hit my tent just as I hear two voices, one belonging to Danielle.

"I'm sorry, Kai. I'm just worried you're making the wrong decision. She doesn't fit into our clique and it would be a shame if she ruined your reputation."

"What I do with my personal life has nothing to do with you, Danielle. We weren't together."

I grab the side of my tent, my pulse racing when I hear Kaiden. I peek around the corner. His back is to me, blocking Danielle from view.

I duck back when he shifts a little, making sure they can't see me.

"I know, Kaiden," she says, adding a sniffle. I roll my eyes. "I always thought we'd be together, get married, but I understand that isn't going to happen now. We grew up together, Kaiden. Doesn't that mean anything to you?"

I hear a frustrated sigh come from Kaiden. "Cut the bullshit, Danielle. I know you too well. I'm sorry if you're hurt, but you knew from the beginning this was never going anywhere."

"I'm not bullshitting," she remarks sharply. "I get it, all right. I really do. Are we still friends though? Or has she turned you against me because we slept together?"

"Whatever," he tells her. "You need to leave Ivy alone."

"I will, I promise. If she means that much to you, I will."

I don't like her tone at all. I've only met her a couple of times, and even I can hear the lie. She's put on the waterworks, tried to manipulate, and because none of that has worked, she's going for the 'keep your friends close, but your enemies closer'.

Fucking bitch.

"Look, I've got to go," he tells her, his voice void of any emotion.

I look around the corner again, seeing her move closer. "Thank you for listening to me, and I'm glad we sorted it out. I couldn't bear us being at odds with one another."

My heart races when she leans up on her toes, wrapping her arms around his neck. A gleam shines in her eyes when she notices me peeking around the corner. Her lips pull into a smug smile as she slowly runs her hands across his neck and onto his shoulders.

She kisses him on the lips, and he turns his head to the side. It doesn't matter. The bitch knew exactly what she was doing.

"I'll let you go. I know how much you love fishing. See you later?"

"Yeah," he grumbles, shaking his head as she walks away. I'm grateful he doesn't watch her walk away and instead turns, startling when he sees me.

"She's full of it."

He grins. "Always has been."

"She kissed you," I state.

"She missed my lips," he tells me, stepping closer, running his hands over my hips. "I came out here to get you some fresh clothes."

I smirk up at him. "You aren't as scary as you first made out."

"Oh, I am. I'm just nice to those I like."

"You like me?"

"Yep, so much so I'm about to show you how much."

"You are?" I tease, pulling away and stepping back, into my tent.

A dangerous glint in his eye warns me he's about to attack, but I'm too slow to escape. And I don't want to. He easily has me over his shoulders in seconds. I laugh, smacking his arse.

"Keep it down!" someone yells, making me laugh harder.

FISHING WAS A DUD. All I caught was sunburn, and I feel like I'm suffering for it. Whoever said fishing was fun, lied.

I shift on the log, where I've been sitting alone for a while, and it pulls at the skin on my back. I wince, biting back a groan of pain. Sunburn sucks. I've never really had it before. Never like this anyway. Mum slept most of the day, which was my only time to enjoy being inside. The second she woke up, I'd leave, and most of the time, the sun had either set or was starting to cool enough to not give me sunburn.

I feel sick to my stomach with each movement, and my skin is tight and uncomfortable. I could cry, but I will not succumb to the sun. I will not be defeated.

I'm going to be known as the girl who cried over a sunburn.

My eyes bug out at the thought. There is no way I'd live that down.

Glancing over to Selina, who spent the day complaining of a hangover, I sigh. She's drinking once again, but not loads like she did last night. The twins talked her into it an hour ago, saying it was the best hangover cure, along with lots of greasy food.

I don't want to force her to leave the party because of me, but I also don't want her to feel like I'm ditching her.

I'm totally ditching her, but I have a valid reason. I feel like I'm going to be sick, my head is pounding, and I'm kind of cold, even though my skin is on fire.

I head up to the hot tubs, where she's got her feet dangling in one. There's no way I can last another minute sitting here without showing weakness around a group of predators.

"Selina," I call, pulling her away from the conversation she's having with a group of girls who turned up this morning. They seem nice, but I've not really had much of a chance to talk to them. And the time I did, they acted like I was going to attack them.

They've been wary all day, not relaxing, but it seems Danielle had other things on her mind than running off a group of chicks.

The top 'to do' on her list was to try and weasel her way back into Kaiden's good graces. After this morning, I shouldn't feel so threatened. I heard his reply, and he didn't even know I was there. That wasn't fake.

They have a history together, something Kaiden and I don't have, and I think that's what's troubling me. They shared something we never would. I'm just some poor girl, raised by a woman who didn't want her, a woman who pushed the first domino, setting off a trail of events that ruined people's lives.

I'm nobody to him.

However, it didn't stop Danielle. I know she's up to something. I can feel it in my gut.

I haven't mentioned my worries to Selina or Kaiden. What would be the point? I don't gossip. I know Selina would listen, but so far, it's just a gut instinct, and I don't want to cause trouble for myself. The other reason is because I know I can handle anything the spoiled bitch throws at me.

"Hey, Ivy," Selina greets, her expression falling when she takes a look at me. "Are you okay? You look a little pale."

"I'll be fine," I assure her, looking away from her friend who is staring at me. "I'm heading to bed; will you be okay? I feel bad for leaving you."

"Of course, I will. I'm heading back to mine soon anyway, so don't worry about it. Did you want me to come back now?"

"No, you stay and have fun."

"Okay, text me if you need me."

I nod, grateful. I'm hurting badly, and every brush of the light breeze, or wave of heat from the sun still beating down, is making it worse. It's getting late into the evening, but at certain points, the sun felt like it was setting me alight when it hit my sunburn.

I didn't think to bring any sunscreen or painkillers, and I feel stupid. But it isn't like I've needed it before. I was never out in it long enough to get burned.

I leave Selina with her friends, chatting about school and what to expect from the Academy. I walk past another hot tub before I reach the stairs. I step to the side to let a group past, looking up when a body steps in front of me.

Danielle crosses her arms over her chest, pushing her tits up. I roll my eyes. She pastes on a fake smile, and I want to slap it off her face.

"Going so soon?"

"You going to miss me?" I ask politely, smiling.

Her happy expression falls a little, but she quickly puts up the pretence, looking around before her attention is solely on me. "Don't think for one second that I'm going to let you have him. He always comes back to me. You're just another piece of arse."

"If he wanted you, he'd be with you. Jealousy really doesn't look good on you." I eye her outfit. She looks good, but I hate the bitch. "Nothing does."

She shakes her head at me, her expression filled with pity. "Oh, sweetie, you have no idea about the things we've done together. He's a beast in bed. He'll always want me. And to be jealous of a washed-up tramp who comes from nowhere…" She laughs, clucking her tongue. "You're just a joke. A big joke. And by the time I'm done with you, everyone will be laughing at you."

"You guys need to work on your threats. You don't scare me. And if you keep pissing me off, I'm going to make sure you fall asleep crying each night. I'm not some prissy rich kid who thinks the sun shines out of your arse. I won't bow down to you. I won't follow you. So get it through your thick head before you make me do something you'll regret."

"You'll see," she hisses. "You're pathetic, and I'll make sure he sees exactly who you are."

"He's seen plenty of me," I whisper, so no one else can hear.

I see her hands rising and react instantly. I guess trying to drown me is high on her to-do list. I push her before she can push me, and I watch with satisfaction as she falls backwards into the hot tub, landing on a couple groping each other.

"Hey," the lad snaps, shoving her away.

She stands up, looking like a drowned rat. She screams, sliding her wet hair off her face. "This is a fifteen-hundred-pound dress."

I wince at the high decimal her voice reaches. "You should wear better shoes next time, maybe then you won't trip," I tell her, a smug smirk on my face.

"You—"

I hold my palm up, stopping her, and step a little closer to the hot tub. I bend down so we're eye-level, her face so red it looks ready to burst. "You messed with the wrong chick. I don't fight fair, and if you keep this up, I'll fucking ruin you in a way Daddy can't fix."

I get up, turning my back to her, and with my head held high, I walk off, heading back to my tent.

I ignore her profanities and high-pitched screeching, smiling as I do.

I'm heading down the path leading to my tent when Kaiden steps up beside me. "You look sore."

I flick my gaze up at him. "I am. I want another shower to get all the sweat and grime off me, but I'm scared it might kill me."

"A thousand bee stings."

"A what?" I mutter, wincing when my top rubs against my back. I could kill Selina for making me wear a bikini top.

He laughs at my expression. "My mum used to say getting in the shower whilst sunburnt felt like a thousand bee stings."

I frown at him. "That doesn't make me feel any better. I've never really been burnt like this before. It fucking hurts like a bitch."

Chuckling, he links our hands together. "Come on. I've got stuff back at the tent. Our housekeeper is forever babying us and chucking it in our shit."

"Annette needs to work on that," I joke, but secretly wishing she had.

We reach his tent without bumping into anyone. He pulls me inside, letting the doors flap shut behind us.

"Go lie down on the bed. I've got some after-sun and ibuprofen."

"My hero," I sigh dramatically, heading towards the room. The bed looks so soft and inviting I could cry. I wince as I pull off my T-shirt and untie my bikini top. I lie on my front, rubbing at the slight burn I've got on my chest. It's my back that got the most of it as I was either bent over the boat or leaning forward, waiting for something to happen in the water. I'll never get that time back.

So, I literally spent the day bored out of my mind, didn't even catch anything and got burnt in the process.

Life.

Kaiden walks into the room, squirting lotion onto his hand.

"Mate, if you think you're getting some after, think again. Hump the sheets."

"Just let me take care of you without the bitching."

"Whatever," I mutter.

Chuckling, he sits down next to me. I can feel him move closer, and my body tenses because of it, but nothing could have prepared me for the cold onslaught of liquid burning into my skin.

"Mother fucker!" I screech, sucking in a breath. "I knew you were going to torture me. I knew it. Last night was too good to be true."

I ignore his smug laughter as he keeps applying more. "Wait for it. The burn will start to ease."

He's right, but every fresh piece of skin he applies that shit to, I feel it all over again.

"You're good with your hands."

"I know!"

"Cocky," I mutter, yet my lips twitch into a smile.

He stops, and I relax into the bed, feeling the cream melt into my burning skin.

"I'm going to grab some ibuprofen and a bottle of water. You need to stay hydrated."

I yawn into the blanket, nodding in agreement. He chuckles, and I hear him move from the bed and out of the room.

He needs to stop treating me like a princess. I might get used to it. Fuck, I think I already am. He's such a contradiction to the guy I first met. I want to know who the real Kaiden Kingsley is. I can't trust him until I do.

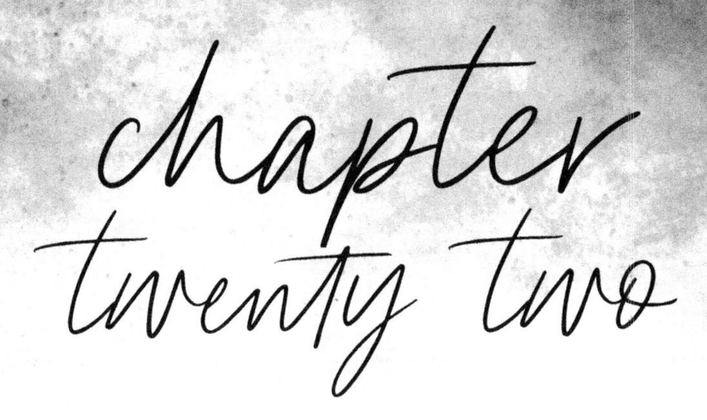

chapter twenty two

I CAN HEAR MUSIC AND LAUGHTER WHEN I rouse from sleep, which surprises me. I thought everyone would have gone to bed already due to leaving early in the morning.

I barely remember taking the tablets Kaiden handed me before I was lost to the dream world.

Turning over, I smile, finding Kaiden asleep on his stomach, his lips parted as he lightly snores.

He looks younger, more approachable with his frown lines gone and his features relaxed.

I want to stay, and it scares me because I know I can't. He messes with my head. Our relationship went from him loathing me, to whatever this is now. He was so sure at the beginning, so adamant in his mission to make my life hell, that I'm unsure what to believe right now.

The more I think about it, the more it terrifies me, because it happened within a blink of an eye.

And if it turns out this is just some sick game he's playing, I'm too invested to come out unscathed, and that bothers me the most. I've always protected myself. Always. And I've let my guard down.

I can't let him in. I can't let him have that power over me.

With that settled in my mind, I slowly slide my legs out of bed, grabbing the shoes Kaiden must have taken off when I passed out, and slide my feet into them.

A small lump forms in the back of my throat when I realise Kaiden had tied my bikini top back up. It was thoughtful, but again, it could be him playing games.

I need to get out of here.

I look around for my discarded top, not seeing it anywhere. I grab the first T-shirt I come across and pull it over my head, grimacing at the slight sting on my back.

I look back at the bed when I reach the opening. Kaiden is still in the same position, none the wiser.

I leave the tent as quietly as I can with such little light. I pat the back of my shorts, happy when I feel my phone still there. I jump down the porch step, onto the grass, and turn to head towards my tent, but a noise startles me.

I spin around, facing the fenced-off treeline. Even in the pitch black, the white horse stands out as it feeds from the ground.

My lips part. I've never seen anything so beautiful in my life. I walk over, ignoring the sting when a few stinging nettles brush my ankles.

He's beautiful, his hair white as snow. I take a tentative step forward. When I draw closer, his head snaps up and he looks right at me.

"Hey, buddy. It's okay. I'm not going to hurt you," I assure him, lifting my hand out to him. He bristles a little but steps closer, bringing his cold nose to my hand. I let out a small giggle, stepping even closer so I can run my hand up his snout. His hair is coarser than I thought it would be. I've seen so many pictures but never a real-life horse.

They're magnificent.

"Are you lost?" I ask, running my fingers over his mane.

He neighs, knocking his head against mine. I laugh, rubbing his snout again.

He rears back suddenly, and I have to take a step back. "Woah, buddy."

Screams and smoke fill the night air, and I spin around towards the campgrounds, my eyes widening when light flickers in the distance, thick, dark grey clouds polluting the atmosphere.

The horse gallops off in distress, and I do the same, but instead of running away, I run towards the chaos.

I pass people coming out of their tents to see what's going on. A sick feeling swirls in the pit of my stomach. Call it intuition, gut instinct, but the need to get to the fire is overwhelming.

The closer I get, the thicker the crowd becomes, and above the yells and cries, I swear I hear my name being yelled.

I push through the crowd, my stomach dropping when I see a tent is up in flames.

Oh my God!

"What happened?" I ask the closest person to me.

A girl around my age with curly red hair shrugs my hand off her arm. "A tent is on fire!"

Way to state the obvious. I try to look around the people blocking my way, to see what's going on.

Another girl standing with the redhead speaks up. "I hear she's seriously poor and has no family to bury her. It's such shame, Shell."

Her accent is different to her friend's. I think she's from Essex. But her words register and my stomach twists into knots.

"I don't think that will be a problem. I think she's burnt to a crisp. I heard she's some charity case Selina Farley's family took in."

Hearing her confirm it, I shove past them, ignoring their insults, and push through the small gap between two people standing in front of them.

It's my tent.

My tent is in flames.

Blinking through the thick clouds of smoke, I try to get closer.

"Ivy!" I hear roared, and this time, I know I'm not hearing things.

Kaiden.

In a daze, I see Grant tackle Kaiden, trying to push him back from the flames engulfing the entrance to the tent. "Stop!"

"Get out of my way," Kaiden spits in Grant's face.

"You aren't risking your life for that bitch," Grant snaps, blocking his way.

The noise around me suddenly disappears, and I hear what Kaiden hears. It finally registers in my brain, and my attention goes to the tent.

Screaming. Loud, painful screaming. I hear the anguish straight to my soul, and I stagger to a stop, fighting for air.

Someone's in there.

The terror in their voice paralyses me, and I know I'll never get the sound out of my head. I don't care about how that could have been me right now. I don't care that it's my tent.

What matters is the person suffering inside, fighting to get out. They sound terrified.

"Help! Somebody help!"

I can't make out who it is as their pleas stop.

I take a step forwards, needing to do something, but become glued to the spot once again when, in a rage, Kaiden punches Grant, knocking him to the floor.

Kaiden storms over to the twins, who run up, holding a knife. My eyes widen when I realise what he's about to do.

"Ivy!" he yells, walking to the side of the tent. His expression is one I've never seen on him before. He looks absolutely distraught and his body is drawn tight. It's hard to see him lose control of his emotions. "Go towards the back."

People follow him, and numbly, my gaze searches the chaos around me. Lads are yelling for someone to get water; others are trying to pat the fire out with wet towels. Girls cry into their friends' arms, staying as far away as they can from the flames, but close enough to see the action.

My eyes stop on a small figure hidden in the background, further away from the group of people trying to get a good look.

Danielle.

It's odd, where she's standing, blending in to the background.

She's with Sophia and Krysten, glowering at the back of Kaiden's retreating form. But before that, there was a smugness and sardonic look upon her face.

Shaking myself out of it, I rush down to the side of the tent, feeling the heat from the flames burning my skin. I need to help whoever is in there.

I cover my mouth with the back of my hand, coughing when my lungs fill with smoke. I hit the back of the tent in time to see a body drop through the hole Kaiden has made.

Everything around me begins to move in slow motion, and I feel like I'm stepping in quicksand.

"Selina?" he asks, his face paling as he quickly passes her off to the guy behind him. My heart stops when he tries to get inside the tent.

The twins help pull Kaiden back while another lad takes Selina, pulling her away from the smoke. I run over to Selina when I'm satisfied the twins have Kaiden and drop to my knees on the ground beside her.

Her eyes aren't open, and her face is covered in soot. "Selina," I cry out, bending down so she can hear me. I look up to the lad who helped carry her. "Call an ambulance."

"They're already on their way," he explains.

I look down at her body, noticing her arm is burnt and her clothing is blackened and torn in places.

"Ivy?" Ethan asks, his forehead puckered as he bends down on the other side of Selina.

We both turn when Kaiden roars, "She's in there. She's fucking in there!"

And it's in this moment I truly see this isn't a game to Kaiden. If it was, it isn't now. The agony etched into his expression cannot be faked. It's real. It's raw.

"Look after her," I quickly order Ethan, jumping to my feet.

"Kaiden," I yell, finally snapping out of my dream-like trance.

He's about to get himself killed, trying to fight his way into the fire. Grant is here now, standing next to Lucca as they block his path.

"Kaiden!" I yell again, louder this time.

He spins around, his fingers locked together on the top of his head. I suck in a breath when I see he's holding back tears.

My feet are moving faster, and before I realise it, I'm running into his arms, wrapping my legs around his waist.

"Ivy," he breathes, holding me so damn tight I can't breathe. "Fuck, I thought you were in there."

"Ambulance, fire engines and police are here," someone calls.

I pull back, gripping his face. "I'm good. But I need to be with Selina. She's hurt."

"I thought it was you," he croaks.

"I know. I'm good. I promise."

He puts me down, and I take a step away, but he pulls me back at the last second—and kisses me senseless.

"I fucking knew it!" Lucca declares loudly. He begins to laugh as Kaiden and I separate. "Looks like you've been dumped, G."

From the corner of my eye, I see Grant storm off, but I ignore it, kissing Kaiden once more, glad he's okay.

I guess people know about us now. The twins don't know how to keep quiet.

"I need to get to Selina."

"Go. I'll go speak to the firemen then meet you at the hospital."

"Okay."

I head over to Selina. She's still out cold, and I begin to worry, running my fingers through her hair.

The annoying morning person has come to mean something to me. I've never cared about anything or anyone since I was five years old and I gave up on my mum. Selina has been there for me, even when I said no. She's been there at my worst, and every day since, supporting me and being my friend.

I hate this feeling; this vulnerability inside of me that I didn't have before. I never had anything to lose, and now I do. And I don't want to feel weak.

She has to be okay. She just has to be. She makes all of this bearable.

"Please be okay."

"I've called Nova. She's meeting us at the hospital," Ethan informs me gently.

When the paramedics come, I get up off the ground, stepping back to let them work on her. I run my fingers through my hair, closing my eyes and wondering how this happened.

How did the fire start?

Was it something I had done?

Why was Selina there in the first place?

I have so many questions.

I open my eyes, and they immediately land on Danielle. Gone is the sour expression. Now she looks faint and ashamed. Sophia heatedly says something to her before storming off.

And it clicks.

She did this.

This was my tent. It's not a coincidence, a stroke of bad luck. This was done with the purpose to hurt me.

And it backfired because I wasn't in it. No, Selina was, for reasons I may never know.

Our gazes lock, and her eyes widen in surprise, fear flickering through them as her face pales.

"You," I growl, even though she can't hear me. She can see me though, and she jumps, acting like I had shouted it in her ear.

"What?" Lucca asks, stepping up beside me.

I push past people, storming over to her. I see the moment when all the doubt and remorse disappear. She straightens herself, twisting her lips together. I don't stop like she predicts. I keep going until we're close enough for me to punch her. I let my fist swing through the air, rejoicing when I see blood pouring from her nose.

"You psycho! Why did you do that?" she screams, stepping forward to attack.

Lucca gets there first, stepping between us with his hands on our chests, pushing us apart. "Woah, ladies, save it for the mud."

"Fuck you, Kingsley."

Lucca frowns at her. "I'd rather fuck a fish."

"Get your psycho charity case away from me," she orders him. "I'm going to have you arrested."

Lucca rolls his eyes. "Calm down, *Susan*." He turns to me, confusion in his expression. "What's going on?"

I fold my arms across my chest; one, to hide the fact my hand is throbbing, and two, because I want to hit her again.

"She started the fire," I tell him, not looking away from her.

"Are you serious?" she asks, forcing a laugh. "So not only will you be arrested for assault, but I'll sue you for slander."

I throw my hands up in the air. "Carry on. You can have my ratty school bag with clothes older than you in. It's the only fucking thing I own."

"Did you?" Lucca asks, his lips twisting into a snarl. He takes a menacing step towards her, and she fearfully takes one back.

"Are you seriously going to believe that tramp over me? I was with Sophia Krysten and Will Owens."

Kaiden startles me when he steps into the circle, bending down in front of Danielle so they're eye level. "If I find out you've done this, Danielle, I'm going to fucking destroy you. I'll make sure Daddy doesn't have a penny left by the time I'm done. I'll take everything you hold precious; your popularity, your friends, your money. Do you think Daddy will still love you when he finds out you're the reason he's lost everything?"

"Kaiden," she whispers brokenly, looking truly scared. "I didn't do this. Ask Will. We were together."

She has the gall to pretend to look upset. Her eyes even begin to water. I'm not buying it, not at all.

In fact, this cements my assumption.

Kaiden looks up at Lucca, silently communicating something. Kaiden turns away from Danielle, and she begins to sob, letting her friends coddle her like she's innocent.

"She fucking did it," I snap when we're far enough away.

"We need proof," he tells me. "Right now, go to the hospital with Selina."

I glance over my shoulder, glowering when Danielle laughs at something her friend says.

She did it. I know she did.

chapter twenty three

I SIT BACK ON THE SOFA, IGNORING THE low hum of the news playing in the background, covering tonight's fire. It's still unknown how the fire started, and nothing has been declared on whether it was set intentionally or not. Something must prove it was started intentionally.

The waiting room is nothing like the hospitals my mum often frequented over the years. There, they had those uncomfortable school chairs and a water dispenser.

This one is more like a lounge. The seating is comfortable, and it has a television bracketed to the wall on the left. On the opposite side of the room is a long table, filled with a mixture of baked goods, tea and coffee and some juice. The only thing that seems out of place is the vending machine in the corner. Everything else looks like a shoot from a magazine, all perfectly clean and placed.

There's been no word about Selina. I'd told the hospital staff I was family, but because I didn't know many personal details about her, they'd presumed I was lying.

Lucca, who had arrived seconds after the ambulance, places his hand over my bouncing leg.

"Nova will be here any second," he assures me, and sure enough, I hear shoes clicking down the hallway.

We turn to the door when it's pushed open, Nova storming through. For half two in the morning, she looks pretty put together.

"Ivy," she gushes out.

I stand to greet her, tensing when she pulls me in for a hug. Kaiden, Grant, and Ethan step in behind her, all with grim expressions.

"They won't tell me anything. I don't know anything about her."

Ethan chuckles. "You pretty much own the hospital."

"What?" I ask, narrowing my gaze on him.

He shrugs, looking to Nova before back to me. "This is your father's hospital. He owns many like this."

I groan, sitting back down. Kaiden moves, sitting next to me.

"Selina's fine. She has a second-degree burn, which is being treated. She's awake but out of it, due to the drugs. She inhaled a lot of smoke, so they're conducting some tests to see how severe the damage is. All we can do is wait for the doctors to update us."

"You couldn't have started with that?" I ask dryly, relief coursing through me.

She's okay. She's awake. She's breathing.

"Sorry. I'm just glad you're both okay," she explains. "What happened?"

I don't like the secretive look Kaiden shares with the others. I can feel the lie before he even speaks. He doesn't want her to know.

"We aren't sure. The firemen are still trying to figure it out. They'll be in touch tomorrow."

He squeezes my thigh, silently ordering me to shut up. And for once in my life, I do as I'm told. I trust him. I might not have before, but I do now.

Nova's phone beeps in her pocket, and she pulls it out, reading a message. She looks nervously at me, indecision written over her face.

"Spit it out," I snark, not in the mood for any more games.

"Selina's father couldn't catch the next flight out. Um, your father, Sam, is here."

"Great," I mutter, closing my eyes.

"I'll be back in a few minutes—to give you time to prepare yourself."

"Whatever."

Once she's gone, I get up from the sofa and head over to grab a drink. Kaiden follows, standing close.

"Are you okay?"

I look up at him, holding the glass close to my chest. "No. She's hurt because of me," I tell him. I laugh and it sounds foreign. "How ironic. My mum hurt the people around her, and since I came to live with Nova, I've spent most of my time screaming about how I'm nothing like her. And now it seems I'm following in her footsteps. I won't be surprised if I'm blamed for the fire."

Grant clears his throat. "Look, I can't fucking stand you."

"Cheers," I mutter, looking away.

"Way to kick a dog—" Ethan begins to say.

"I'm not a fucking dog," I snap.

"Sit!" Lucca barks, grinning at me.

I roll my eyes, turning my attention to Grant, arching my eyebrow. "What were you going to say?"

He rubs the back of his neck. "I don't trust people. It doesn't come easy—to any of us. We have things people want and would do anything for."

"This really isn't helping," I tell him.

He shrugs. "I'm not trying to help. But we were wrong. We've blamed you from the start for being like your mum. All of us are guilty of it," he explains, eyeing Kaiden for a moment. "None of us are our parents. And who they are doesn't define who we become. I can see that now. Tonight wasn't your fault, and you shouldn't feel responsible."

I smirk at his pained expression, enjoying how clearly uncomfortable he is with apologising to me, letting Kaiden pull me into his arms. I ignore the way Ethan's mouth drops open and answer Grant.

"But it was someone's, and we know who that someone is."

"We'll find out. She has a solid alibi though," Lucca explains.

"Is no one going to comment on the fact Kaiden is acting like a loved-up puppy? He's practically humping her leg!" Ethan cries out.

"Old news," Lucca comments, patting his brother on his back.

"She did it. I know she did."

"We need proof. Will was drunk as fuck when we spoke to him, but he was certain she was there, as are her friends."

"She could have gotten someone else to do it," I mention.

"Could be. We'll find out who. We always do," Kaiden explains.

"Yep, there's always someone willing to sell secrets for exam papers or answer sheets," Lucca comments.

"I feel disgusted with myself," Ethan says, plopping down on the loveseat. We all turn to him, questioningly. "All this time I thought you were fucking with her, giving her shit still, and all along, you were *fucking* her."

"Get over it," Lucca orders.

"How you doing?" Kaiden asks, once they all start bickering over the channel.

"Okay. I just wish I could see her. We aren't close like you guys, but she means a lot to me. I guess I didn't realise how much until tonight."

He leans down, giving me a peck on the lips. "She'll be fine. We'll see if you can see her after."

I sigh, staring at his chest. "Thank you for being here."

He tilts my chin up, his startling green eyes blinking down at me. He searches my face, trying to read me. "What's changed?"

I look away for a moment. "What do you mean?"

"You know what. You don't have that guarded look anymore. Why?"

Fucking hell.

Why does he always want to get inside of my head?

I don't want to make a big thing out of this. I liked what we had. But his actions tonight changed that. It changes the dynamic between us. And I'll never forget him fighting those around him, thinking I was inside that tent.

The least I can do is give him something.

"I saw you."

"Saw me?" he asks, his eyebrows scrunching together.

"You thought I was in that fire. You were willing to risk your life to save me. Those aren't the actions of someone who is playing mind games."

He shakes his head, his lips twitching. "I really was a dick to you when you arrived."

I nod in agreement. "Yes. Yes, you were."

He leans in, stealing my breath away when he captures my lips in a kiss. I let go of all the emotions pouring through me, losing control of all senses.

"Kaiden, have you lost your goddamn mind!" a voice explodes.

I jump away from Kaiden, feeling flushed, and turn to find Royce storming over to us.

"Oh shit," Lucca mutters.

"Get away from my son!"

"Don't touch her," Kaiden warns, pushing against his dad's chest. My eyes widen at the rage in his expression when he looks at his son.

"Go home, now!"

Kaiden forces a laugh. "You want to start parenting now?"

"I won't have some washed-up whore get her claws into my family's legacy."

"*My* family's legacy. You mean *mine*. You only have control because of the state Mum is in, but once I turn twenty-five, Dad, the business automatically transfers to me." Kaiden steps closer to his dad, until they're facing off. "And if I hear you talk like that about Ivy again, I'll get Mum to sign it over now."

"I will not have you doing this, Kaiden. Have you forgotten what her mum did, who she is? You'll soil your reputation being with that—"

"Careful," Kaiden warns, his voice deadly.

"Maybe I should go," I mumble, moving to step around them.

"Yes, you should. Keep away from my son. You'll not get a penny from him."

I narrow my eyes at him. "I wouldn't take it if he offered, *sir*. And do not order me around."

"Someone needs to," he snaps sharply. "I've just had a phone call from Mal Holden, who said you assaulted his daughter."

"Danielle's dad needs to put a leash on his own daughter," Ethan pipes in from the sofa, crunching on some crisps.

Royce throws him an annoyed look before his attention comes back to me. "You are easily discarded, just like your mother, so don't get too comfortable. I won't have you do this to my family, our lives. You are a nobody. How much longer do you think Nova will let you ruin her family's name?"

Kaiden takes a step towards his dad, but I stop him, pulling him back. "No offence—"

"That's slang for 'fuck you,'" Lucca calls out.

I roll my eyes. "No offence, but I couldn't care less what you think of me. If Nova ever wants me to leave, I will."

"Kaiden, boys, we're going home. Now!" he orders them.

"I'm staying here with Ivy," Kaiden tells him shortly.

Royce's face turns red. "You will do as you're told, Kaiden. I mean it. I won't have you frolicking with this girl any longer. She will ruin your name, your future."

"Will she now?" a deep voice rumbles. I stagger backwards into Kaiden's hard chest when my dad—Sam—enters the room, his expression tight and filled with anger.

"Sam, old friend," Royce greets, forcing a smile.

"Don't 'old friend' me, Royce. That's my daughter you're talking about."

"And my niece," Nova bites out.

Royce scoffs. "You can't claim her as your daughter, not with who her mother was."

Something passes through Sam's gaze, something painful. "Let's not bring Cara into it," he says tightly. "And damn right I claim her, test results or no test results."

Nova's eyes focus on me, nerves filtering through them.

What is going on?

"She's a menace to society. In her short time here, she's been arrested, and tonight, she assaulted Mal Holden's daughter. And I was informed by my house staff that she caused a commotion at the twins' birthday party."

My gaze meets Grant's, who has the nerve to look guilty, since he was the one who caused that commotion, not me.

The adults keep arguing, and Kaiden's hands hold me tighter. He leans down, his lips grazing my ear. "Let's get out of here."

"I'm not leaving Selina," I whisper, worried the adults will turn their attention to me.

His chuckle vibrates against my back. "Let's go see her, then."

"But the nurse said—"

"You're biologically a Farley. Tell them you own the hospital."

I feel him give a nod to the twins. Ethan, who is paying attention, nudges a clueless Lucca, who looks away from the arguing adults, grinning like a mad fool. When it clicks, he jumps up, and he and Ethan move over to us.

"Let's go. I hacked the hospital's records and found out she's in room 1105," Ethan explains.

Shocked, I can only stare. Lucca grins. "What, did you think we were brainless idiots?"

I nod tightly. "Yes. Yes, I did."

Ethan chuckles, shaking his head in mock disappointment. "You have a lot to learn, little friend."

"Let's go see Selina," I mutter.

The adults are too busy arguing and pissing on each other to notice our departure, let alone stop us. I needn't have worried they would.

"Um, guys," Grant begins when we're out of the room.

"Get over it, Grant. They're fucking and you weren't invited," Lucca teases, making me giggle.

Grant's jaw hardens. "Fuck you, dickhead. I thought you'd want to know my dad is on his way. He's pissed. It seems Katrina decided to spread some lies and told him we were sleeping with Ivy."

I snort. "I barely survived Kaiden," I blurt out.

Kaiden chuckles. "Good to know."

I roll my eyes, ignoring the guys as they congratulate him. I follow the signs to Selina's room, taking a deep breath when I reach her door. I look through the window, seeing her awake, laying in the bed with an oxygen mask on her face.

I push open the door, and her eyes immediately find mine. "Ivy?"

Shit, she sounds awful.

"Hey, girl. How are you feeling?" I ask softly, feeling the others pile into the room after me.

She blinks up at me, her eyes watering. "I think I inhaled weed because I'm seriously high right now."

I laugh, sitting on the edge of her bed. "I think that's the drugs they've given you."

She looks up at me with a sombre expression. "What happened?"

"I don't know. I—I've got no idea. Do you know what happened? How the fire started?"

I feel Kaiden move closer as I watch pain flicker over Selina's features. "I'm not sure."

"What were you doing in Ivy's tent?" Kaiden asks, keeping his voice low, gentle, which is bizarre for him.

She stares accusingly at me. "Why weren't *you* in the tent?"

"You will never fucking guess," Ethan starts, his eyes gleaming with excitement. He's dying to tell people about me and Kaiden.

"Focus, Selina. Tell us. Start from the beginning," Kaiden orders.

She blinks slowly, tiredly, and then her narrowed gaze turns to the twins. "I left my pod because these two were murdering some girl, and I couldn't stand listening to the sound."

My lips twitch when the boys grin. "Trust me, the only thing being murdered was her vagina. She enjoyed every second."

"Her arse will be sore tomorrow too." Lucca grins, and my lips twist in disgust. That's just too much information.

Selina coughs, holding the mask tighter to her face. Once she recovers, she turns to me. "I couldn't listen to another minute, so I went to sleep with you, but you weren't there. At first I thought I'd got the wrong tent."

"Take it slow," I tell her, rubbing her good arm when she begins to wheeze.

She drops back onto her pillow, her hand on her chest. "When I saw your clothes, I thought you wouldn't mind me crashing. I fell asleep and woke up to voices. I don't know who, whether it was a girl or a boy, anything. I just remember smelling smoke, and then feeling the heat of the flames."

"It's okay," I soothe when she begins to choke up. Her expression fills with pain as she tries to stop herself from letting go, from getting it all out. It doesn't work, and her chest begins to heave.

"I-I t-thought, I-I was going t-to die," she chokes out.

"It's going to be okay. I promise."

A nurse rushes in moments after her machine starts going crazy. She startles when she sees us crowding the room.

"You aren't allowed in here," she tells us, but doesn't seem angry about it.

"She's my cousin," I tell her.

"She needs her rest," the nurse tells us as she looks over Selina. "You should come back later."

I feel conflicted. I want to give the nurse room, Selina time to recover, but I also want to make sure she's okay.

"Let's go home, get some rest," Kaiden announces.

The door behind us opens, and I tense, thinking it's Royce again. When I see Nova, she gives me a small smile. She sees Selina is awake and heads over. "How are you feeling, darling girl?"

Selina blinks sleepily. "Tired."

I look to the nurse, who rolls her eyes at my accusing gaze. "I've given her something to help her sleep. She's going to be in a lot of pain when she wakes up. It's better she gets some rest."

"Is she going to be okay?" Nova asks.

The nurse nods. "Her throat is a little raw right now, and we'll have to keep an eye on it. We have a plastic surgeon coming in, as requested by her mother."

"Her mother?" Nova questions, her voice tight.

"Yes. She called and asked how bad the injuries were."

"You mean how bad her daughter looked," Nova scoffs, shaking her head in disgust.

"She'll be out till late morning at the earliest. It's best you get some rest, ready for when she wakes."

"Okay. Thank you again for everything you are doing."

The nurse smiles warmly. "It's my job."

I cling to Kaiden, tiredness overwhelming me. Nova turns, looks at our close proximity, and sighs.

"Did you not put any sun cream on, Ivy?"

I'm caught off guard by her question. I thought she would mention what Royce said, or say something about our relationship, but she didn't.

"I didn't have any," I murmur.

Guilt flickers in her eyes. "Next time, I'll make sure you have everything."

I yawn, and Kaiden holds my weight. "Let's go get some sleep. It's been a long night."

"Your father wants you home," Nova tells him.

"I don't care what he wants right now. I'm not leaving Ivy."

She sighs, looking from Kaiden to me and back again. "Come on, you guys can all stay at mine. No funny business," she warns, giving Kaiden a pointed look.

"Will Annette cook us some breakfast?" Ethan asks, batting his lashes.

Nova rolls her eyes. "No. She's asleep. But I'll make you breakfast."

Ethan winces. "I'll grab something on the way home."

We reach the door, and I freeze, biting my bottom lip. "Where's Sam?" I'm not ready to see him, even after what he said to Royce.

Nova's gaze softens. "He's waiting until we leave to come in to sit with Selina. He knew you wouldn't be ready and is happy to wait until you are."

I give her a short nod, letting Kaiden steer me out of the room. I feel physically and emotionally drained.

And I have a feeling this is just the beginning of something much bigger.

chapter twenty four

THE NIGHT BEFORE SEEMS LIKE ONE huge blur. None of it seems real now that a new day has begun. It's hard to imagine that just last night, Selina was stuck in a burning tent, scared for her life.

My tent.

I still haven't wrapped my head around the fact the fire was set because someone thought I was in it, that someone hated me to such a degree they wanted to kill me—or attempt to.

Danielle either lit the fire or had one of her friends do it. Now, it's just proving it that will become a problem. But I know it was her.

Nova doesn't yet know that it was intended for me, to hurt me. I'm unsure how she will take it, and from Kaiden's reaction last night, he wants to keep it quiet from the adults so he can dish out his own form of punishment.

I shiver at the thought, knowing first-hand how lethal Kaiden can be. I don't feel an ounce of remorse for what is to come. Spoilt little rich girl thinking she can do what she wants, deserves everything she gets.

A wide smile spreads across my face when an arm wraps around my waist. Kaiden pulls me against his chest, burying his nose in my neck, breathing me in.

"You smell like apricots," he comments, his voice raspy, still filled with sleep.

"It's better than the smoke smell I had going on when we got back last night."

"How are you feeling this morning?" he asks gently.

I roll over until I'm facing him. "I wasn't the one burned."

Something passes over his features. "It could have been you. It could have been worse," he grits out. "When I find out who did it, they'll wish they were never born."

I rub a hand over his chest. "It was her. I don't know how, but I just know it was Danielle. She has to pay for what she's done."

He sighs, running his fingers across my hip. "If it was, I'll find out, and I'll fucking ruin her. I promise you that. Not just for the attempt on you, but for Selina. My brothers love her like a sister."

"Do you really have the power to do that to her father?" I ask, kind of scared of the fact. He's young. No one should have that kind of influence over people.

His expression is sombre. "Yes—with time. Her dad is wealthy, with nearly as much as we have. He's a snake, and just like his daughter, he's good at being one. If she warns him about my threat to her, it could give him time to prepare. I can't touch Danielle, but her father I have no qualms about hurting."

"You touched me," I remind him.

"Never really in anger. I would never have physically hit you," he explains, guilt lacing his voice. "You took me by surprise when I first saw you. I hadn't expected you to be so beautiful."

I grin at that. "You had a funny way of showing it."

He rolls his eyes. "I still wouldn't have hurt you, but you're right, Danielle needs to pay, and I'll take away everything that means something to her."

I don't like seeing him stressed. I know it's bothering him to know he can't do anything. "We'll find a way to get justice for Selina. Maybe we should go to the police."

He scoffs. "You've spent the night there. Do you really think they'd care?"

He's probably right. But I hate not being able to do anything. I just don't want to be the fall guy the cop who released me mentioned. "Yeah, you're right."

A light tap on the door startles me. "Ivy?"

My eyes widen as I look at Kaiden, and I try to shove him out of my bed. He doesn't budge, his lips twitching in amusement.

When we got back last night, Nova gave the boys rooms to sleep in. None of them wanted to go back home, since their dad was there, so they decided to stay over. Nova had said it was because they wanted to stay close to me, but I wasn't buying it.

"Yes?" I squeak out, causing Kaiden to chuckle. I slap his chest, pulling the blanket up a little more in case she walks in.

"I'm popping to the hospital to check on Selina. Did you want to come with me or get dropped off later after you've had breakfast? I can have a car waiting to take you."

"I'll come as soon as I'm dressed and had something to eat. I'll grab some of Selina's things."

"You're a sweetheart," she calls through the door, sounding exhausted. "I'll see you there."

"Okay."

"See you in a little while," she calls. "Oh, and good morning, Kaiden. Help yourself to food."

I'm mortified, and slap Kaiden on the chest again when he begins to laugh. "Thank you, Nova," he yells as we listen to her footsteps retreat down the hallway.

"Oh my God! This is embarrassing."

Kaiden presses a kiss to my forehead, chuckling. "We're good. It's not like she heard me fucking you last night."

My cheeks heat as I glare at Kaiden. He fucked me hard in the shower, and then again when we got to bed. "Seriously not funny."

"Although, Ethan sent me a text, telling us to keep it down."

"I'm going to kill them," I groan. We'd left them in the cinema room watching some action movie. They shouldn't have even been near my room.

"I'm going to pop home and get changed," he informs me.

I groan, not wanting him to leave. I'm too cosy, and I was hoping we could have a repeat of last night before we got out of bed. "You're leaving me?"

He smirks, his dimples showing. "I thought you wanted to see Selina?"

Why does he have the power to make me forget?

"Yeah, I do. I'll get dressed and grab something to eat."

"I'll be thirty minutes. I just need to sort some things out. I'll grab the twins on my way out. I bet they crashed downstairs."

I nod, pulling away from him. "I'd best get in the shower. I swear I can still smell smoke."

After rising from the bed, I walk Kaiden to the door, letting him pull me into his arms. He takes my lips in a hard, fiery kiss, stealing my breath. Running my hands over his broad chest, over his wide shoulders, I press myself firmly against him, kissing him deeper.

Those flames he always manages to ignite inside of me, burn, and I want him. I always want him.

He pulls away, and my lips feel swollen and bruised. I blink up at him, seeing his gaze filled with heated desire.

"Later," he whispers huskily.

"Later," I repeat, swaying slightly when he lets go of me.

The door shuts behind him, and I want to collapse to the ground. It's not fair how much he affects my body.

Since I decided to trust him, to give him a part of me no one else has ever had, I've felt this rush pulse through me. It's like I feel free for the first time in my life, like I don't have a weight on my shoulders, too heavy for me to bear.

And in part, that's because of him, because of the power I feel whenever I'm around him.

I just hope he doesn't break my trust. I don't know if I could ever recover from that.

I'm so incredibly fucked.

Showered and dressed, I make my way downstairs, seeing Annette on my way down. She looks flustered, rushed, which is so out of character for her.

I step to the side a little, blocking her path. "Are you okay, Annette?"

She jumps, causing me to frown. "Miss Ivy. I-I just need to make the rooms. Breakfast is in the kitchen."

"Wait!" I call out, reaching for her when she slips past me, her expression tight with worry. She moves out of the way but pauses a few steps above me, looking back at me.

"I'm sorry, Miss Ivy."

What on earth?

"Sorry for what?" I ask, but she leaves, her head lowered, her shoulders slumped.

I watch her go, wondering if I should go after her or not. A noise from the kitchen distracts me, and a grin forms on my lips.

Kaiden.

He must have finished whatever he was doing early. I rush down the last few stairs, a swing in my hips. As I near the kitchen, I slow down, collecting my thoughts before I make a fool of myself.

I walk around the corner, stopping short when I find Royce leaning against the kitchen counter.

Great, just what my morning needed.

"We really should stop meeting like this," I mutter dryly, not moving from my spot. Something is off, and it's not just the haggard, rough look Royce has going on right now. His tie is hanging from his neck, the top buttons on his shirt undone, and his hair isn't combed to its usual perfectly still style. It looks like he's been running his fingers through it all night. And even from here, I can smell the whiskey on him.

"Let's cut the pleasantries, shall we," he snarls.

"I wasn't being pleasant," I tell him, crossing my arms over my chest.

Is he the reason Annette ran upstairs?

I narrow my eyes at him, watching him closely. He steps forward, reaching into his suit jacket, and I force myself not to take a step back.

He pulls out a piece of paper, handing it out to me. I take it, confused, until I look down and see the large sum of money printed on the cheque.

I snort. "Please tell me this is a joke."

"Quite the contrary, Ivy."

"What is this?" I ask, still wary. He isn't giving me this from the kindness of his heart. I don't think he has one.

"*That* is your ticket out of here. Leave and don't come back."

I force out a laugh. He can't be serious. "All because I'm sleeping with your son?"

His jaw hardens, and he steps closer, before bending down until we're at eye level. "I'm giving you this warning once, Ivy, so listen very carefully. I'll not have you destroy everything I've worked all my life to build. You will leave today and not look back."

I tilt my head to the side, studying him. "And why would I do that?"

"Because nobody wants you here. Nova is keeping you close so you don't soil the family name by revealing who the real Cara Monroe was to the press. My son is playing games with you and will be done with you once he has his revenge. He loves pussy, and yours is available. Take the money, Ivy. It will be the only time I offer it."

He really has lost his goddamn mind. But a part of me wonders if that is why Nova brought me here. I don't want to believe it; in my heart, I don't, but in my mind… it's screaming 'what if' at me.

"It still doesn't explain why you are the one giving me this. You aren't doing it to help me, so don't play games."

The veins in his temple pulse as he grits his teeth. "I don't want you here messing with my son's future. I know what you're after, and this is the most you will get from us."

He's lying; it's written all over his face. I don't know what his game is, but I'm not playing.

I take a step closer, loving the reaction I get when he takes a step back. Clenching my jaw, I lift the cheque in front of his face—and tear it in half.

"Then I guess you wasted perfectly good ink, because I don't do well with threats and I don't want your money."

He reaches out, gripping my bicep so tight I wince. "You little bitch. You will leave, Ivy. I'll make sure of it. I will end you before I let you—" I watch him carefully when he stops what he's going to say. It's only a second before he composes himself. "Before you ruin my son's life."

I try to shrug his hand off me, but it doesn't work. "I suggest you take your hands off me, Mr Kingsley, before you make me do something that's going to hurt."

He seems to think about it for a moment, and the veins in his neck begin to bulge. He shoves me away, and I knock into the counter, my hip smacking off the side. I bite my lip to stop myself from crying out.

That's going to bruise.

"You've been warned. If you aren't gone within the week, I'll end you," he threatens, turning without another word and slipping out the backdoor.

"Ivy?" Kaiden calls, and I jump, turning to face the kitchen entrance. I straighten myself quickly, not wanting Kaiden to see me like this.

"In here," I call out, my voice a little shaky.

He looks so happy when he walks in that I don't have the heart to tell him about his father's visit. I don't want to be the catalyst for any problems between them.

Liar. You're scared he'll take his side.

Shaking the thoughts from my mind, I paste on a fake smile. "Hey, you ready to go?"

He looks at the kitchen counter where Annette has left out the food. "You not going to eat?" He pulls me into his side, and I wince when his hand grips what has to be the bruise forming on my hip.

I look to the food, my stomach rolling. "No. I'm not really hungry anymore. Did you want to take something to go?"

"Yeah, can do." I wince again when he squeezes over the bruise.

"You okay?"

I nod, forcing a laugh. "I'm so out of it this morning I walked into the counter. I think I'll have a bruise."

I turn away before I can read his expression, not wanting to see if he believes me or not. "You want me to look?"

"I'm good."

"You sure?"

I nod once, stepping away from him. "I just need to grab my phone and a bag of stuff for Selina."

"I'll be here," he mumbles around a mouthful of food.

I chuckle, stepping out of the room before heading upstairs. I quickly grab my phone from beside my bed before poking my head inside Selina's room, ready to grab a bag for her.

I pause when I find Annette nervously folding clothes into a bag sat on Selina's bed. She jumps when she sees me, relief written all over her face.

"Did he hurt you?" is the first thing that falls from my lips.

She shakes her head, her eyes watering. "I'm sorry, Ivy. I didn't know what to do. Mr Kingsley can get very angry."

I walk over to her and rub my hand down her back. "I'm not scared of him."

She grips my hands, fear written all over her face. "You need to be. He's not a good man, Ivy. Promise me you'll never be alone with him again."

Hearing the terror in her voice scares me. "Annette, you need to tell me what's going on. What did he do?"

"I can't. I'm just a maid, Ivy. He's a wealthy man who has too much power."

I squeeze her hand. "He's just a man, Annette. And you aren't *just* a maid. You are a human being."

"Oh, Ivy," she says, pulling me in for a quick hug. "Please stay true to yourself. Never let wealth corrupt you."

"Please, Annette—what did he do?"

I'm worried for her, my stomach rolling with it. I've become close to her over my time here. She's practically the mum I never had.

And she feeds me. Anyone who feeds me should be worshipped in my book.

She shakes her head. "Just remember he's a bad man. And what you think he'll do to you is not as bad as what he will do to you. Just be careful."

I sigh. Clearly, I'm not getting anywhere. "Damn riddles," I mutter. "Does Nova know what he's like?"

"Miss Monroe is scared of him too, but you can't let her know I told you."

"Nova's scared of him?" I ask, needing answers.

The door opens, revealing Kaiden. "There you are. Are you coming?"

Annette snatches her hand away from me, placing the rest of the items in the bag. "Miss Ivy is ready. Here you go," she tells me, handing me the bag. Her expression implores me not to say anything, to keep quiet. I give her a subtle nod, taking the bag from her.

"I'll speak to you later."

"Car's ready," Kaiden tells me, and I sigh, glancing at Annette one more time. I don't want to leave her like this.

I'm fed up of not getting answers. I need to talk to Nova, and I need to talk to her now.

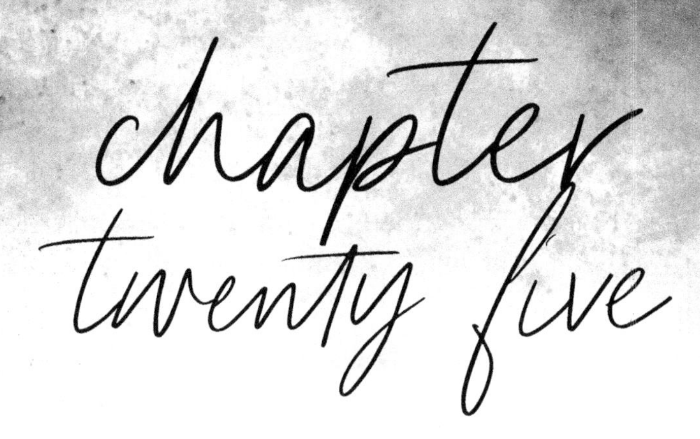

"GET ME OUT OF HERE," SELINA WHINES, her throat still raw.

She's been in the hospital for just under a week. The day I went to confront Nova, once and for all, and demand the truth about those around me, I found out Selina had been intubated. Her lungs and throat had inflamed overnight, leaving little room for her to breathe. She was on it for nearly two days, yet it felt like a lifetime for me.

I'll never forget the moment I walked into her room and saw her like that on the bed. She looked pale, lifeless, and for a moment, I thought she was dead.

My heart was in my throat, and I'd wanted to scream out desperately, but nothing would come out. Kaiden had been my support, emotionally and physically, holding me up when I nearly fell down. I don't know what I would have done without him there.

I lived with Mum for just over seventeen years and didn't shed a tear when they announced she had overdosed. All I felt was loss.

The second I walked into Selina's room, tears streamed down my face, and I felt like I had lost a limb. I hated the vulnerability I felt, hated that someone had the power to make me feel that weak, but Selina had come to mean so much to me. She wasn't malicious, she wasn't fake, and she was everything I wasn't. She was kind, bubbly and filled with life.

She's made a full recovery, but Sam—my dad—isn't taking any chances with her health. Her own parents haven't even been by to check on her as far as I'm aware. It's only that part of her life I can relate to, and I wish there was something I could do to make it better for her. She's tried to play it cool, acting like she isn't affected, but I could see the desperation every time someone walked through the door, and her head would bow with defeat every time it wasn't them.

There was nothing I could do. I knew that from experience. But I could distract her, visit her, and hope I can fill a little of that void like she's done for me since I arrived.

I laugh over the phone, watching her face scrunch up. Whenever Sam is there, I'm not, so we Facetime to catch up. Nova said he didn't mind leaving for a while to let me come in. He's been staying in the VIP rooms to stay close to Selina.

"They said two more days."

"I'm going to miss your eighteenth birthday," she whines. "And I'm fine. Look!" She takes in a deep breath, looking ridiculous. "I can breathe perfectly fine."

I roll my eyes. "It's two more days, and it's not like you'll be missing much. I don't want a party."

She snorts. "I was going to do a girly night and have someone come in to give us facials, wax and tint our eyebrows, and all that girly stuff. School starts in a week, too, so it's perfect timing. We have to start planning."

I grimace, kind of glad she's stuck in hospital. If I weren't still avoiding Sam, I'd hug him right now. There is no way anyone with a wax pot is coming near me. I've seen videos on the internet at school. It looks more like torture than a beauty regimen. I'm pretty sure stuff like that is meant to be relaxing, soothing, and the girl I watched didn't look relaxed. In fact, she looked worse than the woman in the birthing video we had to watch in our health and social class.

Music continues to blare next door, and I inwardly groan. The twins are clearly having another party, and it's getting rowdier by the minute. I'm pretty sure someone just turned it up.

"Is that music?" she asks, making me laugh when she tries to move her head to see around my phone, like that will work.

"Yes. I'm going to go and see what's going on. Kaiden didn't say anything about having a party."

"I still can't believe you didn't tell me about you two. I knew something was going on."

"I said I was sorry," I tell her, chuckling.

"I had to find out from the twins. I'm missing everything. I want to come home."

"Two more days," I remind her again.

She falls back on her bed, holding her phone closer to her face. "I hate being here."

"You'll be fine for two more days," Sam rumbles.

My expression turns to stone, and Selina looks at me worriedly, biting her bottom lip. She knows I don't want to be around him, even if it is through a phone. It's just too much.

"I've got to go. Annette's calling me," I tell her.

Selina silently nods, knowing I'm lying. Annette hasn't been around much since the day Royce cornered me in the kitchen. It's only the two of us who know about the encounter, and I'd rather keep it that way until I figure out what he's up to. There's no way this is about me and Kaiden sleeping together. I could read it on his face when he was threatening me. His issue goes deeper than that, and I want to know why. But there is no way I can go to Kaiden for help. I don't want to be the girl who causes that kind of drama. I'll become my mum if I do.

Cheshire Grove is filled with mystery and cover-ups, and I want to discover what they are.

I end the call just as Sam's face comes into view, cutting off what Selina was saying. My heart races, and I take in a deep breath.

I can't forgive him for what he's said and done, but I guess the little girl inside of me wants to have a father in my life, a parent.

I just don't have a good track record when it comes to parents. I never trusted my mum, not as far as I could throw her.

Sam, however, is in another league, but at least she was honest about who she was. For the most part anyway—she did hide where she came from for all my life.

I just wish I could work him out, what makes him tick. He seems all business, but at the hospital, I saw a different side to him. All of it is driving me crazy.

I flick off the television, slide out of bed and head and downstairs, intending to see what the guys are up to next door. I'm not in the mood to be around a bunch of drunken idiots, but I want to see if Kaiden will take me to the hospital in the morning so Selina can see me for my birthday. Why she wants to make a big deal out of it, I don't know. I've never even received a card or celebrated it before. But it will make her happy, so I'll suffer and let her do the birthday thing.

People mill around outside, clear cups in their hand filled with alcohol. I wave back to a guy I remember from camping, but don't stop to talk to him and his group of friends.

Someone knocks into my shoulder on my way up the stairs to the front door. "Hey, watch it," I snap. I turn to face the tosser who bumped into me, sucking in a breath when I see it's Danielle with a group of her friends. "What the fuck are you doing here?"

She smiles sweetly up at me. "Kaiden invited me. You didn't think you meant that much to him, did you?"

My heart stutters to a stop, but I don't let it show. "Get over yourself, Danielle, or better yet, get over Kaiden."

She laughs, flicking her hair over her shoulder. "Or get under him. He likes being on top. He can fuck harder."

I tap my chin, tilting my head. "Funny. He likes it when I'm on top. Maybe you were just doing it wrong."

Her jaw hardens, her eyes nearly popping out their sockets before her lips lift into a smug smile. "How's Selina?"

I take a step forward, but Grant grabs me. "Inside."

"Did you hear—"

He rolls his eyes at me. "Just go inside to the twins."

Too tired to start another fight, I shake his arm off me and storm inside, ignoring her taunts. I see the twins cornering a guy I recognise from camping. I'm about to interrupt them when I stop, hearing them mention the fire. I step a back so they don't see me.

"Were you with her or not on the night of the fire, Will?" Ethan asks, stepping closer. "Don't lie to us. You know we will find out the truth."

Flustered, Will runs his fingers through his hair, pulling at the ends. "I don't know. I was with her, but it was a blur. There were a few of us hanging out, drinking, and we were hooking up, but I don't know, man. I was drunk, and I passed out. I was so out of it. I did a little too much weed."

Ethan shares a look with Lucca before turning back to Will. "Did Danielle ask you to lie?"

Will's eyes widen. "Nah, mate. One minute we were hooking up and the next she was telling me what a good time we were having, and she loved what I'd done to her. That's all. She didn't even know about the fire. I don't think. I can't remember. Is Kaiden pissed we hooked up? If he is, I thought they were broken up."

"Wait, so you black out and Danielle gives you a run-down of what you'd been doing when you came to?"

Jittery, he nods, looking scared. "Yeah, kind of, man. She said we stopped when she heard the commotion and went running over to help."

"Has she spoken about it since?"

"Look, man, I don't know what this is about, but I'm not getting involved."

Lucca steps forward, gripping him around the throat and slamming Will against the wall. "You are already involved. Can you, for certain, say she had nothing to do with the fire?"

Will's eyes begin to bulge as he shakes his head. "N-no. Like I told you, man, I was out of it."

Lucca lets him go, and Will gasps for breath. "Don't speak of this to Danielle. You know what happens to people who snitch."

Will nods, reaching for the wall for balance as he makes his escape.

I step in when he leaves. "Why was Danielle here?" I bite out.

Both spin around to face me, grimacing when they see my thunderous expression. "Ivy," Lucca murmurs.

"Nope. Don't try to be cute. Why was that slut here?"

"Kaiden wanted her here," Ethan admits, not bothered by how much his words hurt me.

Okay, now I'm feeling stabby.

"Why would he want her here?" I ask.

"It's not what you think," Lucca adds.

"What do I think?"

"That our brother is giving someone else what should be your orgasms," Lucca answers, grinning.

"Where is he?" I ask dryly, giving him a dirty look.

"It's really not what you think. He's doing it to keep her close. He wants answers, and the only way for us to get them is to make her believe she's gotten away with it. She might be a bitch, but she's a cunning snake and knows how to work those around her. Kaiden knows that and wants to use it to our advantage."

I relax somewhat, not feeling as stabby anymore. "Where is he?"

"I think he went upstairs to get something out of Dad's office. I'm not sure."

"Where's that?" I ask Ethan.

"Up the stairs, down the hall, take the first left and it's the first door on the right."

I nod, leaving them to do whatever it is they're planning on doing next and rush up the stairs. I get a quick glance of Grant talking to Danielle and her friends, and my stomach rolls.

Moving quickly, I head to where Ethan directed me, pushing the door open. Kaiden is nowhere in sight, but a picture on the desk captures my attention, and I move over to get a closer look.

It's a picture of Nina—Kaiden's mum—cradling Kaiden in her arms as she lies in a hospital bed, Royce stood stiffly next to her.

He's not really spoken much about his mum, and I've never seen her, not until now. She's beautiful, radiant as she smiles down at the new-born baby bundled in her arms. She has the same features as Kaiden, including stunning green eyes that just seem to pop out.

My attention focusses on Royce, seeing the same blank, soulless expression he constantly wears. It seems there was never a time he was happy, not even for the new arrival of a baby.

I sigh, feeling sad for the boys. Their mum looks so happy in the picture, so full of life, with the potential of a bright future. What did my mum do that took that away from her? What broke this woman to the point she took pills to forget, to forget she had children?

I place the picture back down on the desk. I'm about to step back to go and find Kaiden when the date on a piece of paper snags my attention.

The thin, scruffy scrawl can only be a man's penmanship. I lift it up, collapsing in the chair when I read it.

Howards block, flat 2b

Our flat.

Why does he have our address?

And why does it have the date Mum died on it?

I look back down at the other papers, seeing a picture of my mum collecting drugs from one of our local dealers.

There's nothing else on the desk. I pull out the first drawer, finding nothing but pens and stationery. I open the next drawer, finding pretty much the same thing but with other bits of junk.

The last drawer is locked, and I look around the room for something to open it with. Not seeing anything, I open the second drawer, pulling out the pocketknife and screwdriver I saw. Once I have the knife through the thin gap, I push the screwdriver in and twist the handle until the lock pops.

I pull out stacks of papers and set them down on the desk, flicking through them as quickly as possible. All of it has to do with a business or bank statements. A large sum of money has been taken out of one account, and I glance at the name of the account, confused when I read 'Randal Ryan'. But it's the date the large sum of money was transferred into another account that draws my attention. It's the day my mum died.

This isn't a coincidence.

My heart begins to race as I continue to flick through the last few pages, seeing nothing that can explain why he has all this stuff. A sick feeling swarms in the pit of my stomach.

I look back down at the drawer, finding it empty. I drop the papers back inside, but as I shut the drawer, something doesn't sit right, so I pull it back open.

The drawer should be deeper.

I lift the papers back out and grab the knife once again, digging into the edge of the drawer's base. My heart races when the thin, wooden panel lifts, revealing a hidden compartment. Inside is an old cassette player, a flip phone with buttons, a disc, and a couple of photos.

My stomach roils at the sight of my mum, around fifteen, naked and passed out on a bed. Her surroundings show she's in someone's home, but not Nova's. For one, it has a photo on the bedside table of an Asian family.

I'm going to be sick.

The pieces keep pulling together when I turn on the mobile phone, looking at the last messages sent.

SENT: Message me when you find a local dealer who will present her with the deal.

UNKNOWN: What if she doesn't take them? I can get this done quicker, just say the word.

SENT: NO! It will be too suspicious. Just make sure they take the drugs.

UNKNOWN: I've told you; I don't think the girl does them.

SENT: It's okay. Once the mum is gone, she'll be alone. I'll make sure she never comes back. Make sure you get the tape before she gets home.

UNKNOWN: Done. Mother dead.

I gag at the photo of my mum's dead body lying in a pool of her own vomit, tears spilling down my cheeks.

He had her killed.

SENT: Good. The rest of the money has been transferred.

Why did he do this?

I look down at the next message, recognising the number as my mum's.

CARA: You got my letter? I want twenty thousand by the end of the week or I'll make copies of the tape and send them to the police, press, and to anyone who will listen. I will ruin you like you ruined me. And I made copies, so don't think I won't.

I grab the bin from the side of the desk before emptying my stomach into it. I wipe my mouth, my chest heaving as the twenty second voice clip plays on the phone. It's a little hard to hear, but there's no mistaking the sound of a young girl begging someone to stop.

The diary.

It was true.

Every word was true.

Rising from the chair, I grab all the evidence before rushing out of there. My vision blurs as I try to make it down the stairs without falling.

"Ivy?" I hear Grant call when the cool air hits my face.

I don't stop, ignoring him and running home. I run upstairs, hitting my room and slamming the door shut behind me. I run over to my bed, throwing it all down in front of me. I grab the cassette player, unravelling the headphones.

I rewind the tape and take a deep breath before pressing play. I need to know. I need to hear it to believe it.

A sob wrenches from my throat when I hear my mum crying out, begging whoever to stop. I turn it off, reaching for my laptop and inserting the disc into the disc reader.

I wait a few moments for it to download, struggling to hear over my heavy breathing.

A soft voice singing, smooth and relaxing, comes through the speakers, and a small smile pulls at my lips when I realise it's my mum.

I wipe at the tears, but they keep flowing, blurring my vision.

"Are you coming to the party? Sam's here," a female voice asks.

"Coming," Cara calls out, right before the tape cuts off.

It's static for a few moments, until the sound of music plays quietly in the background.

"She's out of it," a male voice taunts wickedly, sending a shiver down my spine.

"I don't care if she's awake or asleep. When we get the Monroe empire, nothing will stop us. Royce Monroe will be the name everyone remembers."

Royce.

His voice isn't as deep on the tape, but I'd recognise it anywhere.

The recording goes static again, and I lean in closer. A scream has me jumping back, my hand covering my mouth as I listen to my mum beg.

"Don't do this. Please, don't do this, Royce. I'm a virgin."

"Good!" Royce sneers, sounding closer to the recording.

"Please! Oh my god! Please, stop! Neil, make him stop!"

"No," the other man says, before telling Royce to hurry up.

I cover my ears when an earth-shattering scream echoes through the speakers. Unable to bear another moment, I click it off, just as another voice taunts that it's his turn.

I gasp for air, fighting to stay conscious.

The diary was right. Everything she wrote, everything she felt… it was true. My mother wasn't who she was by choice. She was who they made her to be. And she had no one at her side to help save her.

They covered it up.

All of them.

Grabbing the cassette and disc, in a rage, I race downstairs, finding Nova in the living area, sipping from a cup of tea.

"You lied," I accuse, breathing heavily, tears streaming down my face.

She turns to me, quickly jumping from her chair. When she gets close, I put my hand up to stop her. "Don't touch me!"

"Ivy, what's happened. Are you okay?" She looks down at my hands, her face paling. "Is that your mum's cassette player?"

"Yes, but you would know that, wouldn't you," I bite out.

"Ivy, what's going on?"

"She was raped!" I scream at the top of my lungs. "She was raped, and you lied to me. You made me believe she was a pathological liar. She wasn't. Royce and whoever Neil is, are liars."

Nova blanches like I slapped her, before composing herself. "Ivy, you need to understand. I lied to protect you."

I force out a laugh, slapping her hand away when she reaches for me. "To protect yourself, you mean. You lied to me. You fucking lied to me. You let that man near me!" I scream at her, clenching my hand into a fist.

"He's a monster," she yells back, startling me for a moment. "Look what he did to her! I didn't want that to happen to you. Our grandparents were strict, they had roles, rules, and we had to abide by them. Cara accusing Royce and Neil, Grant's father, was frowned upon. They were men with a lot of power, power to order us what to do. So we were forced to keep it quiet. We didn't have a choice. I was scared of what he would do to you."

I look at her in disgust. "Do you fucking hear yourself? You *always* have a choice. You let her go off into the world, knowing she was hurting. She had her power stripped away from her, her *choice*, in the worst possible way, and you let her wither into the ground like ash. You let her waste away."

Nova shakes her head sadly. "I didn't find out until the night she told Flora and Nina what they did to her. I didn't believe her until after I caught her in bed with Sam. She was so far gone by then that everything that came out of her mouth was a lie. I didn't know.

"Sam explained what happened, why he got drunk that night with her when he never drank before. I didn't know. I tried, Ivy. I tried. I knew something was wrong. Looking back, there were times I think she was trying to tell me, but I wouldn't listen."

"So why did you lie and say she was lying?" I ask, anger pumping through me.

"I needed you to believe my lie. I needed you to stay as far away from this as possible. He's a dangerous man, Ivy. He has a lot to lose with this getting out, and I was afraid of what he'd do to you if you knew. He already stands to lose a lot by you being here."

"Why?" I ask.

"Sam's business has a clause in it. If his heir—his daughter—doesn't claim his fortune, the business gets transferred to Royce when Sam dies or decides to leave."

I laugh. "So not only did he kill Mum, he wants me dead too."

She rears back, shaking her head in denial. "He didn't kill your mum. He didn't."

I grab the phone out of my back pocket, giving her the proof. "Try explaining that to me. And, Nova, if you delete any of that before I have a chance to hand it to the police, I will kill you myself."

"Ivy, where are you going?" she calls out when I turn to leave. I pause at the door, tears streaming down my face.

"I'm leaving."

"No, wait, don't—oh my lord," she gasps, and I turn, watching her sway on her feet as she reads the messages.

She looks up, pain filling her features. I don't care. I don't feel anything right now. She betrayed me, lied to me. She let me get close to her, all the while lying to my face.

I can't bear to look at her.

There is one thing I need to know before I go. "Tell me one thing—did Kaiden know?"

She shakes her head, still in a daze. "No. I don't think so."

I walk out, and a moment later, I hear her high heels pattering on the floor as she chases after me.

"Ivy, please don't go. We need to sort this out," she yells.

I spin around to face her when I reach the door. "No! You lied to me when I asked you to be nothing but truthful. About my own mum. You made me believe she was a terrible person," I yell, hiccupping. "You made me believe she wasn't someone capable of love, but she was. She could have been a different mother had the people who were meant to love her stood with her." I stab my finger into my chest. "I could have slept at night not having to worry about the man she was in bed with. I could have gone to school with fresh clothes. My mother could have gotten married, had more kids, been happy. But she wasn't. And why? Because you guys are too concerned about your precious reputations. Money isn't everything, Nova. People survive without it every single day. What you did was worse than what they did. You should be ashamed of yourself."

"I'm sorry," she sobs out. "There's no excuse. None at all. And I wish every single day I had done things differently. She was my best friend until that happened. She was everything, the other half to who I was. I loved her, and I failed her. I'll never forgive myself for it. I might not be able to make up for my part, but I can make certain the same thing doesn't happen to you."

"I can't trust you," I tell her. "I never want to see you again."

"Ivy, please, please don't leave," she begs. "What about Kaiden? What about this?" She holds the phone up, pleading with her eyes for me to stay.

I ignore the phone in her hand, keeping the cassette and disc on me as I grab my bag from the hook by the front door. "I'm going. I need to be away from you, away from this. Away from it all. You lied to me, Nova. You lied to my face and told me she lied."

"I'm sorry. I'm so sorry."

"So am I," I tell her, leaving the house.

I quickly run to the garage to grab my bike, ignoring the stares coming from the partygoers next door. I must look like a right state with the tears running down my face. I put the disc and cassette in my bag and pull it over my head, before getting on the bike and pedalling the fuck out of there.

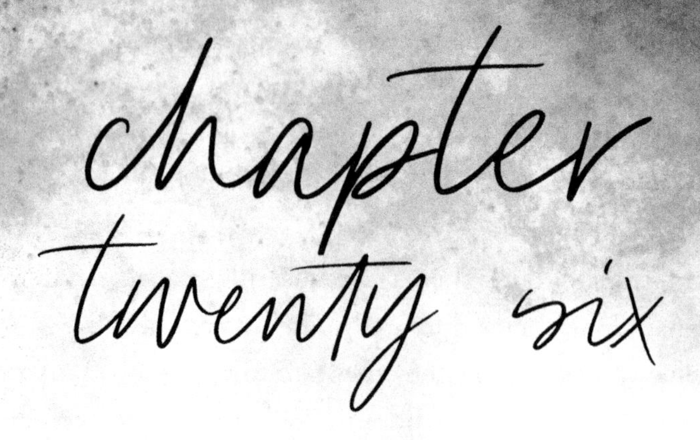

chapter twenty six

It isn't until I pass the gates that have trapped me inside the gated community that I realise I have nowhere to go.

I have no one.

He killed my mum's spirit, her soul, when she was only fifteen years old, and had the rest of her murdered.

Were they all in on it? Am I the only one who didn't know?

I still don't know if Kaiden knew, and that betrayal is the worst of them all. I gave him a part of me I've never given anyone in my entire life.

I gave him my trust, despite the beginning of our relationship.

And if he knew, he stomped all over it like it meant nothing.

I don't know who said it—my mind is a mess—but the words, 'keep your friends close, and your enemies closer', keep repeating in my head. Does that mean Kaiden was keeping me close, so I didn't spill what his dad had done to my mum? Was everything a lie?

I can't breathe. I can't think. I need to get out of here.

I skid the bike to the side of the road, gasping for air. I feel like I'm being sucked into a black hole, my chance of keeping my grip on reality being as likely as escaping its event horizon.

And my mum… God, what she must have gone through. She was still a child, and she was violated in the worst possible way. Not once, but twice. Then had to live with those men in her life with no support from her family. They didn't protect her. Not one person. No wonder she turned out the way she did.

Her behaviour makes sense now; how, after each man she let have control over her body, she would withdraw further into herself. She would take more drugs, drink more alcohol. She'd disappear further away from me.

I need to talk to someone who can make sense of every jumbled thought in my head. I just need someone, anyone, to tell me everything will be okay. Someone who isn't related to a Monroe or a Kingsley.

Mrs White.

Elle. She will know what I should do, what to say to make this not seem so bleak. With a destination in mind, I push off, making my way towards her home.

The road blurs in front of me as tears fall freely down my cheeks. When a car revs behind me, startling me, causing me to jerk the handlebars, I quickly straighten the wheels. I take a quick glance over my shoulder, my eyebrows scrunching together when I see a black Mercedes parked in the middle of the road, its windows blacked out.

I peddle faster, breaking out in a cold sweat, alarm bells ringing in my head. I'm right to be fearful when I hear the tyres screech on the road, the smell of burning rubber filling the air.

My eyes widen when I glance behind me, seeing it coming at me, fast. My legs burn as I try to outrun the car, fear filling my veins.

I'm not being paranoid; this is really happening. Someone is coming after me.

Is it Kaiden? Did he find out that I know what his father did?

My bag is a heavy weight on my shoulder, the contents more important than ever.

Up ahead, a motorbike roars, coming towards us, and panic begins to take over.

I'm going to die.

It's only moments when the car reaches the side of me, but it feels like hours. It swerves, and I scream, twisting the handlebars to the right. My wheel hits a stone, and I fly forward, skidding across the gravel, jagged pieces of stones slicing into my hands and legs. My chin knocks onto the ground, and I immediately feel warm liquid run down my neck.

I roll over and try to sit up the second I stop, pain shooting up my left arm when I put weight on it.

The motorcyclist skids to a stop in front of me, whipping his helmet off.

Carter Remington.

He looks back, further down the road, his eyes wide as he stares at the car growling to a stop.

"Ivy?" The car engine revs, and I glance at Carter, fear stricken. "Get on the bike! Now!" he yells, grabbing the helmet off the back.

On wobbly legs, I quickly make it to my feet and rush over to him, snatching the helmet out of his hands and swinging my leg over the bike as I place the helmet on. Adrenaline pumps through my veins, and I no longer feel the abrasions and broken arm.

Carter doesn't waste time waiting for me to place my arms around him. The second my arse hits the seat, he's shooting off.

"Why is someone trying to kill you, sweetheart?"

I jump a little at the sound of his voice through the speakers in the helmet. "Could be anyone," I mutter, ignoring his deep chuckle.

"We're going around a bend. Follow my body," he yells.

Follow him? Where the fuck is he going to go?

When his body leans to the side, I get his meaning, moving with him. The car behind is close, gaining speed.

"Did you see who it was?" I ask, since he drove straight past the car.

"I didn't get a clear look, but it was definitely a male."

My heart pummels in my chest. "Kaiden?"

"No, I'd recognise that twat anywhere."

"Faster!" I scream. The car is nearly touching the back of the motorbike's wheel. It swerves in the road, trying to get at the side of us, but Carter moves smoothly, blocking its way as he revs the throttle, going fast enough to make my stomach turn.

I grip him tighter as I brave another glance behind me, squinting to see the shape of a man in the driver's seat.

"Fuck!" Carter hisses, forgetting I can hear him.

"What?" I ask, sounding petrified for the first time in my life.

"He's getting close after each bend," he explains.

"Shit!" I hiss.

"He's going to fucking kill us," he grits out, sounding pissed.

"No shit! I can't see who it is."

"You've been here five minutes from what I've heard. Who could you have possibly pissed off?"

I force out a laugh. "Can you concentrate on the road?"

"Sweetheart, I've been doing this since I was four."

I growl, making him chuckle as we grow closer to the car up ahead. "Everyone. Pretty sure you're on that list. Don't think I didn't see it was you who called the cops."

He laughs. "As much as I'd like to take credit, I didn't. I just wanted to see what you would do if you thought I did. You didn't tell the Kingsley's."

"Can we chit-chat when we don't have a car trying to ram us off the road? I'm not feeling secure right now." He laughs, but when it suddenly cuts off, I begin to panic. "What?"

"Fuck! Fuck! Fuck!" he roars, before the sound of a phone ringing echoes in my ear. If this wasn't a life or death moment, I'd be amazed he has Bluetooth attached to his helmets.

"Yeah?" a male voice answers.

"You couldn't wait to call your boyfriend?" I yell, holding him tighter.

"Who's the girl?" the voice teases.

"Ry, I need you to come out to Hartbury Lane. We're coming up to the crossroads near Halewood."

"Why?" he asks, losing the humour.

Carter feeds my panic with how nervous and worried he sounds.

"Because I have Ivy Monroe on the back of my bike and someone trying to run us off the road."

He ends the call as Ry begins to rant down the phone. "Please tell me we're going to be okay," I plead, squealing when the driver of the pursuing car holds down on the horn.

"Ivy, I need you to do as I tell you. In about a minute, a van is going to be driving towards us. I'm going to try and get around it, but to do that, I need to slow down."

"You can't slow down!" I squeal, my heart racing.

"We've got no choice. Be prepared to crash."

"Oh my God," I whimper.

"This is my favourite bike," he whines.

I look over his shoulder, scared to death when I see the large van heading towards us. The road is narrow; there's not enough room for the two of us, even if we are on a bike.

"Oh fuck!" I chant, closing my eyes.

I feel the bike slow down and open my eyes, locking gazes with the driver of the van. He breaks hard, not far in front, but it's no use as the car behind knocks into the back wheel. Carter has no chance of gaining control of the bike. The wheels lock and we're both flying off, into the middle of the road, bouncing once, twice, before rolling through the gravel. I try to stay conscious, my head feeling heavy.

I blink, the sun blaring down, blinding me when I hear a car door open.

"Hey, what are you playing at?" I hear yelled.

My head tilts to the side, and I force myself to stay awake as I watch the person approach. From this angle, all I can see are their legs, black suit trousers and polished shoes. I blink, looking just past him to see Carter, closer to the bike, out cold.

I shiver, my teeth rattling together as the anonymous feet step into my line of vision. I struggle to see who it is, finding it harder with each second to stay awake.

My body jerks when someone roughly grabs the strap of my bag. "No," I croak out, my vision blurring.

The man laughs, bending down until he's shading me from the sun.

Fear runs down my spine when I see his face, shaded by a baseball cap. I blink, watching as he reaches out to me, his hand covering my mouth.

My eyes widen as I try to struggle, my entire body on fire.

"Hey!" I hear yelled, right before my world turns black, the last breath escaping my lungs.

TO BE CONTINUED...

Acknowledgements

I just want to say thank you to all who have taken a chance on Wrong Crowd. This story is nothing like anything I've ever written before, and I hope you enjoyed reading it as much as I did writing it.

Please, if you've read Ivy and Kaiden's story, leave a review on the appropriate platform. I love hearing what you guys think. Always.

I want to take the time to say a massive thank you to Stephanie Farrant, who once again worked her magic getting Wrong Crowd completed. She goes above and beyond, and I'll never be able to thank her enough. I sometimes feel like editors don't get enough credit, so I hope she knows how truly grateful I am for her hard work and dedication. You are an awesome person, an incredible friend, and the perfect woman to have as an alibi if I ever need one. I loves you.

To Cassy Roop, for another amazing cover design. This cover is perfect; it's loud, colourful and out there. It's everything I was looking for and more. Looking forward to the next one.

To all bloggers, readers, and authors who have shared the release or reviewed Wrong Crowd… Thank you. It means everything to me. You guys ROCK! Like, seriously rock! Keep up the good work.

Keep reading.

Keep blogging.

Keep sharing.

We love you for it.

To Melissa Teo, thank you for helping me when I was struggling the most, for giving me advice on what step to take to get this book published and how to go about it without upsetting readers who aren't into this genre. You are completely nuts, but you are one of the kindest people I've ever met. Thank you for organising an amazing beta team, who I'd like to thank from the bottom of my heart. You guys read a sample first, where most readers don't like to. It meant everything to have your feedback. You ladies are awesome, so thank you.

If you'd like to keep up to date on what's next from me, follow my author page on Facebook. It's Lisa Helen Gray Author.

Looking forward to hearing from you.

Printed in Great Britain
by Amazon